mature and powerful'
Montreal Gazette

'well-crafted and imaginative . . . Snyder's tone
and style is vivid and compelling'
Globe and Mail

'a moving story, beautifully told'
Quill & Quire

'Fans of *The Poisonwood Bible* by Barbara Kingsolver and
Paul Theroux's *The Mosquito Coast* will love this one'
Chatelaine

'excellent . . . Snyder has an uncanny ability to make the
unfamiliar intensely knowable . . . [*The Juliet Stories* is] pitted
with a surplus of lovely land mines of revelation,
aha moments exploding into wonderful,
sometimes profoundly sad, insights'
Telegraph Journal

'subtle and deft'
National Post

'Snyder is phenomenal here, crafting some of the most
striking images and beautiful sentences that you will likely
read all year. *The Juliet Stories* is not to be missed'

THE JULIET STORIES

CARRIE SNYDER

www.tworoadsbooks.com

First published in Great Britain in 2015 by Two Roads
An imprint of John Murray Press
An Hachette UK company

First published in paperback in 2015

1

A CIP catalogue record for this title is available from the British Library

ISBN 978 1 444 79268 3
EBOOK ISBN 978 1 444 79267 6

Printed and bound by Clays Ltd, St Ives plc

Hodder & Stoughton policy is to use papers that are natural, renewable
and recyclable products and made from wood grown in sustainable forests.
The logging and manufacturing processes are expected to conform to the
environmental regulations of the country of origin.

Hodder & Stoughton Ltd
Carmelite House
50 Victoria Embankment
London EC4Y 0DZ

www.hodder.co.uk

B000 000 016 4279

For Christian, Clifford, Karl, and Edna,
my sibs

There is the house we all inhabit
the house which is the body and only the body

Where ghostly families in the corridors of the blood
record their odd abbreviated histories

Then there is the yellow house and the doorway and

The child standing in a pool of yellow sunlight
the bright blood shed by the sun at sunrise

— Gwendolyn MacEwen, "The Yellow House"

PART ONE

AMULETS

RAT

Somewhere between Texas and Managua, their bags go missing.

The Friesen family steps off the plane into a wall of heat. They are unencumbered by toothbrushes, diapers, and fresh underwear. They cross cracked tarmac to a flat, squat terminal and the children wait with their mother on gritty tile while their father sorts out visas and donates American cash to armed officials in green uniforms. They wait for hours. At last, a man named Simon, a stranger, arrives to collect them in his silver pickup, to ferry them across this new city, beneath this new sky, wavery with dust. Juliet and Keith rattle around the open truck bed like loose teeth, amazed and elated by all that's here to be seen. Their mother, Gloria, hammers on the glass and tells them, "Get down!" Baby Emmanuel hammers too, but Bram, their father, waves expansively out of the open window. He feels as they do: *Look at this*.

The city is falling down, or already fallen. Dark green canopied vehicles, spilling with soldiers, cruise the streets.

3

Among shacks and shanties run skinny dogs and loose pigs. Children dart towards the truck to touch Juliet's hand, fingers scratching, papery and dry, as they cross her knuckles.

Managua smells like cooking fires, like the sultry burn of incense.

It is dusk when they arrive at Simon and Renate's house. The gate swings shut and Renate shows them to the room in which the Friesen family will temporarily camp: Renate's office.

Renate is a missionary from Canada, and so is her husband.

Juliet knows all about missionaries; that is what Grandma Grace and Grandpa Harold used to be. Two days ago they kissed goodbye outside Washington's National Airport; the wind blew jagged sparks of snow into hair and eyelashes. Grandma Grace said to Gloria, her daughter, keep your purse strap wrapped around your wrist; there are bound to be pickpockets. To Juliet she said, don't forget to say your prayers. Jesus Christ, I don't even *have* a purse, Gloria said to Bram, laughing, as they waved through the closing glass doors and Grandpa Harold helped Grandma Grace into the front seat of his Cadillac: American built with American pride. Nobody cried, not then. The crying part was over, and the questioning, and the lectures.

Missionaries tell other people what to do.

"I've removed any papers of importance," says Renate, standing in the middle of her office, "but I trust you will keep the children from touching anything."

"We thank you for your hospitality." Juliet's father clasps Renate's hand between his own, warmly. "The Roots of Justice thanks you."

Juliet's mother drops to the floor all that they possess: a carry-on backpack containing two paper diapers, four mini cheeses pilfered on the Washington-to-Dallas flight, a box of broken crayons, and a colouring book. In the front zippered pocket Gloria keeps a pack of gum, *in case of emergencies*. Juliet loves to imagine the type of emergency her mother might solve with a balled-up wad of pink stickiness: split pants? broken car part? severed finger?

If her family has nothing, Juliet doesn't know it. She isn't waiting for something better to arrive: not for the luggage, not for her father to find them a home of their own, or to begin his new job in earnest. Juliet can plop herself onto a blanket on the floor, stretch out, and — there, she's settled.

Juliet and Keith have interrupted Renate's nap, and with fallen palm leaves and sticks and industry, they are destroying her backyard. Renate's face appears bisected, glaring through the black bars over her bedroom window as she opens the slats of glass she'd carefully closed to keep out the heat and the dust.

"There is a park down the street." Renate drops each word down onto Gloria's head. Gloria, cross-legged and silent under the window, nurses her baby and watches her children play in the blazing sun. "Go," says Renate. "You will enjoy it."

The yard is not a secret garden. The secret is a city unseen that sprawls outside the yard's concrete walls, which are spiked on top with embedded glass shards but can't keep out the tantalizing squawk of neighbouring chickens, the shouts of children and women, smoke wafting, oily from cooking fires.

"Can't we go, oh, can't we, can't we?"

Gloria lifts Emmanuel off her breast and staggers to her feet. The baby lolls, heavily asleep. "Yes, let's," she says, drawing a circle around the four of them — their father is not here. Simon has taken him to meet someone who knows someone who is selling a motorcycle.

It is early afternoon: the worst hour to venture out. The sun stares mercilessly through leafless trees, dust rising and swept about by a rough wind off the lake below. Nor is the park at the end of the street as promised; instead, they meet a highway noisy with ox carts, and motorcycles spewing black clouds, and elderly school buses crammed to overflowing with passengers and livestock, and little Russian-made cars darting like toys.

As if falling from a great height, Gloria grabs the arm of a woman slowly picking her way along the road's narrow shoulder. "*¿Direcciones? ¿Parque?*"

A wide plastic bowl, laden to overflowing, rests on cloth wound into a circle on top of the woman's hair, and the bowl does not slip, even as the woman gestures vividly with her lips: *Over there, over there.* Juliet suspects magic.

"*¡Gracias, gracias!*" Gloria squeezes the woman's hand in thanks, but to Juliet's ears everything her mother is saying is wrong: her flat American vowels crashing against leaden American consonants, her *r*'s sodden *l*'s.

They tumble downhill. The mirage of a park shimmers and appears before them. "Ta-da!" cries Gloria, as if she's invented it from scratch. She punctuates the moment with a dance of delight performed in her stained white dress. Juliet watches as if from a distance, as if she's taken a step and then another and another away from her mother.

At home in Indiana, Gloria was just her mother, warming homemade soup on the stove as Juliet and her best friend, Laci, burst through the front door for lunch, or standing framed in the front window watching Juliet climb to the top of the school's monkey bars and walk across, the only girl in grade three who dared. But here, in this strange city, Juliet glimpses the stranger Gloria could become, giddy in her jubilation, separate and apart from her children; hardly a mother at all. A novel sensation grips Juliet's gut — shame. She is angry at herself for feeling this way, but mostly at her mother, for making her feel this way.

She can't run fast enough away, to the stripped-down ghost of a playground, metal structures flaked to dim apparitions where Nicaraguan children climb despite jagged edges and corroded-out holes through which entire limbs might plunge. There are swings, and slides no longer slippery, and the remnants of what might have been a merry-go-round. Giant trees grow out of concrete-rimmed knolls, silver bark peeling to white skin beneath.

Juliet darts to the tip-top of a metal-barred apparatus. Something sharp rips her inner thigh, opening a gash, but she ignores it. Her knees are orange with rust, palms dusty as she swings down. Her brother Keith is sprinting towards a real train engine that sits on a concrete platform bereft of track on the far side of the park.

"Ahoy, matey, ship ahead," he shouts, and Juliet yells after him, "That could be an island. Let's pretend it's an island."

"Treasure," Keith pants.

"Wait for me!" Gloria is hampered by baby Emmanuel's bulk.

As she runs, Juliet sees without seeing the old men sitting idle and watching them, and the stillness of the other children, sees without seeing the scene they are making, helplessly.

Keith and Juliet straddle the engine's nose. Juliet is riding a wild horse and Keith is surveying a jungled mountain. Both could be true.

The heat hits Juliet and Keith all at once, and they dismount and slump on a tree root the size of their father's torso: expansive.

"What's that on your leg?" Gloria asks Juliet.

"What, this? Oh, nothing." The cut flames red.

"Tetanus," mutters Gloria. But everyone's shots are up to date. Proof is on the immunization cards, which are in the luggage, which is lost.

"I'm thirsty," says Keith.

"Not right now," Gloria snaps in a tone Juliet recognizes. She is mustering herself.

Before them loiters a boy. He eats ice cream out of a paper cup with a stick, licking, staring, patient, as if he has been watching them for a while. His cheekbones are broad, his eyes' cast is green, strange wide freckles cross skin that is almost pale, and his hair is as red as Juliet's, though tougher, textured like weeds.

"¿Helado?" Gloria asks, thumping hard against the final syllable of the word for ice cream, one of the few in this new language known to Juliet and Keith.

The boy is clearly thrilled to escort them to a small wooden stall on the dark and shady side of the park. Painted white, it could be any concession stand anywhere in the world. Before Gloria can give permission, the boy has ordered on their behalf. Gloria fumbles for the cloth moneybag that swings on string around her neck, dropped down inside her dress. The boy hands them each a paper cup, the dull green metallic-flavoured sweetness within already melting even as Juliet laps it up. The texture is granular on her tongue, swallowed and gone.

Around them a chorus of children is gathering, spilling out of an invisible source, drawn in this direction like filings to a powerful magnet, feet crusty with dust, clothing ripped and repaired and ripped again. Girls much smaller than Juliet carry baby brothers or sisters in their arms or on their backs, tending to them, casually responsible.

With authority, and without consultation, the boy places another order at the window. Gloria and the children watch the woman behind the counter pour the contents of a glass bottle of jewel-red pop into a small plastic bag. The woman secures the bag with a knot on top. The beverage is for Gloria, who does not want it. The boy offers the bag to Keith instead, and mimes instructions. Keith chews, spits a triangle of ripped plastic, wipes it off his lower lip with his wrist, and spills red pop down his chin, staining his only shirt.

The crowd of children cheers.

"It's not fair," says Juliet, feeling this deeply. "I'm the oldest."

"This is it, Juliet. I'm out of money." Gloria buys a second bag. No more, she tells the boy, waving her hands. The pop, called Fanta Roja, tastes like cream soda, a flavour Juliet loathes. But she knows better than to complain again; she sucks the pliant plastic breast dry.

Gloria settles on the ground, unties her shoulder strap, and smiles up at the boy who has helped them, as comfortably as if she were seated on the rag rug in their former kitchen; she doesn't seem to notice Emmanuel's restless head exposing her nipple. In Spanish she asks the boy, "What is your name?"

"Freddy." The boy stands out from the others. Discreetly belching Fanta Roja fumes, Juliet can't stop examining him: his green eyes glitter; he swaggers.

"Freddy?" Gloria repeats his name with surprise. They have not been in the country long enough to know that foreign names pronounced with a Nicaraguan accent are commonplace — Freddy, Edwin, Clifford, Millicent. Who knows what else outsiders have left behind?

"Freddy," the boy repeats, and from behind him comes the call "El Chelito," the nickname repeated gleefully. A girl with a cardboard box tied around her neck points to Juliet — "Chelita, chelita," she says, like a little bird calling. The flat box sticks out like a tray on which the girl displays what she is selling: cigarettes and gum.

"What does it mean?" The children press so near that Juliet can smell their breath, see where they are missing teeth and how their hair shines, unwashed, with grease.

But Gloria doesn't know either and is not paying attention to Juliet. Her eyes are locked on Freddy. "¿Donde vives?" she asks him. Where do you live?

Freddy gestures generally: Over there.

"Freddy." Gloria tilts her head in appeal, says, "Ayudanos." Help us.

Fear alters every angle. Juliet understands: they are lost,

and Gloria has chosen this boy, Freddy, to rescue them. Noise rises, the buzz of disorientation.

Keith's back presses Juliet's. She would never tell him, but she is comforted by the irritating warmth of her brother's proximity, by his sturdiness and height — as tall as she is, though she is nearly two years older. He takes after their father, as she takes after her mother; everyone says so. Between them they share the same wish: that their mother tie up her dress strap, that she cover herself, that she rise.

Puzzled and delighted, Freddy points to himself as if to say: *Me, help you?* And he bows. *But of course.*

"*Casa*," says Gloria; she may not know the word for lost. She waves her free hand, clutching for her high school Spanish. "*Grande. Blanca. Americanos.*"

The girl with the tray wags a tiny rectangular maroon packet of gum at Juliet. She singsongs a word that Juliet does not understand. *No, no, no*, frowns Juliet, and though the girl understands, she refuses to believe, shaking the packet, *rattle, rattle, rattle*, like a handful of little stones.

The girl doesn't know that Gloria has spent all their money on ice cream and soda pop; she doesn't know they aren't rich. They aren't rich, are they? Or does the girl know better than Juliet what they are, what all of the gringos are, no matter what they think they are? The gringos have passports and American dollars; they have another country to call home. They can come, and they can go, and they do, and they will.

They make a ragged parade out of the park, a confusion of followers and pursuers led by Freddy, who dances them down different streets from those they came on, past shacks with dark interiors and dirt floors, chickens scraping in front yards, stray dogs and pigs prowling ruts of soapy garbaged water. This is the smell of a city with inadequate sewers, yet it's a smell that will always remind Juliet of something good — something lost and something good. Because she is ten years old under an open blue sky, because there is no reason ever to arrive anywhere, because she has never felt exactly this way before — this loose in the world, this capable of escape.

Nothing can shift this feeling of goodness, not even the man in black pants stumbling through his gate. Juliet sees his feet in torn plastic sandals, his damaged toenails. She sees that his zipper is down, perhaps broken, and she sees the exposed and flaccid flesh within, pale as a dried cob. There is a whirring in the air, a collective gasp, as the man reaches heavily for Gloria. Her body spins sideways under his weight, baby Emmanuel loosened from her grip, slipping, falling.

Freddy: running past Juliet like a shadow, running at the man, fists shoving gut. *"¡Vayate, viejo!"*

The man's cheeks hang pouched. He staggers a step and collapses. The children — the others, not Juliet, not Keith — explode with laughter. Boys pelt the man with pebbles.

Gloria's body hunches, pinched shut. Time abandons them to one steeply turning moment, slowly, slowly, pinning them here until they wake — it is like waking — to Emmanuel's howls in the dirt. Gloria cannot lift him: her hands shake, her wrists, a shudder that shoots up her arms and rocks her whole body. Juliet tries. She will carry him the way the Nicaraguan girls carry their little brothers and sisters; but Emmanuel is not a Nicaraguan baby. Livid, veins popping from his neck, he kicks Juliet and yanks her hair. She talks to him in a baby voice — "No, no, bad boy, bad Emmanuel" — and renders him ever more furious. His uncut nails scratch her face.

"Put him down, for the love of God," Gloria says. "Stop trying to help." Being angry at Juliet steadies her, and she grabs Emmanuel into her own arms and squishes him to her chest. "Poor baby, poor baby, poor little dropped soul."

Emmanuel's tantrum continues unabated. This soothes Juliet.

They step over the man, around him, away, Freddy's hand in the air near Gloria's shoulder, but not touching her skin. Her long, dark hair hangs loose and smooth all the way to her waist, a veil behind which she hides, and Juliet thinks: She's crying.

"¡La casa de los gringos!" Freddy waves his arm in grand offering.

But the gate is padlocked shut. Emmanuel is a glowing force field of rage. Gloria wrenches the metal catch and wails: "Could this possibly be right?"

Freddy frowns politely. He has delivered them. Confusion spills all around Gloria, that is what it seems to Juliet. Only a moment has passed. The gate is locked, but there is the wicker sofa on the porch, the clump of coconut palms growing out of a raised bed in the otherwise bare front yard, the walled back garden. This is the right house.

In confirmation, Renate staggers out, hair askew. "Good God!" Because she is a missionary, she makes it sound like a prayer, not a swear.

"The gate was locked, Renate, it was locked!"

"I see that." Renate turns a key and they file past with their crumpled clothes, their dusty legs. "The maid must have locked it. I could hear you from a mile away."

The gate swings shut on Freddy. He is cool, sparkling water. He winks at Juliet. "*Adios, chelita linda.*" But he loiters, as before, watching them.

"What's this?" Renate snaps the padlock shut. What, not who.

Perhaps Gloria cannot hear over the screams. Gently she lays Emmanuel on the tiled porch, strokes soaked hair off his forehead.

"His name is Freddy," offers Juliet. "What's a *chelita*?"

"*Chel-ita.*" Renate breaks down the word. "*Chele* is the root; *ita* means little; ends with an *a*, feminine form — so, 'little girl.' Little white girl. It's not very nice, you shouldn't say it. They use it for people who look like him: different." She claps her hands, off you go, as if shooing away a bothersome animal, turns and says loudly, "You have to be careful. Set clear boundaries. You can't let them take advantage."

Renate is not addressing Juliet, but who else is listening? Keith hangs on the fence, waving goodbye through the metal grating. Emmanuel has wrung himself out, and Gloria lifts and cradles him in her arms, carries him into the house without a backward glance.

Juliet finds them in their bedroom. Gloria kneels beside Emmanuel, who sleeps, utterly relaxed, on Juliet's bed. Gloria's hands are on her knees, palms up, head erect.

"Mom," says Juliet from the doorway.

"Shhh," Gloria frowns.

"Renate wants to know if you want a drink."

"In a minute."

Juliet waits.

"I said, in a minute, Juliet. In a minute, for the love of God." Gloria is not a missionary. Her prayers are swears.

In the kitchen, Renate pours fresh lemonade squeezed by the maid. "Does your baby brother often scream like that?"

"I guess so."

"Did you have fun at the park?"

Keith is not helping out.

Juliet darts a glance at Renate, and away; no one has warned her that this looks sneaky. "I don't know," she says finally, speaking the truth. But what she really doesn't know is that there are questions grown-ups don't want answered truthfully; grown-ups will accept a polite yes, but what they really want is confirmation of their suspicions, suspected moral failings guilelessly revealed, though this will bring the child no favour. Nothing will. In this context, the child is immaterial to the grown-up, useful only as an unwitting spy or pawn.

Renate turns to Keith and observes, "You have spilled something on yourself. The maid will wash it for you."

Keith obediently removes his shirt. He hasn't got another.

"Oh, but you shouldn't have, you shouldn't have," Gloria grieves when informed of Renate's action. She is not upset that Keith must spend the rest of the day half-naked, Juliet knows. She is offended that the maid should have to do anything extra for them.

"Don't be ridiculous!" says Renate. "How else would we get our work done? You've no idea, Gloria."

Renate adds in a confiding tone, "You mustn't pay your girl too much. She will be more than pleased to work for a nice American family. It's cruel to pay them more than they will be able to earn when you are gone."

There is silence.

"Work!" says Renate, emphatically and cryptically. She is finished, and Gloria has made no reply.

Juliet never expects to understand fully. She listens, she squints down dark-walled passages lit by cracks of flitting sunshine, following through intertwining tunnels her mother — in conversation with another grown woman. Mystery is a shroud over words, phrases, entire paragraphs, over facial expressions and gestures, over inexplicable laughter, chilly quiet. Usually, though not now, cups of coffee are involved, and a dreamy exhaustion, kitchen chairs pulled up to the table, sugar spilled and brushed onto the floor, interruption and return, laughter, a hushed "Now when did this happen?" to alert Juliet's ear. This exchange is different, because Gloria and Renate are not friends. They are not leisurely. But it is somehow the same, because they are women. They are speaking, with words or without, of puzzles that do not yield to easy solutions.

It is February, 1984.

Ronald Reagan is the president of the United States of America. He is fighting the commies. Commie is short for communist, a thick plank of a word that is used often and ominously on American television; on American television communist means evil. But Juliet takes her definition from Gloria, who says that communists are people who share everything. (Imagine fighting against people who share! It is the punchline to a joke. Juliet writes a skit on the subject, and Keith plays Ronald Reagan with gusto: "I declare a war on sharing! There will be no more sharing!")

Juliet loves and craves definitions. What is the specific meaning of each heavy word that falls from the sky? But a definition is not an answer. It is temporary shelter, a camp that is put up and broken down. The more she knows, the frailer the originally stable definition, as its meaning comes stamping into her brain shadowed with everything it has been and will ever be, everything connected to it.

Nicaragua is a country shaped like a triangle where it is hot and never snows; also, they are having a war. Managua is the capital city, where it is safe to live except for the volcanoes and the earthquakes. The Sandinistas are in charge and they might be commies, but that would be okay — see definition of a communist. The Cold War is America versus the USSR; somehow this matters, even though Nicaragua is neither of those places. The CIA are scary Americans who sneak around and do bad things, playing nasty tricks on people; they might be anywhere, even pretending to work for the Roots of Justice. The Roots of Justice is going to stop the fighting in Nicaragua; Juliet's parents work for the Roots of Justice. They will bring Americans into Nicaragua to protest against the Contra war.

Freedom fighters: what Ronald Reagan calls the Contras. The Contras: masked men who stab Nicaraguan babies with bayonets, which are knives attached to the ends of their guns. The Contra war: the Contras are fighting against the Sandinista government. Ronald Reagan is paying, but nobody knows. Everyone needs to know. A protest is a way of telling, yelling when no one is listening.

Pay attention!

In Indiana, Juliet marched in a protest and got on television, carrying a sign decorated with a crayoned blue and green ball beneath a rainbow: PLEASE DON'T BLOW UP MY WORLD. It was a spring day, sunshine and a chilly wind. They walked down the middle of the street and stopped for speeches in a park. Juliet was excited, and then bored, and then hungry, and then she had to pee, and then she was excited again, and mildly jealous, because her best friend, Laci, had been chosen to speak at the microphone. Laci was supposed to read a poem about flowers, but her voice shook and she forgot and instead cried, "Please stop making bombs, please stop making bombs!"

Others were crying too. But they are still making bombs, as far as Juliet knows.

Juliet's parents believe they can stop the Contra; at least, they believe they have to try. That is why the Friesen family have come to Nicaragua. They have come to stop Ronald Reagan. They will take ordinary Americans to the border towns where Contras ambush and murder ordinary Nicaraguans. The ordinary Americans will not let that happen. They will stand, peaceful and strong, in between. They will wear matching green T-shirts and they will hold hands and sing songs. They won't get hurt.

Ronald Reagan and his freedom fighters won't want to hurt ordinary Americans.

Juliet would like to go too, to stand in the line and hold hands and sing. Juliet's mother says she won't be able to. Juliet will stay with her brothers in Managua, where it is safe and no one is being killed.

"But what about you?"

"I will stay too."

"But what about Dad?"

Tonight the Friesen family sleeps on the floor, in the room like a womb sheltered and dark, lit by the glow of mosquito coils, orange in the breeze. Tomorrow, and tomorrow, and tomorrow, the Friesen family rises to eat dry toast and drink *café con leche* (even the children; Gloria says they may) and to clog Simon and Renate's toilet because they've forgotten that paper is not to be flushed: more work for the maid.

In the afternoons, no water flows from the taps. The quick-falling evenings summon enterprising swarms of mosquitoes; Renate promises it will be worse in the rainy season. For every meal of every day, even for breakfast, the maid prepares and serves *gallo pinto*, red beans fried with rice, yet no one grows tired of eating it.

Finally, an evening that stands out from the blur of temporary routine and heat-stupored stasis: Renate hosts a dinner party and invites the three other Roots of Justice team members, who live in Managua too. At last they have something to celebrate, especially Renate and Simon: the Friesens have found an apartment. The maid serves buttered squash and fresh corn tortillas and a vat of *gallo pinto*, and for dessert, Renate surprises everyone by preparing her specialty, baked Alaska.

When the moment arrives, Renate switches off the lights and emerges from the kitchen balancing a mounded confection lit spectacularly on fire. In the glow of blue flame, her angular face floats pale and eerie. The smell of burning rum pervades the air.

An impromptu cheer erupts from the emaciated Roots of Justice team members: Andrew, Jason, and Charlotte.

"I've never had a baked Alaska," says Gloria. "Everyone tell Renate thank you, please." She is speaking to the children, who understand.

"Thank you," Keith and Juliet echo as the flame burns into nothing.

From Gloria's lap, baby Emmanuel emits a dull rumble. His bedtime bile is rising.

"What an unexpected treat! And here in Nicaragua, who would have imagined it. Tell Renate thank you," Gloria repeats, as if deaf.

"We did," says Juliet, and Renate frowns as she dishes out miraculously unthawed ice cream revealed beneath meringue topping. Juliet senses displeasure, distaste, but she does not know why.

Renate passes the first bowl to her husband.

"When exactly are you able to move out?" Simon wonders, licking his spoon before anyone else has been served.

"Imminently," Bram promises. He has rented them several rooms on the second floor of a seminary located in the broken downtown core. He can't sit still. He plucks Emmanuel from Gloria's arms, pacing the room and hurling the fussy baby into the air until Gloria warns he'll be sick. But the rented apartment is only the beginning, a shining omen of all that's to come, and Bram's list grows with each toss, grand and grander: "And we'll find ourselves a real office, and a proper house for you volunteers. We'll buy desks, furniture, a truck, a bus. We'll need a bus driver. We'll get these kids into a Nicaraguan school, learning Spanish — right, kids? And our office will have everything we need. Telephone, typewriter, computer, tape recorders, cameras, walkie-talkies . . ."

Everyone looks at Juliet's dad, and their faces are flushed with sweet sugar and sweeter promises. Like Juliet, they believe him. They do not doubt.

"Bedtime," says Gloria, ending it all. She takes Emmanuel from Bram. "You've gotten him all worked up."

Juliet and Keith sit still, hoping their mother won't notice them too.

"Bedtime!" She snaps her fingers. "Juliet. Keith. Say goodnight."

"Just a little longer, please? We'll be quiet."

"Enough. Say goodnight."

"It's not fair!"

"Say goodnight."

"Goodnight."

"Goodnight. Sleep tight. Don't let the mosquitoes bite." One of the volunteers, the one with the moustache — Andrew — smiles at them.

It *isn't* fair. Juliet and Keith know this for a fact: no one else goes to bed at seven o'clock, no one but babies. They whisper in the dark, the throaty snores of their brother sighing inside his pen of overturned chairs in the corner. Through open windows they hear other children playing in the street, the sound of firecrackers — or is it gunshots? The blare of a radio, the motor of a passing car chased by a pack of dogs.

A warm breeze deepens the orange of the lit mosquito coils on the windowsill, the scent of citronella drifting on a line of smoke.

From the dining room, laughter bursts in high-pitched waves — could it be real when it sounds so fake? Juliet and Keith resent its existence: fun that excludes them. They are not sleepy. They will not sleep.

Juliet tiptoes to the door, pulls it wider, Keith on her heels. Shhh!

Candlelight flickers down the hallway, tossing shadows. They crouch against the door's frame, conspirators clad in underwear. Smoke from cigarettes floats overhead, thick and blue. They hear the clink of glass on glass. They hear the squeak of borrowed guitar strings. More laughter, as their mother searches for a song — they know the sound of her — trying out an opening, and another, chording sugges- tions; and then, her discovery of the song itself, lonely before it fills out with other voices that ride in, uncertain and stum- bling, till the chorus gallops by and they all catch hold, and the song swells full up, and they are vanished inside it, in an- other room in the mind.

Juliet inches across the tiles, naked from the waist up, her hair hanging long and unbrushed for days, a scramble at the back that will take persistence and bitter struggle to comb free. The grown-ups slump on chairs around the table, with eyes that do not care what they find — even when they alight on her. They are lost somewhere else, in song and drink, in cause and dream.

Gloria's back is to Juliet, her shoulders bent over Simon's guitar. The instrument slips out of tune, and Gloria fiddles with the pegs on which the strings are wound. Beside her, Simon slowly sips a bottle of beer while Bram tips his chair back on its hind legs, his expression animated, the wild brush of pale orange hair rising off his scalp, skin peeling in flakes; *yes, yes*, Simon nods seriously. Around the table dances Andrew, an elfin man, nimbly topping up glasses from a bottle of white rum; as he passes, he inclines his head and winks at Juliet.

No one else spies her.

Jason, another volunteer, is a man of many twitches; one of his eyes wanders independent of the other. Juliet takes a shiver of pleasure in her fear of him. He only sets down his burning cigarette to take in a bite of food, or to drink.

The last of them is Charlotte, her round face as softly appealing as the moon's, angled upward, her eyes half-closed as she tracks a path through her private forests.

Gloria has found another song.

Charlotte's timbre rolls low under Gloria's, honey spilled on the floor, sticking; Juliet's palms are caught in it. They are similar, Gloria and Charlotte: long, dark hair, and powerful voices. But Gloria has her back to Juliet, and Juliet prefers it that way. Gloria's face is like the sun. Do not gaze upon it. If Gloria were to see Juliet, she would send her away, back to bed, impatient with being a mother; in turn, Juliet is impatient with Gloria, for being unfair and dismissive, but most of all, for being her mother.

Juliet does not see Renate, offering black coffee, watching her.

"*You* are a little rat," Renate tells Juliet.

Juliet, who is on her way to the backyard with good news to tell. Juliet, who has just seen by accident — by slippery, stand-in-the-doorway-and-stare accident — Renate in their hushed bedroom (her office) silently kicking and trampling the Friesens' bedding and meagre belongings.

The two of them stand alone in the hallway, brilliant sun flashing through the open back door, making of Renate a silhouette.

"*Rat*." Renate speaks in a whisper, menacing, in Juliet's face. She anticipates betrayal, tattling, though Juliet has no intention of telling. What to tell? Her family is living in a state of such untidiness — Gloria incapable of picking up after them or demanding that they do so for themselves, Bram oblivious — that Renate's tornado can neither create damage nor leave behind evidence. But Renate is right.

Juliet is a little rat.

Just for now, she's a packrat, adding to her piles, her secret stash; but one day, someday, she will be that other kind of rat, she will *tell*, in her own way, wearing the sheerest of disguises, quite remorseless. And none of it will be true; and all of it will be. And even that is not true, because there is nothing absolute about telling: there are only fragments, shards, the rare object retained whole, ciphers removed from original context, hoarded by shifty, impecunious memory.

Why is one thing taken and put away and another not? And who is to place value on the worth of either? The thing that is lost may have mattered more than the thing that is saved, and there is no way to judge.

Silence.

Renate whirls past, and Juliet thinks it might have been a dream. She makes it into a dream. It becomes one. It was.

Juliet wakes, blinks, and she is running down the hallway, chased into the white-hot backyard by the good news she's come to tell. She shouts at her mother: "Our bags are here! Our bags are here! Dad says!"

By the time the Friesens pile themselves into Simon's polished pickup for another drive across the city, the scratch on Juliet's leg is just a scab and she has brushed her hair free of knots. The truck enters Managua's ruined core, speeding Juliet away from *You are a little rat*, from the boy called Freddy and the children throwing stones and the smell of burnt rum, as if these have vanished forever.

The air swarms ripe, thick as nectar, closing around them like the seminary's iron gates. Gloria hauls Emmanuel and a heavy rectangular suitcase up the clean-swept concrete stairs to their new apartment. Juliet follows behind.

Imagine that someday everything in that suitcase will no longer exist. Everything that made its journey, lost to found, will be used up, discarded, replaced, forgotten. Into that someday, imagine Juliet. Imagine that she has found these other bags, ones she has no memory of packing. They seem to belong to her.

Imagine that she has gotten around to opening them.

BORROWERS

The seminary stands encircled by a chain-link fence and surrounded by the remains of less fortunate buildings felled in the earthquake of 1972, crumbling cement skeletons occupied by those who refuse to leave what once was the bustling downtown core. But Bram says there's a library nearby. He's scooted past it on his motorcycle.

Juliet scrapes the corner of a book against her two front teeth: it's borrowed from a Canadian family living in Managua, not-quite-acquaintances. Juliet chose the book for the horse on its cover, only to discover that horses are peripheral to the plot, an adventure story about a forest fire and a daring rescue. The Canadian family has two boys, older.

"I need more books!" Juliet begs, but Bram leaves a trail of breakfast crumbs on his way out the door, and Gloria can't decide whether to attempt an adventure before or after the maid is to come. Before would be ideal — it is scorching by mid-morning — but the seminary director has been unwilling, or unable, to pinpoint the maid's arrival time. A shrug, a smile, a "what does it matter?" Because it doesn't, in this country, in this heat. Time is a liquid, improvisational substance that only a foreigner would attempt to freeze into symmetrical cubes. Tomorrow morning, the man said.

"Mañana, en la mañana," Gloria mutters. Sunlight licks thin, dirty curtains. "Besides," she argues with herself, "Emmanuel's napping."

Plastic institutional breakfast dishes crowd the sink, stale crusts uneaten. The Friesens supper in the cafeteria among the seminary students, and otherwise fend for themselves. Their kitchen consists of a miniature fridge squatting beside a gas-fired hotplate, and a sink set in a scrap of rotten countertop. Mouse dirt spills from drawers and cupboards; cockroaches the size of toy cars beetle freely about the floor.

Gloria disappears through the curtain of beads that separates her bedroom from the main room. Cigarette smoke drifts lazily.

Keith pens on the inside of his wrist and watches Juliet chew the borrowed book. "I'm telling," he says.

"Keith's drawing on his arm!" Juliet counters.

"Juliet's chewing on the book!"

"Am not."

"Are too."

There's a rap on the door. The mop handle bangs as the maid enters, bucket dragging behind. Emmanuel flares from the towel on the floor where he's been left.

"Out of the way, children," says Gloria, hurrying through the chiding beads. She plucks up Emmanuel.

"Ah, what a pretty baby," says the maid in Spanish. She is thin, bony, young — not youthful. Juliet sees that she is missing what looks like an important front tooth.

"*Now* are we going to the library?" she asks her mother.

"I have four of my own," the woman continues. She bends and waves her hand close to the floor. "Little, little ones." This is only the beginning of all she has to tell. Juliet understands the new language like a haze on the horizon, like she's hearing without seeing, understanding without interpreting.

Complaints.

Patchy elbows exposed, the maid runs cold water (there is no other kind) and washes dishes, wipes them dry, casually stacks them in the dark, bug-ridden netherworld behind the rickety cupboard door. Gloria's face contorts in protest — she's been storing them on the table when cleaned and not in use — but she stands frozen in the middle of the room, staring, as they all stare.

The maid fills her bucket at the sink, grunts as she lugs it past Gloria, who rouses herself as if speaking in a dream: "What is your name?"

"Bianca." The woman laughs without smiling and enters the children's bedroom.

Juliet licks loose a fragment of flame-illustrated paperback cover, chews it to pulp, spits it out discreetly onto the back of her hand. She sees Bianca at her cot, folding and tucking the sheets. She mops backwards across the bedroom, long grey tentacles swiping the tiles, *swish, swish, swish*, until she is back in the main room.

"Lift your feet," Gloria says to Juliet and Keith.

"Oh, how hot it is." Bianca's ropy arms strain. "What heat."

She props her mop, wipes her forehead, and advances upon Gloria's bedroom, where Gloria stands guard before the veil of beads.

"Your clothes, your clothes," Bianca demands, snapping fingers with impatience.

Gloria's eyes dart.

Bianca explains: She will take home their dirty laundry and return with it, cleaned, dried, and ironed, in the morning.

"Wonderful, wonderful!" Gloria dashes about, her pleasure all out of proportion: perhaps because she hates doing laundry, or perhaps because she's kept Bianca out of her bedroom and wants to compensate for the imagined offence.

Bianca stuffs their soiled clothing into a plastic bag and gathers her supplies. She is going. Gloria holds the door. It doesn't seem possible for Bianca to transport on her person everything that she must.

Gloria calls anxiously down the stairs, "Is it okay?"

"Yes, yes, it is fine," Bianca calls back.

"Mom? The library?"

"Not today," says Gloria. "Just play outside. Now. Take Emmanuel."

"We need to make a trip to Jalapa," says Bram after supper.

Juliet and Keith, freshly showered and wearing T-shirts for pyjamas, dart around the main room, scaring into oblivion the mice and cockroaches. Gloria's reply goes missing beneath Keith's rattling cough.

"It has to be done, and quickly," says Bram. "The first team arrives next week."

"By 'we'," says Gloria, "you mean you — don't you."

"We could all go." Bram scratches the back of his neck.

"On your motorcycle?"

"We're getting a truck."

"Over the land mines?"

Bram inhales deeply, his chest broadening with breath. "So stay," he says.

"You don't want us to come," says Gloria.

Bram opens the fridge, removes a bottle of beer. His shoulders slump fractionally and the underarms of his shirt hang damp. But he is revived by his first sip.

Gloria cries, "Brush your teeth!"

"You heard your mother," Bram says.

"He's going to leave us here, all alone!"

Juliet blinks at her dad. His face is crinkled with sunburn, and she can see all the way to his crispy scalp. They share the same thin red hair, fragile skin, but there the comparison ends. Nothing scares Juliet's dad, not even her mom.

"So come," Bram says lightly.

Gloria begins to cry, which everyone hates, including Gloria, but most especially Bram. "It's nothing to you to leave us, is it."

Juliet understands that no one is listening.

In the bathroom, Keith coughs again.

"Your germs are all over my toothbrush!" Juliet punches her brother in the arm; she can't say why, but she must. He aims for her shoulder. She tackles him and they roll on tiles scented with Bianca's vicious lemon Pine-Sol.

"My glasses!"

"Disgusting!"

"Stop." Bram is visible in the doorway for a solitary beat of time before the electricity fails, extinguishing the buzzing light overhead, emblazoning their father's outline on Juliet's retinas: he stands solid as a tree trunk, strong as stone. At the apartment's core, the windowless bathroom is black and it hums in the wake of machinery fallen silent: no fan blades rotating and exhaling, no refrigerator murmuring, no radios blaring outside. Juliet feels herself lifted, like a child much smaller than she actually is, and pressed to her father's chest, Keith mashed next to her.

"Apologize." Bram smells sharpish.

They hear the grunt and slurp of Emmanuel suckling at their mother's breast. They hear and feel with disgust each other's half-brushed breath, hear and feel the lonely beat of their father's heart against their cheeks.

"Sorry."

"Sorry." Juliet turns her head away from her brother. Faint moonlight ghosts the curtains in the main room. She can't remember what she's trying to forget — something specific dissolved into an emotion, a crack of fear opened in the wall of her rib cage, a splinter of cold fingering its way inside.

Sweat pastes them together. Something has to.

It is dawn. The children and Gloria rise early to admire the new truck. The men are on their way.

"Call as soon as you get there," says Gloria.

"No phones," says Jason from the driver's seat, his face sectioned into nerve endings, cigarette burnt down to the filter as he lights a fresh one off the old.

"No phones?"

"No phones."

"But how will we know you've arrived safely?"

"Assume the best!" says Bram, squashing Keith and Juliet like bugs against his ribs. "Always assume the best."

"Don't worry," Andrew says to the children. "We'll look after your dad. We'll take good care of him."

"Okay," says Juliet. She would agree to most anything Andrew says.

"It's going to be fine," Bram whispers into Gloria's hair, fingers tangled, stroking. The grown-ups gaze the other way, but not the children, for whom every scene is open, yet closed. "It has to be done. It's a routine trip, nothing to worry about. You're strong."

"I'm not." So quietly Juliet might be wrong.

"You are."

"The sooner we go," says Jason, "the sooner you're back."

"So long! Farewell! *¡Adios!* Goodbye!" Andrew leans across Bram to call out the window as Jason taps *beep-beep* on the anemic horn and the white truck bumps down the potholed street and around the corner, ignoring a broken stoplight.

Goodbye, Juliet waves in return, practically frantic.

"Can we look for the library?" asks Juliet.

"No." Gloria paces. After she's gone around the room a few times, she disappears into her bedroom.

The children gnaw stale bread. Gloria purchases it fresh from a bakery just beyond the seminary gates, but it arrives out of the oven dry and rough-textured, tasting of the mould it promises to grow.

Keith places his slice on the tabletop, one hole gnawed into the centre, and rests his head on his wrists.

Cigarette smoke trails through beads. What is she doing behind there? She is reading a book — not the Bible but like the Bible, given to her by her parents, Grandma Grace and Grandpa Harold. Juliet has opened its sunrise cover and skimmed its soft pages. One entry for every day of the year, a passage of scripture, a meditation on which to reflect, ending with a suggested prayer, each sounding very much like the others: God, greatness, goodness, love, Jesus, spirit, forgiveness, obedience. Something else about the book: Bram would never read it, not because he doesn't like books about God or Jesus, but because this book is a book written for women. Only a woman would read it, ashes and tears marking the cracks between the pages.

Keith coughs tenderly. Juliet wishes for jam or peanut butter or honey. Emmanuel renders his slice inedible, crumbling it into minute fragments, seeding the hairs on his head.

Someone should tell someone something, but when Juliet says, "Mom?" there is no reply.

By noon, Keith's face and chest will have broken out in red dots. Before suppertime, Gloria will discover that her favourite red blouse is missing from the pile of clothes returned by Bianca. Near midnight, Emmanuel, speckled and inflamed, will thrash off the bedsheets. Gloria will wake at three in the morning to rise and compulsively count the cloth diapers, twice. She will meet Juliet, stumbling to the bathroom, and tell her that some are missing.

The smell of a burning cigarette wreathes Juliet's dreams.

"I think this is a pock." Juliet thrusts her wrist under Gloria's nose. Gloria glances with disinterest. Emmanuel lies naked on her bed, spattered red from the crest of his scalp to the fat soles of his feet.

"It's very itchy," says Juliet. She's finished the adventure story about the fire and the horses. She's read a book about a boy detective named Encyclopedia Brown and has nearly completed a third, set in the Arctic, in which two boys become lost and build their own log cabin to survive a long winter. She wishes the Canadian not-quite-acquaintances had girls instead of boys.

"Can we go to the library today?" she asks, already knowing the answer.

"Don't scratch it." Gloria's hands wearily fold the corners of Emmanuel's diaper and she talks around a pin held between her teeth.

"Mo-o-om," calls Keith.

"Coming!" Gloria cries and the pin falls out. "Juliet, see what your brother wants."

"But what about my pock?"

"Juliet!" Gloria's forehead shines with beads of sweat. She pushes a hank of damp hair behind one ear. "Go, now!"

Juliet stands in the doorway of the room she shares with Keith. "What do you want?" Their room is several steps closer to the flat zinc roof, several steps closer to the sun, and the sun just won't stop staring.

"I want Mom." Keith scratches his chest with socked fists, teeth gritted.

"Mom's changing Emmanuel."

"I'm thirsty." Without glasses, Keith's eyes look shrunken in his tanned brown face.

Juliet comes closer. She picks up Keith's arm.

"What are you doing?" he says.

Silently, Juliet rubs Keith's arm against her own. It isn't fair. She wants the pox too.

"Mo-o-o-om," Keith hollers. "Juliet's touching me!"

Dust settles on every surface. Juliet drops Keith's arm. They look at each other in a silence that is neither hostile nor challenging but worn out. After a while, they hear their mother calling hoarsely, "Juliet?"

Juliet finds Gloria lying slumped on the bed. Her slender body looks even smaller curled around Emmanuel's plump baby flesh, brushing his dimpled thighs.

"It's so hot. Pull the curtains," whispers Gloria. But there are no curtains in the little bedroom.

Juliet touches her mother's wet forehead. It burns. Juliet's heart pounds hard.

"I never got the chicken pox." Gloria opens her eyes and gazes despairingly at Juliet. "As a child. When you're supposed to."

They hear Keith crying, "I'm thirsty."

Gloria lets her eyelids fall. Emmanuel sucks crankily at one exposed breast. Juliet conjures her dad. He's in Jalapa by now, far gone, way up north near the Honduran border (Keith has looked it up in his travel-sized atlas). He's in Jalapa, where there are no telephones, even if Juliet knew how to find one on which to call. He's in Jalapa, where they are fighting the war. He's where the Contra fighters attack villages and farms, running out of the trees to shoot and to burn. The roads are mined with bombs. Helicopters fly overhead. Soldiers launch rockets at green and black planes sent by the Americans.

Juliet pours clean water from the container in the fridge, boiled by her mother and set there to cool.

She carries the cup to Keith. "Mom's sick too," she says.

She picks at the pock on her wrist and knows, sinkingly, *It's just a mosquito bite.*

The maid clucks her tongue to discover Juliet alone, crouched at the table with her book.

Juliet looks at the maid but doesn't see, just as she looks at the page but cannot process the words; inside her skull is a muddle. She tracks a thought towards possibility but disaster swoops, tricks her, traps her, sends her scurrying behind a rock where she huddles, waiting to be devoured. The boys in the book have survived wolves and polar bears, but Juliet, ramrod straight with paralysis, sits in a sheltered room, in a large city populated by people who seem to be friendly, with a cafeteria one floor below, and contemplates dying of starvation.

Then it comes again: low, nonsensical words rising in a crescendo behind the beaded curtain.

Panic weaves invisible threads, ties Juliet to her chair.

The maid, muttering like an untuned radio, pauses to listen, turns, eyes Juliet.

Bianca. Juliet mouths the maid's name.

"*¿Tu madre?*" Bianca demands. Feet slap tiles, beads chatter like fevered teeth. Juliet hears Bianca shouting to her mother — her volume, her certainty and impatience never falter — and then, *swish-swish*, she's back.

Snap-snap, her fingers say to Juliet, who rabbits herself hunched and blinking.

"Come here!" Bianca rubs together the fingers of one hand to indicate money. *"Dinero, dinero,"* she points, and Juliet, confused, obedient, allows herself to be propelled to the cupboard beside the sink, to open the peeling door, to discover, in a plastic glass, a rolled handful of American dollar bills.

Bianca claps: "Now. Quickly. Hurry."

Juliet upends the glass and holds in her palm the slick, greasy-feeling fortune.

Bianca calls to Gloria: "We'll be back." Or: "Don't worry." Or: "You'll never see your daughter ever again."

There is no time for *Help!* as the apartment door slams behind them.

Bianca clamps Juliet's wrist, drags her through the seminary's gates; no one questions this. They scurry the busy, dusty street, and already Juliet, squinting under the steadfast sun, is lost. They veer into a dim and crumbling *tienda*. The woman behind the store counter grins as Bianca produces Juliet with a flourish. The women's hands flag the air expressively, they are emphatic, their lips pucker and purse: *¡Ahh, sí, sí, sí, que no, aye que lástima!*

Juliet could cry.

From darkness behind the counter, the woman produces a chicken. Plucked and pimpled, it is mercifully headless, but Juliet recoils. Bianca taps the hand in which the dollars are clasped, unfolds and counts bills, licking her thumb: mostly ones and fives. A bag of rice, half-filled, is thrown onto the counter, a jug of dark cooking oil, salt, sugar, eggs. The women argue back and forth, but in the end Bianca insists on only the chicken. She pays and returns the change to Juliet, who doesn't trust her, and who cannot refuse the still body, placed into her arms like a brand-new baby wrapped in plastic, smelling of something disturbing and recognizable, almost human: faint rot, flesh.

Everything is a peripheral blur as Juliet chases Bianca's smudged heels in pitted flip-flops along the rutted road, through a break in a knocked-down wall, into a tiny courtyard where four small children, partially clothed, play in dust beneath a laden clothesline. Juliet feels her lungs expanding, contracting. The building is four storeys tall, its face entirely ripped off, each floor and its contents — flapping sheets and cooking fires — visible from below.

Emmanuel's diapers swing on the line overhead. Beside the diapers hang her mother's red blouse and a pair of shorts Juliet recognizes as belonging to herself, though all are so removed, flapping in this location, that she feels no attachment.

A thought bursts, collapses: She imagines herself pinned to the clothesline.

Bianca unbuttons her dress and grabs the smallest child, who feeds and squirms, craning his neck to examine this pale stranger. Juliet is obvious, and reduced. She hides behind herself because she is both naked and disguised in broad daylight; she is only what she appears to be, all surface.

Bianca is shouting names: her children's, which she wants Juliet to repeat. An old woman materializes with displeasure from the building's bowels, like a dried-apple doll brought to life. For no apparent reason she slaps one of the children, and the little boy stops his howl with his thumb. For this he is slapped again.

"*Mi madre*," says Bianca. The woman offers Juliet a triangular pastry. "*Pico, pico*," she repeats. Juliet will cry now. She will cry.

"Psst . . ." With her free hand Bianca snatches a frayed cloth off the line and the old woman wraps several pastries, then balances the package atop Juliet's chicken. Juliet's chin holds everything in place, and she is helpless as the old woman draws money from her fingers.

Bianca pulls the baby off her breast, still sucking. He screams, but not for long; maybe he expects a smack. He cannot crawl, but sits on his bottom and tugs his penis.

Pico. It is a sweet glazed bread, filled with soft cheese. Nothing could taste finer, no dough could be more tender, melting on Juliet's tongue. Over the blue gas flame, a pot of salted water and one whole chicken boils and bubbles and fills the sweltering rooms with the smell of a far-off home — in another country, where this is winter's comfort food. Bianca is satisfied, and gone. She is gone.

Gloria swallows four tablespoons of hot soup; she does not ask where it has come from, and Juliet does not think to tell. Keith drinks two bowls. Juliet tears both drumsticks off the carcass, with some effort and spilled broth and flaring flame. The sigh of gas hissing and alight accompanies their sleep. Around midnight the tank runs empty; for the first night in a while, the apartment quiets.

By morning, the *pico* has staled. Emmanuel will not be content to lie beside his mother for even one minute more, and Juliet trails behind as senseless instinct toddles him towards electrical outlets and dangling cords and open windows and exposed fan blades.

Bianca doesn't come. The thought occurs to Juliet while she wearily gnaws a cold chicken bone, but Emmanuel, neglected, tumbles down the steps into the main room, and Juliet doesn't think of it again.

He bounces upright and stares at her, chin smeared in blood.

"Mom!!!" yells Juliet, clutching him, trying. Wet washcloth. There is no ice. Cold water.

"Goddammit," cries Gloria. Spots of blood dribble to the floor, down Emmanuel's bare chest, onto Gloria's sheets and her greying T-shirt and Juliet's shoulder. "Nobody else is allowed to say that."

"Then why are you?"

It's just a split lip, but Juliet is to blame and she hates being to blame.

"Stop feeling sorry for yourself," says Gloria, prone. She is weak, but that does not stop her from being withering.

"I miss Laci." Juliet feels her lips tremble. It is the closest she can come to saying: I want to go home. Laci, her best friend in Indiana, loved playing with Emmanuel, cradling and swaddling him like a living doll, and Emmanuel adored her right back.

But his feelings towards Juliet are ambivalent. When she tries to entertain him in their sweltering rooms, he fights and fusses. He snaps her crayons in half and rips up drawings for the fun of it, and he can't drink anything out of a cup without spilling.

There goes the rest of the day.

It is dusk when Bram arrives. He appears out of the half-light: they'd forgotten him. He is jaunty from his journey, slap-happy, brimming with jokes and camaraderie and dust blown through open windows, sights unimaginable. He walks into this forlorn place a foreigner in a distant land, and just as unwelcome.

"Fix this mess!" croaks Gloria from the bedroom, and Juliet hates her. Hasn't she, Juliet, tried? Hasn't she done her best? And all her mother sees is a mess. Ambushed, Juliet becomes a furious projectile: she runs roaring around the table, bashes a chair and knocks it down, sprints past her father and out of the apartment, leaving behind an echo of confusion.

"Juliet?"

She pants in the wide-open courtyard. In crashing darkness she searches for the fort she and Keith have built out of fallen palm leaves against the chain-link fence. In luminous darkness she destroys it, and feels much better. Peaceful. Stars prick the night sky. The city's lights pale by comparison, yellowed, stinking of diesel fuel.

"Juliet?"

She squats under a bare tree and watches him standing in the seminary hallway staring out. Her father is nothing but shadow, cut from a piece of purple construction paper. He can't see her.

"I know you're out here," he says. "Juliet, let's not give your mom more to worry about."

Silence.

"Come out, come out, wherever you are."

Juliet slinks beneath shadows until she's close enough to yell, "Boo!"

Bram doesn't twitch. Juliet wants something on his face that he won't show her: fear, apology, relief, anger?

"I know it's been tough." He squeezes her shoulder. They climb the stairs to the apartment. "But I'm home now." They open the apartment door to discover — Emmanuel peeing in the corner of the main room, Keith propped in a chair, idly observing.

"This is not okay," says Bram. He does not raise his voice. He lowers and softens it, making of it a gloved fist of disappointment. "I left you in charge, Keith. I expect better."

Keith freezes, Emmanuel dribbles, and from the bedroom Gloria yells, "Leave them alone, coming in here like a big bully . . ."

Calmly, Bram spanks Emmanuel, one whack on bare speckled bottom, as if he hasn't even noticed the fat lip or the pox. He would do the same to Keith, but there isn't time: Gloria propels herself through shrieking beads towards Bram's throat.

"If you ever ever ever —" she cries, but Bram holds Emmanuel out to her.

"Stop yourself, Gloria," he says.

Juliet doesn't know if her mother would actually hit her father. She has seen Gloria pitch at him half a loaf of unsliced homemade bread, across the dinner table, an act not meant to be funny that instantly became a family joke; but Juliet cannot make this into a joke. It won't fit. Like Keith, Juliet is nothing but eyes, watching her mother yank Emmanuel from her father's grasp, watching her squeeze Emmanuel fiercely until he squeals in protest. He's already forgotten the spank; bewildered, he beats Gloria's shoulder, kicks her soft belly.

Holding him, she passes through the beads, a mama bear entering unnavigable black forest. The beads sway and whisper, sway and swing, and, finally, hang silent too.

"Your mother —" begins Bram, but he takes one step backwards and splashes into the puddle of urine, and this is the moment that recasts the tumbling moments that came before, this is their rescue and delivery. Bram pretends to skid, threatens to slip and fall, arms comically spinning, until Juliet and Keith are goaded to laughter, and even Gloria drags herself out for a look and a snort.

"All better?" says Bram.

"You always think so." Gloria crawls back to bed.

"It always is."

Juliet is down to the last book in the pile from the Canadian boys — about a hunting dog — and she has not forgotten the library.

"Maybe today —" she says as her mother collapses into a chair on the other side of the table, but the door bangs open, and Juliet is first to see Bianca. The blouse hangs loose on her narrow shoulders, but red is the colour Bianca is meant to be wearing, red like painted lips, like candy; she radiates vigour and health.

Gloria, too weak for coffee after a cold morning shower, turns and gasps. "My blouse," she says in English.

Bianca, bustling, chatting, filling the sink with water, cannot understand, and has no warning.

"My blouse, my blouse." Scarred with dried pocks, thin and pale, Gloria is a record player skipping, her voice rising with her body. Her fury flowers. It blooms, explodes. Petals scatter.

Bianca pauses, cocks her head to listen.

"Mine." Gloria points. Fury cannot calm itself to be translated. "That's mine. You stole it. Thief!"

"Mom!" Juliet runs around the table.

"And our diapers," says Gloria. "Where are my baby's diapers?"

"Mom." Juliet tugs her mother's arm. Keith stares at his plate and Emmanuel chuckles, but Bianca only dries her hands on her skirt, puzzled.

"Get out! You're not welcome here. Out!"

"Please?" whispers Juliet.

"She's taken advantage of us, Juliet. You don't understand. You stay out of it."

In this blouse Bianca is fearless, if ever she were anything but. She dries her hands again, lifts the bucket and the mop, though she does not shut the door behind her. Juliet wishes to run after her and explain, but there is nothing to be untangled by explanation, nor are Juliet's silent pleas addressed to Bianca. Bianca is a thief, this is true. The diapers are gone, this is true. But Bianca's baby will get to wear them; but you should see her house, Mom; but she made you soup. You got better.

Gloria grips the back of a chair, the eloquently carved wood under her fingers dark with vines. She is thinking, hard. She goes to the cupboard and swings the door.

"The dollars," she says.

Juliet opens her mouth, closes it.

"She stole the dollars too."

Juliet studies the unmopped tiles, identifies a print that matches her own foot. She is trying to remember what happened to the leftover bills. Were there any? Stealthily she feels in the pockets of her shorts, the same pair she's worn for days, and removes her hand as if it's touched fire.

She licks her lips.

"It wasn't much," says Gloria. Petals sink to earth. Stillness settles in the breezeless room. "It wasn't much, but I should have known better. I'll speak to the director."

"Mom?"

"Not right now, Juliet. I need to think."

Juliet senses a deeply sad ending, one she feels unable to bear, yet craves. She begins weeping while there is still hope, and staunches her tears with pages of the book.

"What on earth?" says Gloria with irritation, not interest. She claps Emmanuel to her hip; she's made her decision, and while she's out, Juliet must be in charge of Keith.

"I'm in charge of me!" Keith yells from the bedroom, but Gloria is gone.

Juliet runs to the cupboard and stuffs the roll of bills into the plastic cup. It takes only a few seconds and she thinks, *There*, as if everything has been put right again, and for a flash it seems so. She returns to the book, picks it up, but an empty restlessness chokes her at the hollow of her neck, where she wants to swallow but cannot. The sensation unspins itself like a cape whirling around her body, envelops her; thins the words on the page, wrings from her the ability to feel.

When she's older she'll know the word for it: *desolation*.

She lays the book on the table, pages spread, cracking the spine.

Gloria charges back into the apartment. Confrontation has had a medicinal effect, flushing her skin with colour, thickening her hair, plumping her lips.

"Done," she says, setting Emmanuel on the floor. She goes to the cupboard for a glass and continues, swishing open the rotted door, "The director has promised me swift action. I actually feel bilingual today. I felt like I could really and honestly speak Spanish. I wish your father had been there to see —"

In her hand is the cup with the wad of American dollar bills. She tips it and the money falls onto the counter. "But . . ." She cannot believe what she is seeing, and spreads the money flat, counts it.

"Six dollars missing . . . but . . ."

Juliet blinks.

"But I didn't see it before? But it wasn't there? She took it. She took it, didn't she? She took it."

Gloria turns to ask Juliet, but only because Juliet is there to ask, not because Gloria expects an answer.

"He's going to fire her," Gloria says, almost to herself.

"But then," she says after a moment, "she did take the blouse. And the diapers."

Emmanuel yanks on the beads hung across the bedroom door, and in his hands, in one smooth movement, they come apart. Their hanging patterns disintegrate and pour like tropical rain on the floor, each jewelled ball landing with a tinkle, a splash, rolling the tiles to the far corners of the room, under the apartment door, down the stairs, beyond.

It is the sound of calamity, and then of quiet. It is the

sound of that which cannot be unsaid, or undone; and the silence afterwards, the immediacy of what seems not so terrible after all.

"Let's go to the library," offers Gloria.

"Now? Today?" Juliet is incredulous.

"Why not?" With her bare foot, Gloria kicks aside a scramble of beads.

After all this time, it isn't far.

They cross one anarchic street, trudge past a low concrete wall painted with martyrs of the revolution. Hats, bandanas, fields, faces, babies, guns; primary colours. Or perhaps these are revolution's children. Gloria isn't certain. She reads the slogans several times but cannot promise that her translation is correct.

"There?" Juliet points to a lone square building, like a child's block, painted bright yellow with windows all along one side.

Gloria's body sags under Emmanuel's weight, and Keith trails behind in silent misery. It is not far, but suddenly it seems they will never arrive. Midday heat streaks down upon them; their hair will catch fire.

They wade through a bare field with grass burnt dead from the sun.

Behind its heavy door, the library is quiet. Its shelves are half-filled; you might say, mostly empty. Juliet kneels and selects a picture book, opens it. Disappointment crests and buries her. She can't read this book. She can't read any of the books in this library. It is like staggering through a desert towards what looks like a pool of clean, clear water and discovering as you kneel to drink that cupped in your hands is sand, that you are washing your face in a pool of sand.

"Mom?" she whispers.

"Yes?"

"It's in Spanish!"

Gloria huffs a small laugh; she knew it all along.

They could walk home the way they came, but Gloria is lost in the jumbled world and today she trusts no one. They cross a different field and another street, dodging cars whose drivers — men — honk and call to Gloria. She doesn't exactly ignore them; she mutters her disgust as they escape into a neighbourhood that resembles a war zone, pitted and scarred.

It is Gloria who sees the diapers flapping from the clothesline. White, thick, triple-padded, absorbent, superior, American-made cloth diapers. She stops in the street.

"Could it be?" she asks, and in confirmation, Bianca steps out of the hole in her wall before them, holding her baby. He is peppered with pocks.

The women face each other.

Gloria doesn't say, *My diapers*, just turns and looks at them.

Bianca does not say, *My poor sick baby*. She says, "You're lost? Come, come. This way."

Gloria and the children obey in dull silence. They are pallid by comparison, blanched of strength, bewildered and weary.

At the seminary gates Bianca reaches with her free hand for Gloria's, clasps it, and Juliet sees what could be: she imagines as if it were happening Bianca removing the red blouse like a snake shedding skin, new skin beneath the old. Imagines her mother's arm sliding into warmed silky fabric in reverse, pocks erased. She imagines her mother saying, *I was wrong*.

But instead, after a moment, Gloria lets go. She says, "*Gracias*," and they leave Bianca and her baby outside the gates, climb the steps to their apartment. It is hot, as always. The rooms smell of an unflushed toilet and underfoot the tiles are gritty.

"Mom," whispers Juliet. What would happen if she were to tell?

Gloria gazes at her, eyes glazed with exhaustion. "Did you find what you wanted, Juliet?"

"Mom?"

"At the library?"

Oh.

"Did you? Sweetheart?"

Juliet nods imperceptibly. Her mother is already halfway to her bedroom, through the now-exposed doorway. Nothing so terrible, nothing so terrible.

Emmanuel pops a bead in his mouth and rolls it across his tongue. When Juliet tries to dig it out with her finger, he screeches, and Gloria calls out blindly, "Whatever you're doing, Juliet, just stop."

Emmanuel swallows; gone.

THE ECSTATIC

"You can endure all kinds of things, but that's not living," Charlotte says to Juliet. "Living is when you're going somewhere with someone you love."

They are in the new guesthouse. They kneel barefoot on Charlotte's mattress: the upper bunk of a bed in a room Charlotte shares with other Roots of Justice volunteers, though it's just the two of them on this soft afternoon. The room is always dark, its lone window shaded by trees, ceiling low over their heads. Squat candles line the metal rails at the head and foot of the bed. Charlotte has taken time to carve out her own space in a place that is always and only a temporary home. Most Roots of Justice volunteers travel frequently; some are sent to live for a month or more in outlying villages, wherever the danger is most present, but not Charlotte. Charlotte has yet to be sent.

Charlotte holds out a candle: "Smell this."

Juliet bends, palms sunk into the thin mattress, breathes a scent smoky and sweet, emanating not from the unburnt candle but from Charlotte herself, her hair swinging past her ribs. The bed sways.

"This is my mother's kitchen. Vanilla. She was always baking something good," says Charlotte. She holds out another. "Close your eyes. When you're blind, your other senses become stronger. Patchouli. This is Mexico, and my first true love. And here's the Jersey Shore every summer of my life except this one. Coconut oil. One more — this is spring in my grandmother's yard. Peonies in bloom."

Inside her mind, Juliet sees everything that Charlotte is showing her.

"Open your eyes. Your turn."

"My turn?"

"You tell me. Where are you coming from? Where are you going?"

Conversations with Charlotte are like nothing Juliet has ever known. She would wrap them whole in scraps of fabric and store them for later examination if she knew how. To Charlotte, Juliet is a whole person who is only incidentally a child. Juliet is free to put her head back and think, to take her time, to imagine, to wait for an important thought to shake loose and float into view.

"French fries with ketchup in the back of the car. The creek overflowed and it smelled like . . . worms. Well, mud and worms. My best friend —" Juliet stops to consider. Her eyes squeeze shut the better to see Laci, as if it were the two of them sitting side by side on Laci's bed, each holding one half of a book about unicorns, and Laci smells like, Laci smells like — "Strawberries. But not real strawberries, strawberries like a Strawberry Shortcake doll."

Juliet waits with her eyes closed. Charlotte does not comment or judge. She does not say, "You must miss her," because the obvious does not need saying. Nor does she remark upon Juliet's brilliance or creativity; she does not flatter or assess. She lingers in the whorls of their shared thoughts.

"Today, this afternoon, smells like sand," Charlotte says. "And we're nowhere near the beach."

"Like *frijoles*." Juliet opens her eyes again. Maybe the guest-house cook is making beans for supper. She adjusts her gaze to the posters thumbtacked to the wall all around Charlotte's bed: golden women, some of them naked, coupled and melting into an embrace with a man, or alone in interior contemplation, or alone and dead, as in Juliet's favourite: ravishing Ophelia, wreathed in flowers and floating down a river. She could fall right in, washed by waves of sweet sadness, as if she herself were cloaked in flowing white robes, her hair streaming, as if she herself were a vision of departed loveliness, pale skin and green eyes.

Juliet wants something when she looks at the pictures. She aches. She cannot name the want because it exists only in evocation. The unicorn's horn and lifted front leg and delicate white hoof. The curve of a rainbow. Fairy wings. Heavy princess gowns. A landscape of misty forest and rolling green hills. Hair. Gauzy imaginary impossible shimmering beauty.

"Stay just like that." Charlotte opens a small black book filled with blank pages. She says, "Your life is a canvas on which you can paint — anything, anything at all, so long as you don't hesitate."

But she herself hesitates, pencil hovering over empty page. "Yes," she says, considering. "Because hesitation is not the same thing as meditation. Because doubt is not the same thing as patience. Where were you going when you ate french fries with ketchup in the back seat of the car?"

Juliet holds still, arms clasped around knees, toes pointing to the ceiling. "Sunday drive," she says.

"Ah," says Charlotte.

"I remember when we drove over the creek," says Juliet. "It sounded like thunder, and the water was washing over the bridge, and we stopped and my mom was mad that we got out and looked, but my dad wouldn't let us fall in."

Charlotte is staring at Juliet as if Juliet were form and shape and shadow rather than girl. The bed rocks under her shifting hips; she settles herself more deeply. "Your dad has his arms around all of us," she says.

Juliet doesn't like this, but it sounds true enough.

"Look." Charlotte holds out the page and Juliet sees herself, curled and floating. In the sketch, Juliet's eyes are closed in her tilted head; her hair is much longer than her real hair and it flows around her body.

Charlotte gives Juliet the book and the pencil. "Your turn. You draw me." She poses with her head on an angle, one shoulder dropped. "Don't lift the pencil. Don't look at the page. Keep your eyes on me and draw with one single line."

I can't, Juliet thinks, but the lone line presses onward, intertwines with itself like thread that will never be unwound. Who would want this thread unwound? It makes a sprawling-here, crammed-there heap of a picture. Part woman, part map.

"The shoreline and the sea," says Charlotte. She rips the page from the book and tacks it low, near her pillow.

When it is time to go home, Juliet sprints from the Roots of Justice guesthouse to her own new house, just down the street. She never walks when she can run. Children who have gathered in a neighbour's yard to watch a television propped in a window turn their gaze to look at Juliet instead.

Both guesthouse and Juliet's new home lie under the shadow of a hill carved with the giant letters *FSLN*, the abbreviated name of the ruling party. But while the yard at the guesthouse is bare dirt shaded by high, heavy foliage, the yard at home is bright and sunlit, the house surrounded by palm-fronded coconut trees out front, a grove of banana varieties beside the kitchen, and spiny lime trees out the bedroom windows. The rooms in the guesthouse are crowded, but at home Juliet and her brothers can run races through the long central room and around the sunken indoor courtyard that stinks of Emmanuel's urine. Gloria has given up trying to stop him. She lets him run naked like any Nicaraguan toddler.

Not everyone approves. The Roots of Justice office has been squeezed, for reasons of economy and convenience, into the front room of Juliet's home. Volunteers come and go, using the Friesens' kitchen and bathroom like their own, and some of them hold opinions about children and hygiene that run counter to Gloria's.

Gloria doesn't fight directly. But she has an expressive absence of smile, a twitching eyelid, a way of grabbing a passing child and thrusting him or her into the midst of a conversation like a pawn into a battle zone: "What was that you were saying about feces? This is useful information, Juliet. Something about pinworms?"

The office is for grown-ups, but Juliet knows what is there to be found: words. Every surface is littered with stacks of field notes, newsletters, clippings, purple mimeographed government forms, yellow pads of foolscap beside the telephone with messages jotted in Gloria's looping hand. Words are like candy, if candy was free for the taking, and Juliet will read anything — signs, cereal boxes, books on any subject; she has no awareness of boundaries, no compunction about snooping, no care for the dangers of evil.

In stolen moments, Juliet reads what must be the worst of it, tracking a volunteer's scrawl across the page. Eyewitness reports from the *campo*, of the war:

We arrived in the village of Limay several hours after the aerial bombing of its military base. A witness, Maria, age 12, reported that she and her sister Lucia-Ana, age 14, had gone to the base to sell pastries. They saw a strange plane in the sky that could fly forward and backward. They knew that it was the Americans and they ran. Artillery was fired. "We are killed!" Maria remembers screaming. Her sister was struck by shrapnel and died instantly, but Maria hid safely behind a low wall. Later, their father and brothers retrieved Lucia-Ana's body parts with a shovel. A Roots of Justice volunteer returned to continue searching when it was discovered that some parts were missing.

As protection, Juliet thinks: It is happening far away from here, it is happening to people who don't look like me. The real Nicaraguan children at school seem impervious to its happening, may not even know that it is — like the foot of a body that does not know its hand has been cut wide open.

"There you are, Juliet. Keith is looking for you. Go and play and stay outside. Emmanuel's finally down for a nap."

Their street is paved, the yards fenced with metal bars standing in poured concrete, but behind theirs are many more streets, of pocked dirt, along which smaller houses of wood and tin crowd to the foot of the hill. Juliet and Keith follow an ox cart around the corner, stepping over patties of steaming fresh dung.

They enter a tiny *tienda* stuffed into the front room of someone's house. Keith has enough for a packet of Chiclets, which they open and share. They examine the shelves in the middle of the room: nothing but jam. Jam is rare. Juliet picks up a jar to read the label, but the words are neither English nor Spanish: an alphabet composed of ordinary letters mixed with backwards *R*'s and *N*'s and upside-down *V*'s and too few vowels.

"Cherry?" She squints at the picture, but they don't have enough money to buy a jar.

The store owner rocks in a chair in the corner, breast-feeding a large toddler. Tongue against the roof of her mouth — *tst, tst, tst* — she shoos away the children crowding the door, who have followed Juliet and Keith in expectation of some light diversion.

The silhouette of Sandino, hero of a long-ago failed revolution, is spray-painted in black on the wall beside the front door, but that won't help them find this store again: Sandino is everywhere in this neighbourhood. He wears a hat. Fifty years ago he was killed by assassination — a peasant who demanded more for the people of Nicaragua than the dictator was willing to give, a story known to poor nations everywhere. A few with all and most with nothing. The Sandinista government is rewriting the story by taking back from those with too much and sharing it out equally: farms, land, food, education.

In this neighbourhood, everyone is a Sandinista, even Juliet and Keith. But at school it is the opposite. No one is.

Mornings mean school, afternoons mean home. Mornings make Juliet's stomach churn and turn, as though she's coming down with the flu, which is always, miraculously, cured by the afternoon. It is like living two disconnected lives.

But then, so much in her every day is bifurcated, split down the middle, parts separated one from the other, never touching, with only herself the link between strange, opposing, untouchable solitudes. American; Sandinista. Rich; poor. Free; constrained. Admired; scorned. Befriended; alone.

Just after six o'clock in the morning, and already the sky is bright and swarming hot. Mingled aromas of hot plastic, rusted springs, and flowering trees pervade this new season as the bus wends its way through Managua's better neighbourhoods, collecting Nicaraguan children born into wealth, children of foreign diplomats and of U.S. embassy employees. Juliet and Keith are the only children of peace workers. (Is that even a profession?)

Despite the school's tidy classrooms and manicured grass and swept stone pathways, Juliet cannot find her way. She is chronically, bafflingly late, searching the campus for a familiar face, disoriented, wandering, and it does not get easier over time. She gets lost on the playground. The ringing bells indicate different things at different times, and she cannot keep their meaning straight — was that the first or the second bell, and is she supposed to be in art class or at lunch? On odd days, at unexpected times, she is removed from her peers to sit with a handful of other children, most of them kindergartners — children of foreign diplomats who are also learning Spanish for the first time.

Placed into the fourth grade late in the term, Juliet will never catch up. Classes are conducted in English, which the teacher speaks with a Nicaraguan accent, but this offers Juliet no apparent advantage. She cannot remember the names of the seven seas, she confuses latitude and longitude; in desperation she checks the test of the girl sitting next to her — cheater. Sick at heart, she rips to shreds a note from the teacher and sends it fluttering out the open bus window. Keith doesn't tell. He has a facility for languages, and no one has suggested he sit with kindergartners.

At dawn, Gloria brushes Juliet's fine hair until it crackles with electricity and clips it behind her ears with pastel green barrettes. The barrettes arrived with an incoming delegation, in one of Grandma Grace's regular care packages, cardboard boxes crammed with small luxuries: homemade granola, Dinky cars, underwear, Black Stallion books, even a potty chair for Emmanuel. In return, Gloria writes long letters on yellow foolscap to send back with outgoing delegations. If the children need something Gloria makes a request, though never for herself.

In the bathroom mirror at home, Juliet believes in the power of new green barrettes. But at school they render her neither less obvious nor less invisible, the impossible reality in which she's trapped. She hovers at the rear of the classroom while the other students push through the open doorway, loose and free with laughter as they greet and compare and bump against Juliet, who might as well be furniture.

"Juliet," says the teacher. "Juliet, sit down. Now."

She has managed to be last, and those same students turn at their desks and stare with cool appraisal. I had lots of friends back home! Juliet imagines shouting at them. It is true, but it does not matter. She can't pick up who she was before and by force carry her across the barrier of stranger.

For phys ed, Juliet's class is herded down to a spacious green playing field, immaculately maintained, where they are split into separate groups of boys and girls. The girls shed uniforms inside a concrete building at the far end of the field. The room is crowded; slits for light are cut into the walls at the top. Juliet wears a poor facsimile of the school's uniform: lime-green skirt instead of navy; white T-shirt standing in for a buttoned blouse, the ironed-on insignia peeling off. She doesn't care but the other girls do, and she understands that she is supposed to too. Not caring makes her even more of a stranger. But if she cared, she couldn't bear to come to school in the wrong uniform, and she has no choice: there is a lag time between letters to Grandma Grace and packages in reply, and she is still waiting for navy, and for buttons.

On the shining grass, Juliet runs fastest, jumps farthest, throws like a boy, but her talents are themselves humiliating, inappropriate. Girls don't try; girls don't sweat.

Back in the change room, Juliet searches the floor and under the bench, but she can't find Grandma Grace's gift.

Hoarsely, in English, she whispers, "Has anyone seen my green barrettes?"

"Has anyone seen my green barrettes?" mimics the girl sitting next to her, dark thigh exposed beneath pink lace panties, and the phrase is repeated, voices rollicking off concrete walls, disappearing into Spanish, which the other girls speak when not in the classroom, where they are required to use English.

She doesn't care, but the teacher does. "Your hair is a mess." The fault is Juliet's. Explanations are worse than useless, holes dug in quicksand, speeding her descent.

But when she lays her cheek against the cool plastic bus seat, hair blowing loose in the wind, she is already on the mend. Mercifully, Juliet and Keith are dispensed outside their fence. They clank through the gate, shuffling their running shoes, tossing their backpacks. It is one o'clock, and the rest of the day remains openly, lusciously theirs.

Today the main room of their house hums with volunteers and religion, cigarettes crunched out in clay ashtrays. From a prayer circle on the floor, Gloria rises and greets them with a handful of coins. "Go and buy yourselves a snack. And take Emmanuel."

The afternoon wants them. Emmanuel is a troublesome pet cajoled and soothed by bribery. The coins are enough for crackers and *crema* at a little *tienda* behind their house, not the one with the jam. At almost every house something is for sale: tortillas, or beer, or eggs. The woman at the window peels a ripe mango and passes the pit through the window for Emmanuel to suck on. It is shady in this yard, comfortable with the murmuring cluck of hens, and Juliet and Keith squat on their heels and squeeze the sweet, salty *crema* onto damp white crackers.

"I hate school," says Juliet.

Keith doesn't have to say anything.

"They stole my green barrettes," she says. "At least, I think so. Maybe I lost them. Maybe they fell under the benches or something. I don't know."

Keith says, "I'm thirsty."

They crave shaved ice drizzled with syrup, sold from the dripping wooden cart that is often at the park. They debate, on their way, the best flavour and the likelihood of finding the cart, and they are almost there before they realize something is missing: Emmanuel. It is too awful to consider him forgotten in the shaded yard, sucking on a mango pit, tended by hens. Juliet blames Keith, who knows their mother will blame Juliet, who is the next thing to hysterical when they are found, as they run down the street, by some children, one of whom holds Emmanuel in her arms. He isn't crying or scared or sad. The girl hops him on her hip; she is lean, her skirt dark, hair carefully brushed; no taller than Juliet, but older. Breasts under her white blouse.

"*Pobrecito*," she coos to Emmanuel, continuing to cradle him as they walk together. "*Gordito. Papacito. Muñequito.*"

She knows them, but they don't recognize her until she steps into context, through the Roots of Justice guesthouse gate and around the back to the kitchen, where the cook greets them with an energy that could be mistaken for anger. The girl is the cook's daughter; the anger, fierce kindness fired by exhaustion.

Out, out, out, the cook whisks the children away from the tiny, sweltering kitchen into the yard. But in a moment she carries out three tall plastic cups filled with sweet, watery milk flavoured with cocoa and thickened with pounded corn — *tiste*. The plastic is rubbery and pliant between the teeth. The corn sifts like sediment to the bottom and whirls amongst melting ice cubes: sand and rocks. Juliet and Keith sit on cement blocks in the damp yard, and the cook's daughter, whose name they now know is Marta, sits on her heels and shares her drink with Emmanuel. Neighbourhood children wait outside the gate, but as the skies darken they begin to drift.

The rainy season is upon them, humidity standing amongst thick greens and fat fruits, clouds filling up with warm rain that wants to pour before suppertime, washing the world briefly clean again: the blessed moment before wet turns to steam.

The cook says that the Friesen children must go home too. The guesthouse is empty now, but soon it will be full of Americans, a new delegation arriving to stay. Her daughter Marta needs to help: Food for many tonight! Juliet understands by inclination, by tilting her head and listening without her ears, but Keith understands every word and replies in Spanish. Thank you for the *bebidas*.

Something special for your supper, the cook promises. That means the Friesen children will eat at the guesthouse tonight, and not in a restaurant or around their own kitchen table, where sometimes they share meals with their mother and their father, though more often, lately, with their mother only.

Gloria is glad to get out of the house. She makes Juliet and Keith wash their faces and she scrubs Emmanuel's until he howls (Juliet thinks there is some correlation between howling and cleanliness, some invisible rule that her mother follows: only through misery shalt thou be made clean). Gloria herself is wearing lipstick and mascara. Juliet watches her in the bathroom mirror.

"There," says Gloria to her reflection, and smacks her lips together.

The rain has stopped and the air sticks to the skin. Gloria hustles the children down the sidewalk to the guesthouse, only to find they've arrived early. Supper is not ready. The guesthouse has not expanded to accept the fourteen newcomers and their oversized luggage; it has contracted, and the atmosphere tingles with nerves and confusion and mile-long questions.

Grown-ups crowd the porch, clutching plastic cups of water or — for the braver among them — of *tiste*.

Juliet swims like a fish into the volunteers' bedroom: empty. She climbs up to Charlotte's bunk and sits on the mattress in the dark. *Snooping.* If she were caught, that's what it would be called. She sniffs the candles, digs her forearms into the pillow and bumps against the little black book. Her fingers travel inside its pages, exposing pencilled naked bodies in parts and whole, carefully drawn bones and muscles, and scattered words that come apart at the seams: *What if freedom calls for anger and not love? Transpose your life. Sunday drive. Here is the skyline; here is the shore; my body and yours, nothing more. Don't think, create.*

Juliet startles as someone bumps into the room in error. Blinking up at her from the doorway: "Is this the bathroom?"

"No."

"Oh."

Perhaps the person cannot see that Juliet is a child; perhaps her eyes have not adjusted to the dim. The woman looks half-blind behind owlish glasses, and terrified, as if a bomb might fall from the sky upon her head at any moment. She is waiting for Juliet to give her some direction. She is one of the fourteen newcomers: protestors from Ohio, all of them milling about, stumbling over backpacks and guitar cases, and quite shocked to discover only one toilet in the house.

DO NOT FLUSH TOILET PAPER, reads the sign on the wall, but someone will, guaranteed.

"It's by the kitchen," Juliet says at last.

"Thank you, dear."

Backing down the metal ladder, Juliet leans and places her face upon the pillow, brushing it lightly with her nose. She inhales Charlotte.

She finds Keith on the porch, where he is alone — temporarily. Certain delegates make a beeline for children; others are oblivious to their existence. All possess a similar look upon entering their new tropical reality, regardless of sex or age: dazed, sweat beading above upper lips, swamped armpits, furry legs, socks with sandals, insistent bellies beneath green T-shirts.

Now one approaches and bends to asks the usual questions, which the children consider scarcely worthy of reply. How old are you? Do you go to school? Do you speak Spanish?

Juliet fakes a Nicaraguan accent; she has practised while gazing into the bathroom mirror at home. Keith doesn't need to fake anything: his Spanish is streetwise and quick and impresses the man, whom the children nickname Old Yeller, after his teeth.

Few of the delegates speak Spanish. They are in the country for only two weeks, reliant on translators, on Bram and the other volunteers, their visas approved by the Sandinista government. They will be driven to the countryside, to the edges of the war zone, where they will mill about on co-operative farms and at health clinics, much as they do now.

It is time to eat at last.

Everyone gathers in the main room around tables pushed together and draped in plastic. Bram blesses the meal with a brevity that reminds everyone that children are present. The cook takes her cue and produces, with a flourish, a feast sourced by ingenious means: one whole fish for each guest, cleaned and roasted with head intact, served on a plastic plate with a single ring of fried onion decorating its browned and crusty upward-staring side.

But the tallest, skinniest, palest pair of people Juliet and Keith have ever seen recoil in horror: they are vegans. The Ghost Twins. (Even after they are revealed to be husband and wife, Juliet and Keith think of them as a weirdly fused brother and sister.)

In a flash, Marta, the cook's daughter, removes the offending offering. "We don't want to make a fuss," the Ghost Twins say, "but there is such a thing as cross-contamination. What are the beans fried in? Is there butter on the vegetables?"

Bram assures them that all is well and unbuttered, but he may or may not be telling the truth. This is not the kind of disturbance that troubles him.

Gloria says, "The cabbage salad is dressed with lemon and salt. You must try it."

The Ghost Twins are a threat only to themselves. They cannot spoil the air of celebration that attends this occasion.

After the meal, Gloria tunes a guitar and suggestions are called out, voices join in. Emmanuel drums on his plate with his spoon. When finally he dissolves, he is plucked up by Charlotte and danced onto the porch, where the liquid air stands still.

The heat in the room expands: everyone wears it. Bare bulbs swing drunkenly, tossing wild shadows onto bright turquoise walls.

Juliet and Keith and Emmanuel are rarities in a closed world. How easily Juliet has adapted to the dangers and privileges: sneaking under the drifting blue haze of cigarette smoke, picking her way through the forest of adult limbs, catching scenes like pictures unfolded, words snagged, bedtime avoided. She steps off the porch beyond the ring of light. Against her shoulder blades the rough concrete wall is cool. The night breathes, alive — *there* — she can hear its breath: a soft moan like a knife carving a cut between her ribs. Juliet scans the darkness, traces a three-headed figure entangled beside chain-link fencing, bodies connected, swaying in unison. In this light, at this hour, in this place, she believes she is seeing a mythical creature, a figure of magic.

The screen door at the back of the house bangs open, shedding a gash of light: Marta tosses a pan of dirty water at the bushes. The screen door slams shut. Juliet kneels and finds against her toe a perfectly smooth mango; its thick skin gives way under her thumb, holding the shape of her print.

"Hey, you." Charlotte stops, barefoot in the shadows. "What have you found?" Emmanuel holds two fists of her dark hair. Juliet turns, but no one stands beside the fence. Charlotte waits patiently for her reply.

"I found a mango," says Juliet.

"Anything else?"

Juliet holds it out. "I hate school."

"Do you?" Charlotte lifts the mango to her nose and inhales the scent of ripeness and sweetness before returning it to Juliet's open palm. The fruit's skin opens along a hairline crack, leaking sticky juice.

"Someone stole my green barrettes today."

"That's not right," says Charlotte.

"I know. But I don't care. Not really."

Charlotte's free hand rises to Juliet's head, fingers stroking hair and scalp, pulling from Juliet a shiver of pleasure so fine it is a thread of pure gold drawing up her spine.

"There she is — there you are. Your mother's looking for you. Time to go home." Bram materializes out of blackness and looks down at Juliet. He takes Emmanuel, who won't let go of Charlotte's hair. The three of them are stuck together as if tied with rope. Bram and Charlotte laugh.

"Let me keep him," says Charlotte. "He'll be mine."

Juliet can hear her mother through an open window. She does not sound like a woman who is looking for her children. She is playing and singing, and she would play and sing until dawn, given an audience.

Inside, Keith guzzles a glass of milk by the kitchen door, watched by the cook, who pets his black hair. Marta beckons Juliet into the kitchen: she has a puppy, almost newborn, and she lets Juliet press it, trembling and frightened, against her heart, tiny black nose cold under her chin, teeth like needles in her skin.

The pieces of the night fall where they may. If a child is clever, loose in a forest of grown-ups, she won't draw attention to herself. She will be forgotten, which is not the same thing as being neglected. It's like going invisible, by choice, like hiding in the underbrush to spy, to explore, to play — untroubled.

"Do we have to go to school?"

"Yes, or you can never stay up that late again. Ever."

"I hate school."

"You don't."

"I do."

"Where are those green barrettes? Your hair is a mess."

"I don't care."

"Juliet!"

"What? I don't, and it's my hair. Why should you care?"

"I have to care. It's my job. I'm your mother."

"That's stupid."

"It is. How about that: I don't care either. My head is splitting and Emmanuel was up nursing half the night and your father's leaving tomorrow for the *campo* with the delegation and I really and truly don't care about your hair. How about that."

Oh.

There *is* something worse to be found, in handwriting, in the office. Here is Juliet, reading about — words, words — torture. She cannot take it in. *Forced to swallow his own tongue, cut out of his own head*. And worse. The children are watching, the fields are on fire, the animals are screaming from a shed where they have been shut up and set alight, and the bayonet digs into the mother's belly and pulls out a baby. Tossed to the dogs. The children are watching. The children are forced at gunpoint to watch.

She cannot take it in, but she cannot take it out.

Strange, she can't guess how the pictures will flicker silently inside, against, and around her, always, nor how she will hold them in her hands — not the way a memory is held of an individual loved and lost, but held lightly between the fingers like playing cards from a deck, dealt for an unknown game.

She can't love the people in the pictures; she does not know them. She can hate and fear the men with their bayonets. She can pity the tortured. But she cannot love. It is too painful to throw love like a rescue line to humans doomed to suffer, already dead and gone. She will remember forever, and yet never well enough, never with the particularity of love: these people whom her parents have come to save from suffering, who continue to be killed, whose killing will not end the suffering of others, whose torture and murder fall like drops of rain and vanish in the punishing sun.

Words. They scrape along her skin, enter, and the wound heals instantly. She appears unhurt. She does not suffer nightmares or wake in a cold sweat or fear for her life, because she does not believe it could happen to her.

That keeps her safe: belief that she is different, her family unique, marked out for protection by their skin colour and their citizenship and, yes, by their goodness, their rightness.

So much of what she believes is wrong, but if it is never proven to be wrong, how will she ever know?

She hears her mother and Charlotte on the porch, talking, in disagreement, and she smoothes the loose sheet of paper, its story, its murdered and tortured, face down on the desktop.

Charlotte says, "All I'm asking is to get out into the *campo*, away from Managua. To do something that matters!"

Gloria says, "I trust Bram's judgement."

"You could put in a good word for me — please, say something to him," says Charlotte.

"I could not," says Gloria. "If he doesn't think you should be in the *campo*, then you shouldn't be in the *campo*."

"I didn't volunteer to hang around an office all day."

Silence.

Charlotte: "Aren't you bored, stuck in the house? With the kids? Left behind? Don't you find it all very sexist? Misogynistic?"

Snort. "Charlotte, ask yourself, why do you want to go so badly?"

"Why wouldn't I?"

"Charlotte, I've been watching you. I'm warning you to be careful. That's all: be careful. Take care. You are the one who will get hurt."

Pause. Juliet sits down hard in the desk chair. It squeaks. She hears her mother walking towards her.

"Juliet, you are not supposed to be in here. Move it. Out."

"You're wrong," says Charlotte, following. "About everything."

"Oh God, that's shit. Watch where you step." Gloria bends just outside the office door and with a leaf scoops a curl of toddler poop off the porch tiles and tosses it under the front coconut palm. "Well, I hope I am," she says to Charlotte. "That would be nice for a change." And then she goes looking for Emmanuel, to wipe him clean.

Juliet feels an overwhelming urge: she wants to touch Charlotte, the edge of her skirt, the back of her hand, the feathery hairs on her arm. She slides closer, but is too shy.

"I don't want you to go to the *campo*," Juliet whispers.

Charlotte turns and gazes with eyes that see shape and form and shadow, but not Juliet. "The only thing we have to fear is fear itself, nameless, unreasoning," she says.

The protestors from Ohio are leaving for the *campo* in the morning. For their send-off meal they will feast outdoors. Juliet, Keith, and Emmanuel walk with their mother to the field at the end of their street, which belongs to nobody. Littered grass is stamped flat under all these feet, and blankets are spread on muddy ground. The afternoon rains have come and gone. The cook stirs a giant pot of *indio viejo*, a traditional stew of cornmeal cooked over a fire, flecked with beef and tomatoes and seasoned with mint and bitter oranges.

It is growing dark, as it does here, early. Gloria points to the belt of Orion, faint and clear against the steady sky.

"What's that hanging from his belt?"

Gloria says it's a knife. A hunting knife.

Bram's head and shoulders loom above the crowd. He is going to the *campo* too, and he seems removed from them, as if he has already left behind his family, and they him, as if they need no further goodbye. Juliet eats where she drops, close to Charlotte, who notices and wraps an arm around her, draws her into a circle of grown-up talk.

Marta walks among the group, gathering plates and utensils in a large plastic bin. The puppy stumbles behind, nipping at her heels.

Bram calls for song, and Gloria lifts her guitar and plays, joined by the pluck of banjo strings, the rattle of tambourines, and by Charlotte's open throat: *Oh, woman, would you weep for me?*

Voices swept together by darkness, satiation. Apart, they come together, in a faraway land, far away from home.

"Let's dance!" Charlotte moves, she moves, she moves with the spirit, but Juliet hesitates. "Never hesitate. Start with your parts. Hold out your hand. Start with this one."

A girl in parts.

One hand. One wrist. One elbow. One shoulder, two, and down the other arm and on, until piece by piece her entire body is in motion. Hips and knees and head and feet and guts, and who is watching? No one. Juliet is entwined, enmeshed with her own body. She is whole, she's forgotten that her spirit is separate, because it isn't, when she's dancing.

Everyone is moving.

Charlotte, neck exposed, holding hands with Juliet's father, swings him into a circular dance, pulling him towards Juliet so that she can join too. Juliet, right hand in her dad's left, feeling his strong, thick fingers wrap and squeeze her own, thinks she will cry.

"Do you have to go to the *campo*, Dad? Do you have to?"

He can't hear what Juliet's asking over the music and the laughter. He smiles down at her, though he is breathing heavily. "Isn't this something else?" he puffs, but he is ready to stop. He is a man of bulk and solidity, not made for whirling.

They are still holding hands, the three of them. Juliet is the first to let go, stranding them together, her father and Charlotte, but only for a blink. Their hands swing back and forth once and then they drop each other.

Bram says, "If you want, you can come along to the *campo*. Why not?"

Juliet thinks he is talking to her, and something leaps like a small furry animal inside her chest.

"Oh," breathes Charlotte. "How can I thank you?"

Not Juliet. Charlotte. Charlotte can come with Bram to the *campo*. The small furry animal in Juliet's chest curls around itself, a weight heavier than before.

Bram shrugs, smiles warmly. "We'll keep you safe."

"I'm going somewhere," cries Charlotte. "We're going somewhere!"

Charlotte grabs for Juliet's hand and kisses it. Her cheeks shine wet in the firelight. She twirls Juliet like a ballerina. "Come. Let's go!"

And now the two of them, Charlotte and Juliet, are on their way, together. Together, they are dancing away from Bram, who mops his brow with a handkerchief, and from Gloria, whose fingers find rhythm no matter how asymmetrical. They are living, really living. They step lightly, delicately, weave invisibly over blankets and past backpacks, out beyond the forest of bodies lit by sparks, through deep and heavy grasses where the shadow of a tethered horse flickers in the dark, stamps its feet, and whickers soft and low.

"Oh!" breathes Charlotte, like they have passed into another world, like they may never find home again.

Maybe, thinks Juliet, we never will.

Her mother's music drifts from the other side of the field, sending them off, and the sky is dusty with stars — the blackness of a sky unlit by electricity, a long-ago sky in which no planes could ever fly, from which no bombs could ever fall. Charlotte pulls Juliet by the hand, dreamily, two train cars rolling silently down a track.

Rolling, rolling, rolling, and we ain't never coming back.

SHE WILL LEAVE A MARK

Across Managua, election posters flutter, graffiti is sprayed, car windows are plastered with slogans, and beautiful murals are painted on walls in honour of the ruling Frente. For five years the country has waited to vote, and in two months — on November 4, 1984 — the people will go to the polls, observed by a legion of foreigners, including those from the Roots of Justice.

With a handful of volunteers, the Friesen family attends a massive rally held before the Palacio Nacional. The building is decrepit and magnificent, its huge white pillars faded grey and spotlit under a humid, porous sky. Daniel Ortega, the slender leader of the ruling party, appears onstage in his olive-green uniform, to a collective thrill.

Juliet and Keith raise their voices deliriously in the party's official song: *"¡Luchamos, contra el yanqui, enemigo del humanidad!"* We will be victorious over the Yankee, enemy of humanity!

Juliet and Keith relish the shared joke: that they themselves are Yankees, enemies of humanity. Ha! They haven't considered taking the words seriously. They haven't considered that it might change them to straddle borders this way, that they might be forever altered, forever unable to choose a side, unable to respond to even the most obvious warning, so utterly confident, so utterly believing themselves to be who they are: multiplicities containing worlds, unpinned by definition, free.

Gloria's sweet soprano caresses the notes like she's attending a gospel tent meeting from her childhood, eyes half-closed, body swaying. But they aren't here as supporters of a political party, says Bram. They come as observers, to experience, to soak it all in.

Fireworks explode in the black sky over the crumbling Palacio, a symbol no longer of exclusion but of a revolutionary nation struggling to define itself. Daniel Ortega wears military fatigues. Beside him is his brother Humberto, the Minister of Defence. The country is at war, and the military and the ruling party are as one.

Within the gathered throngs, smaller, fiercer firecrackers explode, cheap paper soaked in gunpowder and set alight by boys and men, whirling and popping and rising.

The crowds push and heave. Juliet begs to buy gum from one of the girls who duck and dart and shout with boxes displaying their goods tied around necks like little shelves — bare feet and tattered dresses, thin arms and legs and faces.

"No," her mother says, and in the next instant she is parted from Juliet. The crowds are suddenly tightly packed, swelling, pushing against Juliet with a pressure as shocking and ruthless as a tidal wave. Juliet feels herself lifted off her feet and carried, breathless, in the wrong direction. She can't see anyone she knows. The smell of body heat is oppressive. No one is watching out for her; no one is holding on.

She feels herself falling. She is slipping under, under the feet, under the weight, knocked to the dirt on her hands and knees. They will crush her without knowing what they've done.

Instinctively, Juliet protects her head with her forearms; she will be trampled in this position. But instead she is grabbed from behind, lifted by strong hands, wrenched free. Her armpit aches, and her shoulder, where he's caught hold. Her father, Bram, bellying bodies aside, pins Juliet against his damp cotton shirt with one arm and with the other clears the way, forcing a path, relentless as a tank.

Together they ride out of the crush. The edge of the crowd, the thin layer beyond which it disperses altogether, is as sudden as its invention. Juliet feels cool night air on her hot face.

"Thought we'd lost you," is all Bram says. Instead of setting Juliet down, he swings her onto his shoulders. She feels younger than she is. Shyly, she lets her fingers brush his crinkly hair.

"What can you see from up there?" If he's worried, his calm tone does not betray it.

Juliet points. There is her mother, pushing towards to the stage, her arms raised. Music blares over the loudspeakers. And here is Charlotte, quite near Juliet and Bram, looking for them, Emmanuel in her arms. Juliet waves and shouts, and relief washes Charlotte's face clean as she comes towards them.

"What about Keith? Can you see Keith?" Bram asks.

Juliet can't. They turn in a circle so that she can scan every direction, but she can't see Keith.

"He's with somebody," says Bram. Their small group picks through the impromptu parking lot towards the white mini-bus, guarded by their driver, Israel Junior.

Juliet slides off her father's shoulders. The crowds are thinning; the people are going home. One by one the other Roots of Justice volunteers find them, each with some small adventure to report, but Keith is with none of them.

Still Bram says, "He's somewhere nearby," and pats Juliet on the head, absently, a touch that chafes. She ducks and he glances at her in perplexity, his eyes distant, unfocused. Worried.

Gloria is the last to know. She's running to meet them, her face shining: she touched the sleeve of Daniel Ortega, revolutionary hero! He leaned down from the stage to greet the people — no barriers, no bodyguards, no bulletproof vest.

"We can't find Keith," Charlotte interrupts.

"What? Where is he?"

"He can't be far away," says Bram.

Juliet feels the weight of her father's palm pressing the top of her head as he says again: "He can't be far."

"Oh God." Gloria claps her hands against her rib cage, her face drained of colour and suddenly still, frozen. "Kidnapped. Someone saw us, someone saw an opportunity. Oh God. What will they do to him?"

"Gloria." Bram's tone is stern. "We will find him. Yuri and Andrew are going around the perimeter of the crowd right now. No, don't move, Gloria." He catches her by the arm, but she yanks free. "Stay here. We can't lose you too."

"We have to tell someone," she says. "The police, someone."

"I'll do that," says Charlotte.

"Sit in the bus," says Bram.

"Fuck you," says Gloria. "You think we're on the sidelines. But we're in the middle of a fucking war."

Keith has black hair. His skin tans easily, his eyes are nut brown. No one would guess him to be a gringo. He slips into a crowd and becomes any boy in a way that Juliet cannot become any girl. She envies her brother his malleability, his deftness at the art of reflection. Wherever he is right now, she knows he is not lonely: he's squatting in the dirt lighting firecrackers with matches, or drinking a bag of pop offered for free by an admiring woman, or playing a game of street baseball with a stone and a stick and a rabble of boys.

He will saunter up, hand in hand with Yuri or Andrew, and shrug: What?

But if she were to slip away, if Juliet were to creep towards the Palacio to see the brass band playing right up close, to touch the nose of a horse, to hop onto the stage and declaim her favourite poem from *The Hobbit* — what would happen to her? She knows the question is without validity. Everyone would see her coming; they would whisper and point and stroke her hair to see if it's real, and she's not brave enough to go.

On top of the minibus, Israel Junior, the driver, jumps up and down with excitement.

"Oh!" Gloria sees them and she runs, her jaw and fists unclenched, her hair unfurling like a flag in her wake: Yuri and Keith.

What?

As they pull out of the parking lot, Gloria turns in her seat and tells all of them, but Juliet especially; "I know I said some things that sounded bad. Did they scare you? I'm sorry if they did. Were you afraid too? I was so upset and worried, it was like I'd lost my mind. Do you understand?"

Juliet nods yes.

Her mother does not ask for forgiveness. She sums up what has happened, rolls down the window, and lets it blow away, like that.

Keith's leg rests next to Juliet's on the plastic seat, bumping up and down as Israel Junior negotiates potholes and ruts and stray pigs. It is a just a leg, like her own, and she couldn't say anything more than that in explanation, looking down on it: so close to hers, so warm, so irritating.

Juliet pinches Keith.

He stares at her and she stares back, blank faced, almost as surprised as he is, and he has to — he pinches her thigh in return — so she has to — she pinches again. Hard, her nails digging. She will leave a mark. *Hey!* Whispered. He punches her arm. She kicks his ankle. He pulls her hair while she digs her nails into his brown thigh.

Neither will let go. Breathing through their mouths.

They hold on in silence, hidden in the back of the minibus from all but Israel Junior, who watches them in the rear-view mirror, sees them carrying a rage that can go nowhere but here, caught, pinned together as the dark city spins past and warm air washes like incense through open windows and the grown-ups talk about who will win, and who should, and what their roles as impartial observers might be.

TIDAL

Adios, Mrs. Friesen. Say goodbye to your house. Say goodbye to your family. The bomb is ticking. Adios, los Raíces de Justicia.

The muffled voice on the other end of the line is speaking Spanish, but badly.

Describing it to the uniformed soldier afterwards, Gloria insists the accent was American. The Friesen family stands in the street across from their house. Two trucks styled in jungle camouflage idle in a diesel fog. The soldier jots notes; his companions amble and smoke. "What were his exact words?"

Gloria does not know the Spanish word for "ticking," and when pressed admits that she cannot recreate the message with precision. "Does it matter? His exact words? He knew my name. He knew the office was in our house. He knew all about us."

"Ka-boom!" The mysterious voice had made the sound of an explosion, and she dropped the receiver and ran, yelling her children's names: Everybody out, get out, get out! Run!

Her hands are still shaking. She holds them out for the soldier to see.

"We'll go through the house." The soldier turns from Gloria and addresses Bram. "You. Show us where to look."

"You're kidding me, right?" Bram speaks an effortless Spanish, acquired through the skin as a child, while his mother attended university classes and he spent his days walking hand in hand along snowy sidewalks with an Argentine woman whose papers were not in order; his mother was resourceful and she was unsentimental.

"Show us where to look," the soldier repeats.

"And if there is a bomb?"

The man shrugs. He is more boy than man, skinny, armed to the teeth. The soldiers with him are boys too, none of them seeming serious enough for the job.

"You can't go," says Gloria.

Bram shifts his weight to his shoulders; he is his mother's son. "No one is going anywhere. We'll let these men do their job." Casually he removes a roll of curled American dollars from his back pocket and shuffles them with his thumb.

The soldiers, these boys, tear the place apart.

Juliet's books are in there, and her collection of shabby figurines that populate the pretend dollhouse under the bottom bunk, and her hairbrush, her clothes, her underwear, her pillow and blankets, her toothbrush.

All clear. The Friesens walk through their house as if it is no longer theirs: items strewn across the floor, dumped like trash, stepped upon, boot prints in dust.

"I will never feel safe in here again," says Gloria.

"Maybe you're right," says Bram. "Maybe you and the kids

should go somewhere else for a while. A little break, a vacation, by the beach."

Bombed into paradise. That's what Gloria calls it.

Gloria and the children take a bus to San Juan del Sur. There is some confusion about making a connection, and they are stranded in a nearby town, inland, until Gloria decides to accept the offer of a ride in the back of a pickup truck.

Hitching to paradise. That's what Gloria calls it.

If she regrets the choice, or resents that Bram hasn't taken the time to drive them himself, she does not say so. In fact, little can be said over the gusts of wind, sitting loose in the truck bed, jolted and jounced and jarred down a road that bears only the rough appearance of once having been paved. The smell of the Pacific comes at them at last, and then the sight of it, as they approach from above and it spreads out below, blue and endless and clear.

They are a million miles from school.

When Gloria tries to pay the driver, he refuses.

Free passage to paradise. That's what Gloria calls it.

Andrew laughs appreciatively; but he laughs easily, he laughs at anything, he bubbles with mirth. He's been waiting all day on the front porch of the Roots of Justice house, here in San Juan del Sur, keeping his eyes peeled — "Like this," he shows them, fingers stretching eyelids wide — for the arrival of Gloria and the children. He's only recently been sent to man the outpost, and "By God, I've been lonely!"

Gloria and the children will stay with Andrew at the Roots of Justice house: it has many bedrooms and a sunny courtyard, and is steps from the sand. The house is used both as a place of rest and recovery for weary volunteers and to host delegations of protestors. Although San Juan is a fishing town, its port has been targeted by American planes for surveillance. A military base armed with anti-aircraft artillery guards the town from atop the hill.

Andrew welcomes Gloria and the children with a monstrous bowl of purplish red fruit called *momones*.

"Help yourselves." He demonstrates the technique. Juliet cracks the shell with her teeth, pops into her mouth the pale, wet, gumball-sized fruit within, and sucks and sucks and sucks until the hairy fibres lose their flavour and the jelly-like remnants come squeakily away from the pit. She is left with a strange emptiness, as if the fruit has parched her mouth instead of moistening it. She will eat until she is sick or until the bowl is empty, whichever comes first.

But this is paradise. The bowl is never empty. The children are never sick. The days are solidly sun-filled. The nights are languid and studded with stars, and the sound of waves through open windows soothes their sleep. Gloria sits on the porch in the dark and picks at her guitar's strings, and Juliet lies in bed under one thin sheet and listens; the songs are in a minor key, but for beauty, not for loneliness.

It is Juliet who sees the other children first, white-blond, walking with their father along the top of the beach. There are three of them; the oldest is a girl, and they are picking their way deliberately towards the Friesens.

"Howdy," says the big, fair man, and he smiles down on

Gloria. He has a softly European accent.

"Hello." Gloria adjusts Emmanuel's limp sleeping body, shades her eyes. Her breast is showing where she has pulled down her swimsuit to nurse. ("I'm going to wean him any day now," she says every time he demands to be fed. "It's time." And yet she doesn't.)

"You are new in town." The man smiles.

"We're with the Roots of Justice. The children and I are taking a holiday from the city."

"You have found the perfect place for a holiday."

"My husband . . ." Gloria stops, looks down and strokes Emmanuel's head, adjusts, tucks herself away.

"But I haven't introduced myself." The man offers his hand, which she accepts. "My name is Heinrich. My children: Isobel, Dirk, and Jonathan. My wife and I work for the Red Cross. We live" — he gestures down the beach — "Big white house, porch goes all the way around."

"We haven't had a chance to look around."

"You will come for a meal, of course. Anytime. I'll tell Clara."

"Oh." Juliet watches Gloria free her hand and gather her hair in one fist at the nape of her neck, her words trailing out. "I don't know how long . . ."

"It was from this beach that many of Somoza's *guardia* fled," Heinrich says after a moment. He takes a cross-legged, very upright position beside Gloria. He is speaking of the former dictator, overthrown in the revolution. The word *guardia* is as evil on the tongue as *Contra*: words that mean terror and murder and death.

"I didn't know that." Gloria is genuinely surprised, her spine lengthening as she turns with interest to Heinrich.

"The ones who were pushed south, who were trapped here, they hijacked fishing boats. It's a story not much told, but if you ask around, people know which fishing boats, which fishermen."

Gloria gazes into the harbour, where vessels rock and bob in the contained port. The untended beach nestles between two rocky outcroppings, beyond which spreads the open sea.

"They say those *guardia* were trained into the Contra. They're the leaders now. That's what they say. Full circle." Heinrich's hand sweeps towards the ocean. "Leave by sea, right here, in the south, and return by land, up north. Everyone wants to go home."

"Do they?"

"Don't you?" he asks her.

"I don't," says Gloria, her face so open that Heinrich might fall in; but only for a glancing moment. Juliet watches Gloria release the full weight of her hair, swing it over her shoulders and around her cheeks, hiding herself again.

The girl named Isobel is watching too, her own hair coiled and pinned.

"I like your bun," says Juliet.

"It's a chignon," says Isobel. Juliet has never heard of one. With a tug, Isobel removes the polished wooden stick that is holding her hair magically in place, and it cascades in pale ribbons around her neck and shoulders.

Isobel has just turned twelve.

"I'm almost eleven," says Juliet.

Isobel disdains driftwood dragged to make a pretend house, nor will she touch the tiny crabs that scuttle over wet sand left behind by the tide, leaving faint tracks, a path any-one with interest could follow.

"You have the most beautiful . . ." they hear Isobel's father tell Juliet's mother.

The most beautiful what?

"Thank you," whispers Gloria. She peers in the direction of the sun; her eyes squint shut.

Here comes the tide. Helped by Isobel's brothers, Keith digs a trench, drags sticks, piles sand to divert water, but the tide overwhelms; Juliet cannot resist, crouching to push walls of sand with her forearms, until even Isobel is drawn into the fight, standing above the tide line, calling out directions.

Heinrich helps Gloria to her feet, bends and lifts her towel, shakes it out, folds it neatly.

"Time to go home," he tells his children.

"Us too," says Gloria.

"It was a pleasure to meet you." Heinrich reaches for Gloria's free hand, the one loosely against Emmanuel's shoul-der; his thumb strokes her knuckles.

Juliet's bare feet sting as they cross hot pavement to the Roots of Justice house, which faces the water. She is thrilled to have met someone like Isobel, and relieved to be away from her.

"Yes, I know them," Andrew is saying to Gloria. "But he's not with the Red Cross. His wife is. She's a physician. Dutch? Danish? Accept all invitations, that's my motto. Take me along too?"

"Oh, leave the dishes," Clara says. "Heinrich will do them before bed."

She is a grand-looking woman who matches her husband, the way some couples do, as if drawn to each other in the mirror. (Juliet's parents are that opposite version of coupledom, pulled together by differences that fold into one another like origami.) Clara and Heinrich are tall, robust, fair, though her eyes are icy pale and his dazzle like the ocean at noon — or is it only in memory that Juliet invents these characteristics?

The mothers flop onto a cushioned loveseat, sloshing wine; Gloria licks her wet knuckles, reaches for a book resting on the coffee table. "I never imagined such comfort in this country."

"We have built this life over many years."

Gloria opens the book as if opening their life, peering curiously at florid line drawings of half-naked, contorted bodies wreathed in vines and flowers, shone down upon by suns with stick rays. Heinrich smiles like a cat. Gloria pauses at a page that demonstrates how to squat in fresh running water and draw liquid in through one's sphincter by means of some interior muscle; Juliet, hovering, will hunt for and examine the same page at the first opportunity.

"What is this?"

"Yoga." Clara is dismissive. This is not her version of their story.

"Wow! Andrew, do you know anything about yoga?"

"Of course!" Andrew hops off his chair and stands with his feet hip-distance apart in the centre of the richly patterned rug. He bends at the waist, places his palms on the rug, and wiggles his bottom as he settles into the pose. "Downward-facing dog!"

Juliet can't help giggling, but she is the only one.

Clara half-lids her sharp eyes.

"Is it Indian?" Gloria turns her face to Heinrich's, and Juliet sees her ear exposed, one hand tucking strands, flushed cheekbone sleek with heat.

"Grown-ups," Isobel whispers to Juliet. She pronounces the word dismissively. She knows where there is an abandoned glass of wine in the kitchen, and between them they drink the red liquid down.

"Are you drunk?"

"I guess so."

"Me too."

And Juliet and Isobel walk around the house like grown-ups do, weaving and laughing and bumping into furniture. Smiling like they have secrets and the secrets are about to spill out. I can tell her anything, thinks Juliet, but she cannot think of anything significant enough to tell.

There is a shark on the beach, but otherwise today is a day like all of their San Juan days. There is nothing particular to do or to be done. Gloria and the children are at leisure, not at wait, drinking up the sun, skin salty from the shallows.

Jellyfish wash up amidst the driftwood, pale and purplish and pliable when poked with a stick. Local boys run into the waves and scoop out fish with their bare hands or catch the shining, flailing bodies with primitive poles made of hooks and line and sticks. Today they run out of the water shouting with excitement. Juliet and Keith come to take a look. Laid out in the arms of a boy is a shark, dead. It is small, but the boy pulls apart its jaws to show them rows and rows of teeth.

Around ten o'clock, the Friesens are joined by Heinrich and his children, who are being home-schooled in an arrangement that has them sending assignments back and forth by mail to a private school in Germany. Their hours are malleable. So long as she excels, Isobel is allowed to stay up as late as she likes, working, and to sleep in as late as she cares to, blinds drawn in her bedroom, the fan purring like a cat.

She is in the equivalent of the tenth grade and intends to graduate by fourteen and go directly to a foreign university. "But I won't break any records. The youngest student ever accepted to Harvard was an eleven-year-old boy, so I'm already too late."

Heinrich reclines directly on the hot sand, his hands cupping his neck, his elbows at angles, exposing tufts of pure white hair in the pits of his arms. "Isobel, this is known as bragging."

Gloria does not glance up from her paperback, on loan from Clara. Emmanuel sleeps in her lap, crashed under his sunhat.

Juliet and Isobel walk in the waves that lick the sand. "Don't follow us," Isobel tells her brothers.

"You're following us," says Dirk. He and Keith are the same age. Jonathan is two years younger and silent.

"Are not."

"Are too."

"Are not."

"Are too."

Isobel sighs. "What were we talking about?" she asks Juliet.

The boys with the shark are ahead of them, down the beach. That's who they're following, all of them, walking

north on sticky sand, allowing the salt water to wash in and
out over their toes.

It doesn't feel like they are going too far, not at all. The
beach looks short from one end to the other, and Isobel says
they are allowed to go wherever they like, but as they walk and
walk and walk, distance becomes an optical illusion, a trick.

The village core is only a few streets wide, and soon they
are past it. Concrete houses are replaced by primitive structures, few and far between; the smell of cooking fires. Wild
greenery grows up to the sandy perimeter. A cow with a
hump, more like a buffalo, wanders loose, foraging for feed.

They hop from stone to stone across a sludgy stream
that feeds into the ocean. Isobel has to turn around to help
Jonathan. She and Dirk debate the annoyance: "I didn't bring
him; you brought him; you take him back." But Jonathan
doesn't want to go back.

Gloria and Heinrich have been reduced to two miniature
figures in the centre of the beach. The children wave and believe they see hands waving in return.

Past the stream, more rocks crowd the sand, tumbled
from the cliff that marks the end of the bay. The rocks are
black and slimy with seaweed. Some they pick through like a
maze, and others must be scrambled over.

"Cool!" Keith finds a pool of water on top of an indented
boulder in which a tiny fish swims, in its own private lake.
The children discover more puzzling puddles atop tall rocks,
high above the water that washes in, but none of them can
read the warning.

They pause between rocks, the five of them, on a sheltered
plot of sand warmed by the sun. They have come to the end

of the beach, beyond which boulders make a gradual ascent up the rock face and curve around into the open sea; but they can't tell from here.

Nobody says: Let's go back now. Nobody wants to be the one to say it.

Dirk's white hair lifts in the breeze. Juliet notices his green eyes. Though younger, he is already taller than her. She fights the urge to grab him and push him. She wants to beat him at something: climb faster, climb higher. It is the only suitable expression for what she feels.

She scrapes her knee in her hurry to climb the next stone, Keith and Dirk at her heels.

Isobel, stuck with Jonathan, falls behind.

The waves are higher, wilder, louder. Juliet pushes on without thinking, following the San Juan boys, who disappear from view, then reappear, always seeming to be just around the corner. The sun stands at noon. The wind rises.

And so does the tide, with stealthy speed. There is no more sand below them. Water runs in between the boulders and eats away their passage to shore.

"Wait for us!" Isabel hollers, and Juliet pauses.

She and the boys stop. They look down, and they see ocean below them, clear beneath frothy waves, limpid green.

Juliet smells smoke, but it is Dirk who discovers its source, above them. He and Keith climb up and up until they are standing on a ledge looking down on Juliet, now joined by Isobel and Jonathan.

"It's a cave! A real cave!"

"I'll never get him all the way up there," says Isobel. "He weighs a ton."

"Do not!" says Jonathan.

The cave is not deep, as Juliet expects, more like a cupped hand of rock, a shallow shelter overlooking the bay. She climbs into it and stands. She can't see her mother on the beach, but perhaps it is too far. Isobel lifts Jonathan and scrambles up last.

"Thanks for nothing," she says to Dirk, but she too is drawn almost instantly into this perfect pocket, this camp improvised by the San Juan boys. It is clear that they visit the hideout often: a collection of dry sticks and driftwood stored in one corner; a vessel of rainwater that can be covered by a lid. Everyone takes turns dipping their hands and drinking from cupped palms.

The three boys, not much older than their visitors, welcome them courteously. One dusts the floor with his hand before offering the girls a seat.

Another guts the shark with a knife and throws the guts onto the rocks for the seabirds.

Over the open fire, several whole fish sizzle, stabbed onto sticks. Everyone is suddenly ravenous. They eat with their hands, carefully, so as not to choke on the bones.

Shark meat is denser than fish. The San Juan boys discuss meals past. They claim to have caught and cooked a pelican, and as proof show off a pelican's skull, but Isobel teases them: You found that on the beach. The conversation is in Spanish, and Juliet's is weakest. She listens in silence until one of the San Juan boys addresses her directly.

"Do you like the fish or the shark best?" Keith translates.

"I know what he said!" But words for a reply slip from her. She shrugs. The San Juan boys laugh and Juliet flushes and says, in English, "The fish."

Dirk tells the boys, "She likes the fish," and Juliet discovers that the question was not idle. The boys wish to offer her more food, whatever she desires.

Isobel prefers the shark. She sits primly upright, her legs crossed at the knee, feet curled around her left hip. Unlike Juliet, she does not lick her fingers but eats delicately off her palm and brushes her hands together lightly to clean them.

Until the tide turns, the San Juan boys tell them, there is no way back to shore. No one finds this news unwelcome.

When the girls need relief, they scramble over rocks around the corner, towards the open sea, until they are out of sight. Perched side by side, trying to pee down a crevice, Isobel and Juliet get the giggles. It isn't anything; it's everything. They want to laugh. They have to. Pulling up their underwear, they are doubled over, weak, helpless. Just a glance at one another brings on fresh waves.

Back at the cave, the bigger boys play a game that involves pairing up and slapping the inside of the other's wrist with two fingers, taking turns — *slap, slap, slap* — back and forth until one boy can no longer stand the pain. The other is the winner.

Keith and Dirk trade slaps until their fingers are puffed and raw. Juliet hopes that Dirk will win, but she is helplessly proud of her brother, his teeth gritted, his tanned, round face set and determined. There is no mercy; this is not a game for girls.

"Give it up," says Isobel. She pulls Juliet down by the wrist and they lie side by side, faces towards the sky. They indulge Jonathan's limited imagination, which can find nothing but trucks and guns in the cloud shapes.

At last, two San Juan boys separate Keith and Dirk: a truce.

Isobel inclines her mouth towards Juliet's ear. "I think that one likes you."

One of the San Juan boys dips his fingers in the bucket of water and spritzes the girls, who sit up and gasp. "Told you," says Isobel, in English. "He likes you."

Another boy punches the first in the arm. They exchange punches back and forth, smiling sheepishly.

"Ignore them," says Isobel. At any moment the weather could change — the clouds could roll, black and tumbling, blown by an angry wind — but it won't. The children are not bored or hungry or tired, and it does not occur to them that a search might be underway.

If Juliet is giddy, if she is bold, if she exudes a vague hysteria, it is because she has no awareness of being afraid. Anxiety flickers deep under the skin, so far down it is interpreted as a thrill, as the hum of unease that accompanies adventure, enlivening the body, and it is with regret that the children watch the tide recede, become low enough for safe passage.

The San Juan boys clean up, kicking out the fire with their bare feet, tossing bones to the birds. One lifts Jonathan onto his narrow back and the descent proceeds quickly.

"Uh-oh," says Isobel, the first to notice Heinrich and Andrew on the rocks below.

Everyone deflates just a little bit. The San Juan boy drops Jonathan gently. Without being close enough to hear what Heinrich is saying, everyone knows it is not good. Juliet spots Gloria on the beach, and is glad that her mother has been stopped by the fallen boulders, Emmanuel in her arms. Wrath pours off her.

The San Juan boys vanish into the landscape.

"Totally unacceptable!" Juliet hears.

"Pappie," Isobel mutters under her breath. Isobel's family speak to one another in English in public, but in private they often use Dutch or German.

"We're fine!" Dirk shouts.

"Just ask us how bloody fine we are!" Heinrich has lost a sandal and his foot is cut. "All of your privileges — gone!"

"What privileges?" Dirk says, and Juliet is impressed by his boldness and stupidity.

Neither family is a hitting family, though for a moment, now that he's near enough, Heinrich looks to be considering otherwise.

"Nice day for a hike." Andrew pulls Heinrich's rage onto himself, gently. He winks at the kids. "Where were you hiding?"

"We weren't hiding," says Dirk.

"This will never happen again," says Heinrich.

Of course it won't. It can't, though it's nothing to do with a grown-up's decree, one way or the other. Escape is like being struck by lightning, as rare and as inexplicable. Being found again? Well, that's nothing special. That happens daily: interruptions that startle children back into the world of time and safety, and the rules that would bind them here for good.

"I'm too angry to hug you," Gloria says, even as she squeezes until Juliet and Keith think they will pop. "Stupid, stupid children! How could you be so careless with your precious lives?"

It is impossible not to feel ashamed. The shame seems unfair, a layer of adult misery burdening their happy day.

Neither Keith nor Juliet wishes to share the details — any part of it — with their mother. She would never understand. And they see, suddenly, that it is her they were escaping, her and all the rest of them: the grown-ups.

The sound of the kettle whistles in the Roots of Justice kitchen, the clatter of coffee being prepared and served, the companionable murmur of voices: Andrew's and Gloria's and Heinrich's. For supper Andrew will make his specialty: omelettes to order, with a choice of tomatoes, onion, and *queso fresco*, a soft white cheese. There is a surfeit of eggs in San Juan's market, and a dearth of much else.

Clara arrives carrying a bottle of red wine, and Gloria and Heinrich join her on the porch. She is not as interested in the story of the foolish children as Heinrich thinks she ought to be.

"They are here and well, as far as I can tell." She kicks off her sandals and tucks her bare feet under her on the swinging wooden bench. "They used their common sense. They didn't attempt to walk back to shore until high tide had passed. Besides, punishment is futile, wouldn't you agree, Heinrich?"

"Not if it prevents future disaster," says Heinrich.

"And does it?" his wife asks. "I should very much like to know."

The grown-ups have not finished eating when the power is cut.

Ahhh is the sound around the table. The children hear it from the porch, where already it is dark. The hunk of moon reflects off the water in the bay, and the rocks and their cave are far away, vanished, though not from the mind's eye. They hear the clink of glass on glass and laughter as someone attempts to pour wine in the dark — no, it is Gloria's laughter they hear.

Clara comes onto the porch. "We are going home," she tells her children, who fail to rise. Heinrich follows and presses against his wife, his fingers kneading her shoulders.

"Stay," he says, but she shrugs herself away.

She's so tired, she says, by the end of the day. Her mind just shuts off.

Andrew lights candles and drips wax to stick them into plastic cups, which he arranges along the low porch wall.

"Oh, please, won't you stay?" Gloria goes to Clara as if to touch her, though she does not.

It is at this moment that gunfire rattles. It could be coming from the street beside them, that is how near it sounds. *Thud-thud-thud-thud-thud*, quicker than Juliet can click her tongue. Automatic weaponry. And then a shrieking sound in the air, wailing, cutting the sky as it falls. Silence. And again the shrieking fall.

Their panic shocks them, the pushing and shoving, Gloria crying for Emmanuel, whom Juliet remembers was near her, sitting on his bottom and playing with a Dinky car, when the gunfire began. She could see him then but not now, though there is no reason for it — has she gone blind? — and she is on hands and knees searching the porch, knocking her head on the swing.

"Gloria," says Heinrich in a clear voice. "Gloria, I am holding Emmanuel in my arms. He is right here with me."

Andrew blows out the candles.

"God, we came here to get away from a bomb." Gloria's voice shakes.

Clara calmly calls out the children's names, one by one, like a teacher taking attendance. She asks them to reply "I am well," and they obey.

Andrew points at the lit sky. "It's not a bomb. It's tracer fire. Harmless as fireworks. It's coming from the army base up the hill. They're looking for something."

Rat-a-tat-a-tat-a-tat-a.

"And what the hell is that?" Gloria is a shadow in the doorway, stroking Emmanuel's head.

"Anti-aircraft artillery, also from the base. Something's come too close to shore. Probably a drone."

"American?"

"We'll never know," Clara says briskly. "This is not our business and not for us to know."

"What's a drone?" asks Keith.

"It is nothing," says Clara. "We have to live here, and you do not."

"Clara," says Heinrich.

"I'm going home," she says.

"The children stay until this is over."

"Fine. I need the quiet." She walks down the porch steps. "Safe." She lifts her arms, offering them her vision of the sky, which continues to rain tracer fire. "Perfectly safe."

"A drone," says Heinrich clearly, so that Clara can hear him as she walks away, "is a plane that flies without a pilot. It is fitted with cameras to collect information. Maybe it is taking a picture of my wife right now. It is known as a Blackbird."

"Like a spy plane," says Keith with some excitement.

Juliet watches Clara disappear into the darkness. She can't see Isobel's expression clearly, lit only by the flickering orange haze, but she senses that Isobel has watched her mother walk away before.

Isobel turns to Juliet and smiles. "Sleepover!" Juliet understands: they are in no danger of being punished further for today's adventure. It is over, displaced in their parents' minds, forgotten like a paragraph in a book that was never meant for grown-ups, that grown-ups could never understand even if they cared enough to try.

Andrew and Gloria wait to take their cue from Heinrich.

The artillery fire appears to have stopped for the moment, but he says nothing about leaving. "Does anyone have a cigarette?"

Gloria shifts her weight but doesn't reply.

"We want to have a sleepover, Pappie."

"Direct this request to our gracious hosts." Heinrich sweeps into a partial bow.

Later, much later, fresh cigarette smoke drifts into Juliet's sleeping lungs. Her feet are tangled in the sheet and Isobel's arm is thrown over her own, making an X across the bed. Her hand is numb but she hesitates to move away.

Later, much later, Juliet pads from bedroom to bathroom. What does she see, like a spy camera, like infrared radiation collected on a fuzzy screen? Two grown-ups on the porch, his hands pushed under her heavy hair, her face turned and closed, soft and wet, and neither giving any consideration to something hanging overhead in the sky, circling, circling, encrypting their kiss with its secret eye.

"I've put in a call to Managua," says Andrew in the kitchen the next morning.

"Let me talk to Bram when he calls back." Gloria pours hot diluted powdered milk from a pan into her cup of coffee.

"Word is," says Andrew, "a Russian cargo carrier offshore has caught the Americans' interest. I'm going to pitch Bram on bringing the next delegation here."

Without thinking, Gloria reaches for the packet of cigarettes on the table and lights one. "I've made a mistake," she says. Juliet thinks that is what she hears as she comes into the kitchen with Isobel.

"Never, not you," Andrew says, and to the girls, "You slept."

He turns off the stove under the pan of milk, and Gloria walks to the open window to blow a stream of smoke away, as if the girls might not notice.

"How would you like your eggs, ladies?"

"Over easy," says Isobel, and Juliet says, "Sunny side up."

Gloria flicks the burning cigarette through the bars crossing the window and turns around. "Scrambled." She is laughing.

PHOTOGRAPH NEVER TAKEN

The Roots of Justice rolls into San Juan del Sur, a travelling circus of Americans spilling from minibuses, waving signs and wafting cigarette smoke, trailed by a pack of foreign reporters and cameramen who anticipate bagging the story of the week: a showdown in disputed waters between a Russian cargo carrier and an American warship deployed to force it to change its course.

Juliet, Keith, and Emmanuel stand on the porch of the Roots of Justice house and watch their beach fill up and spill over. They are looking for their dad, and when he bursts from the milling crowd, they shout and wave. He jogs across the stretch of pavement and up the steps and they wrap themselves around his massive limbs and breathe him in. He smells of apple cider, slightly soured.

"Holiday's over," says Gloria from the open doorway, and she goes to the kitchen to start washing dishes. There is no cook and she will be in charge.

Bram follows, children hanging off him like monkeys off

the branches of a tree. "Can we start bringing folks in?" he asks. "Beds all set up, everything ready?"

"Hello to you too," says Gloria.

"I love you." Bram doesn't hesitate. He places his hands on her face and kisses her warmly.

"Yuck!" The children drop to the floor.

"Everything's ready." Gloria's smile fights against itself.

Emmanuel screams frantically, arches his back, beats his mother's legs. She bends and lifts him. "Did you bring Charlotte?" she asks. "I could use some help with this one if I'm going to get a thing done."

In moments the house where they have been staying for weeks, rattling around its empty rooms, is transformed by the presence of a crush of guests. Sand crunches underfoot. A toilet is clogged, and the woman responsible churns frantically at its handle. Armpits leak odour. Wet towels dangle on lines strung across the courtyard. A radio crackles. Smoke drifts. Feet shuffle.

On the front porch, Gloria offers a mid-afternoon snack of cut fruit. Juliet and Keith circulate with a sign-up sheet asking for volunteers to wash dishes, cook, go to market. They return the page, filled with names, to their mother, who is in the kitchen mixing up punch dosed with a generous slug of rum.

"You should have added cleaning the bathrooms," says Andrew, who has just spent half an hour applying his negligible plumbing skills to the problem of the overflowing toilet.

"I'm just getting started. I'm easing them into it — just you wait." Gloria hands him a drink and sends Juliet and Keith outside to play.

Their beach has been overrun, not just by Roots of Justice but by a swarm of organizations and non-profits, all come together to protest against the United States of America and its warship. The ship can't be seen, though Juliet imagines she sees it, a mirage on the horizon, a flash of white. The other ship is out there too, invisible: if Ronald Reagan is to be believed, it carries a shipment of Soviet-made fighter jets, though the Sandinista government says it is merely dropping into port to receive a load of Nicaraguan shrimp. Either way, the protestors argue that it has the right to dock, to move through a sovereign nation's waters unchallenged.

Juliet and Keith tread like spies. English is the dominant language, pronounced in the accents of America: the Southern drawl, the flattened Midwestern grade, the West Coast wave and the East Coast punch.

Charlotte is easy to find amidst the throng, kneeling on a white bedsheet spread flat over the sand, its edges held in place by stones. Emmanuel busily dips his fingers into paint and whacks the sheet. Charlotte is writing the words *Boat of Justice* in large, looping letters across the fabric.

"Come and help!" She waves to Juliet and Keith. She wants them to stamp their handprints and footprints in primary colours around the words — messy and deeply satisfying work.

At four o'clock the sun looks as if it might stay forever perched above their heads, like a benevolent god. No matter how long you've been there, it is always a surprise when it begins to fall, and how precipitously, crashing into the sea and leaving behind the blackness of a primitive sky, nothing but stars and moon.

Charlotte hangs their creation over the porch wall to dry.

The house is candlelit. It lacks a central gathering room with ample table and chairs, so guests line up through the kitchen doorway to load plates with beans and rice, tortillas, salad, before perching themselves in odd improvised places to eat, heads bent over plates balanced on knees: in the hallway and courtyard, on the porch, down the steps, and even on the curb along the street.

"This is going well," Bram tells Gloria as he passes by. She is eating with the children in the kitchen, at the breakfast bar, on stools.

She lifts an eyebrow. "You say that like you're surprised."

"I've found a Nicaraguan school that will take the kids. Private but not exclusive. Classes entirely in Spanish," he says. "If you'll come back to Managua."

Juliet and Keith hold themselves perfectly still. Silently their mother wipes Emmanuel's mouth with his shirt. He is standing on her lap. Whatever she is thinking, it cannot be read on her face.

On the beach, the flames of a bonfire rise. Bram circulates through the rooms of the house, reminding delegates of the early-morning prayer meeting, though they are free, of course, to join the party on the beach.

It goes on through the night.

Emmanuel and Keith race Dinky cars down the hallway, on hands and knees, crashing them into walls with exploding sound effects, a game they share despite their age difference. Though the hour is early, their father permits the play: anything to rouse the volunteers, young and old, fuzzy with booze, some of whom glare with unguarded hostility at the boys, though others chirp unconvincingly, "How cute."

Early-morning prayer meeting is a quiet affair. Gloria serves *café con leche*.

It has been decided that the group will gather at a hut on the beach that serves a generous — and cheap — breakfast of eggs with *gallo pinto* and tortillas. Following the meal, a press conference has been planned, and then the Roots of Justice will launch the "Boat of Justice," a fishing vessel hired to carry protestors out to sea, into disputed waters, to float between the American warship and the Soviet freighter.

"I'm going on the boat." Charlotte slides into Juliet's chair, pushing against her thigh so that they both fit.

"We're not." Gloria sits with the children at a round table off to one side. The children devour a plate of *platanos*, thick, gummy fried bananas, licking caramel stickiness off fingers. Above them the roof is of thickly woven dried palm leaves, populated by sleeping bats.

"I want to go too," says Juliet.

"Don't be ridiculous," says Gloria.

Surely this is not a scripted moment: after the press conference, Gloria walks the children towards their father, into the ring of cameras, and he touches each on the head and says goodbye. He kisses Gloria. Later today, footage of the family will flicker briefly on American network television. Bram will appear, hair blowing, backed by the ocean: "This is not a publicity stunt. Our job is to witness. We also serve who only stand and wait."

"All aboard!" calls Bram, and the waters throng with Americans churning towards the little motorboats, called *pangas*, that will ferry them to the larger vessel anchored in the deep waters of the bay.

Charlotte runs past them, wrapped in the colourful painted bedsheet. It flutters around her shoulders like a superhero's cape. She is barefoot, so it is a mystery what trips her up — the sheet, her own toes, her flowing yellow sundress? She stumbles, tumbles, splashes all the way under the waves and then gasps to the surface, helpless and struggling with laughter.

Bram grasps her outstretched hands and pulls her upright, and she leans into his bulk, still laughing, though her face is upset, humiliated — young. Juliet sees the paint smearing, dissolving off the sheet. Bram speaks to Charlotte gently, pulling her wet hair into his closed palm, wringing it out at the nape of her neck.

It is a shred of a moment that adheres to the curved rear of Juliet's eyeball: the shape the two of them make could be a different day, another woman gazing up at Juliet's father with wide eyes, asking for something it seems only he can offer.

Before Nicaragua, before *here*, the Friesens are Americans in a small town in Indiana. Of a Sunday they go for a drive in the country, but no matter how far they drive, they are never far from somewhere: from a tidy farm property, from a well-tended orchard with shacks to house migrant labourers during the picking season, from the bell tower of a church in the next town over.

The conversation from the front seat flows musically over the children's heads, drawn out by the movement of the world outside the windows. They pass a wooded lot with a FOR SALE sign nailed to a rotten fencepost.

"When we find our fortune," says their mother, "we'll live right here." (But they won't.)

"We'll build our house out of trees we'll chop down with our bare hands."

"We'll have chickens."

"And a horse!" says Juliet.

"We'll clear a spot for a big truck patch," says their father. He slows the car and performs a three-point turn in order to drive by the property again, letting them drift past the rutted laneway and idle to a stop in the road. "There's room for a horse," he says.

"I'd like one too," says their mother.

"Then we'll have two." (But they won't.)

"Goodbye, see you soon," the family waves out the windows to their imaginary log house in the woods, the mare and the stallion and the foal, the truck patch of vegetables, rows lined with straw to keep down the weeds.

(They'll look, but they'll never find this place again.)

Spring wind crashes against eardrums and the children can't hear a word their parents are saying.

Crunch. Something darts out of rotting weeds and ends underneath their tires.

"What the hell was that?"

"Oh God. We hit a dog."

"We have to go back."

The car reverses slowly and stops at a laneway. Their father gets out and walks to where the dog lies. They watch him shake his head. It is not a big farm dog, but smaller, like a terrier. It is not in a state to be picked up or delivered to its owner.

Slowly they drive up the stranger's lane. Their father says: "Come with me, Juliet, Keith." They don't want to, but obey. He knocks on the door. A woman opens it, young, in cut-off jeans and a man's T-shirt, paint-spattered like her bare arms and legs.

Their father explains the accident.

The woman says, "I knew this house was a mistake."

She holds the door open for them and they stand in her gritty kitchen and eat one burnt cookie each. "He was just a puppy," she tells them. She presses fists against her eyes, which look dry, hot, itchy. Juliet is still chewing when the woman flings herself in a crashing motion through the standing silence at their father, who opens his arms and braces her against his chest.

They stand like this, as their father stands now, feet in the ocean, breathing.

The woman lifts her head from their father's chest and gazes up at him, anointing his Sunday clothes with wet paint; as Charlotte soaks him in salt water.

Everything he offers emanates naturally from his eyes, the calm assurance of his encircling arms. Of course she would want what he can give to her. Of course he would give it.

Their mother waits in the car; waits in the sand, on the beach.

They can hear Emmanuel howling, but he is different now, older. He is muttering to himself. He sits at his mother's feet and stirs himself a hole.

Bram releases Charlotte, all but her hand, and she gathers her sodden skirt and accepts his assistance into a waiting boat. Carefully, Bram swings his bulk in beside her, the last to board. The engine putters, the *panga* turns, and they are off in a slur of wake.

The beach is deserted. It seems twice as quiet as it did before the protestors arrived, the way a house feels abandoned after a party, and dirty, and forlorn. They stand and look out into the bay for a long time. The tiny *pangas* skitter around the larger fishing boat, eventually fluttering and dispersing, and the big engine chugs and the Boat of Justice is dispatched, like that, out to sea.

Gloria sinks into the sand behind Emmanuel. She sets her face into her palms and lets her thick black hair drape and hide her like a blanket. Juliet and Keith bite their lips and glance at each other.

"Mom?"

But she doesn't reply. She allows herself to tip sideways, to fall into the sand, to collapse. Her knees curl in towards her belly, her feet bare beneath a simple dark skirt, and her elbows and wrists curve before her face. Her chin tucks, her ribs rise and fall, and her eyelashes flutter against her cheek.

Ever so subtly, the children, even Emmanuel, remove themselves from her and begin digging a hole that will become a pool as the tide rises. No one sees the two men approaching, laden with equipment, until they are very near: gringos with tanned, roughened skin and ruffled greasy hair, and kind eyes that are yet not gentle.

One smiles at Juliet and Keith and raises his hand for quiet, though they have said nothing.

The other, the photographer, does not ask permission. He lifts the heavy eye of his camera and bends and circles, calculating the angle of the sun and the opening of the aperture. He shoots. He is not interested in the story or its context, only in the tableau made by the lovely fallen woman and the wild children who hold themselves apart from her.

He alone sees what Gloria has become, fallen onto the sand: she is iconic. He steals from her an image that will give a man a name for himself. It will win prizes.

But Gloria will despise it, and pretend it never happened.

Many years from now, Juliet will go looking for this photograph that has fallen into myth and that she cannot confirm exists. Seated at a library carrel, she will sail through rolls of microfilm and arrive, dizzy and nauseated, at this particular take on portraiture: unrelated to either real disaster or real deliverance, while appearing to portray both.

She will not quite believe that what she's been hunting still lives to be found.

Sweating inside her winter coat, in the pulsing heat of the library's overworked radiators, Juliet will look upon a beautiful figment told in black and white, a compressed image that speaks to the eye and calls to whatever it is missing. She can't remember why her mother was fallen on the beach — perhaps she never knew — but not remembering gives her permission to see what a stranger saw and captured, and she will be washed by profound emotion, stabbing into the heart this truth: some grief cannot be touched.

Gloria sits up, resting on the heels of her hands. "What's this?" Her eyes are dry.

The first man names the newspaper for which he is freelancing. "Could we ask you a few questions?"

"You've missed the boat." Gloria's hair is thick with sand. She frowns at the photographer, who lifts his lens to the harbour.

The other laughs and taps a cigarette from a packet, lights it. As an afterthought, he offers the packet to Gloria. She flicks her eyes at the children.

"No, thanks."

"Yours?"

"Believe it or not," she says.

"You are American."

She nods, expressing disinterest in his questions, turning her gaze to the water.

"More Americans." The man points up the beach. "More blond kids."

Heinrich and his children are walking towards them, and Gloria sighs. "Dutch. They've nothing to do with anything."

"But you are with the protestors?"

"Gloria!" Heinrich waves as his children run to meet their friends, except for Isobel, who never runs. She arrives cool and composed.

"You will excuse me." Gloria stands and shakes sand off her skirt. She goes to Heinrich and they speak to one another in low tones. Her arms are folded across her chest, and so are his; though he smiles, she does not.

The freelancer turns to the children. "What are you kids doing in this town?"

"I live here," says Isobel. "My mom is a doctor."

He nods.

"My dad is on the Boat of Justice," offers Juliet.

"The Boat of Justice," the man repeats.

"To stop the American boat," says Juliet.

"So you're an American Sandinista," says the man.

"No." Juliet hesitates, her tongue curling around the *o* sound, lengthening it.

"Isobel! Dirk! Jonathan!" Heinrich is calling his children, and his voice has an edge. "We are not staying to play. Come. Now."

Surprised, the children continue to dig, half-heartedly.

"Keith, Juliet, say goodbye to your friends." Gloria's artificial lilt does not disguise her command.

Isobel stands.

"Bye," says Juliet.

"Um, bye."

"Bye," says Dirk.

"Bye," Juliet says again.

Their parents are telling them to say goodbye for good, but they do not know this.

Gloria is not sober. She has gone to the bathroom to splash her face before returning to the party. Upon exiting she is met by her husband, who hands her a bottle of red wine, a going-away present: "For you, from the European fellow, the doctor."

Her expression is fixed as she stares up and down the hallway and into the courtyard and kitchen, thronging with people.

"I didn't invite him in, should I have?" says Bram.

Juliet and Keith press themselves, camouflaged, against the kitchen doorframe; they have already been tucked in once. The Friesen family is sleeping in a cramped room originally intended for servants, just off the kitchen — about as close to the party as actually being there. Noise, laughter, a sprawl of light as the door is opened by someone who thinks she's discovered an extra bathroom.

The opened door is the kicker. They've left Emmanuel snoring softly at the soggy centre of the double bed where he will be joined later tonight — much later — by their parents, when the party's over.

It is their last night in San Juan del Sur. Tomorrow they will rattle home to Managua with their parents to become schoolchildren once again. They have not been consulted, only informed of their changing circumstances: "All good things must come to an end."

"For what it's worth, it didn't look like he wanted to come in," says Bram to Gloria.

The children watch their mother accept the bottle.

She hesitates, then turns and walks slowly past, not seeing them. She is balancing the bottle in the cup of one hand like someone performing a trick, though she moves tentatively, as if struck and dazed. At the threshold to the porch the bottle teeters, and she seems to stand aside and watch it slip, its smash terrific, instantaneous, glass striking tile and shattering to splinters and blood-red splatter.

Juliet feels droplets spray her own legs.

Gloria's feet are bare. Her hairline is soaked. She stands at the centre of the mess, a light smile tugging at her lips.

Andrew dashes towards her with a broom. "Now it's a party — something's been broken!" But Gloria isn't in the mood to laugh.

Bram thinks he understands. He walks across broken glass and his arms wrap and hold her. Gloria looks up at him, and Juliet sees the other women looking up at him, and she sees that her mother is not the same. She is asking for something different, something her father may not have it in him to give.

She wants him to leave her alone. She wants him to let her stand unprotected in the middle of her own mess. She wants him not to tell her what to do or how to fix it, but just to let her be.

That is what Juliet takes. If she could slide back through time with a camera, she would point it at this, and she would shoot it for all to see. *Bang*.

DEAR RONALD REAGAN

Juliet is always writing.

She writes to her best friend Laci back home in Indiana. Her mother tells her to write to Grandpa Harold and Grandma Grace and to Oma Friesen, and she does, without complaint. She also writes letters that will never be sent, words tumbled into a lined notebook received as a Christmas gift, along with a set of fancy pens, *The Encyclopedia of the Horse* pocket guide, and a stationery set decorated with kittens, too fancy for any ordinary letter.

Dear Isobel, I miss you. I'm growing my hair out. My mom pierced my ears with a needle. She almost stopped after the first side. They're kind of infected.

Dear Charlotte, Dad says we can come see you in Jalapa!!! Mom took us to a volcano, but mostly it's school, school, school.

Dear Juliet-Older-Than-Me, Are you still living in Managua? Have you been to the beach again? Have you gotten to ride a horse?

Juliet and Keith's new school is private, evangelical, with classes conducted entirely in Spanish. Rather than riding the bus, which is overcrowded to the point of comedy or tragedy, depending on one's point of view, they are driven each way by their mother.

The school's classrooms are painted turquoise or fuchsia or sunflower yellow, and are connected by corrugated zinc roofs that shelter concrete walkways from the sun but not the wind. Goats roam the weedy playing field, trimming the grass with their teeth.

At recess Juliet sits under a tree and writes.

Her classmates ask to see what she's writing so diligently, so *constantly*, and they admire the pages upon pages of words in English, which none of them can decipher. Some of the girls stroke Juliet's fine, fiery hair, and Juliet pinches the carved wooden cross hanging around her neck on a thick blue string, head bent, until the girls go away.

What's wrong? they ask. They aren't mean. They are curious. If anyone should recognize and sympathize with the impulse, it is Juliet. But she hates being the object of interest, being defined and misunderstood. She shakes her head and waits for them to leave her alone.

At home, Juliet works on a magazine. Juliet assigns Keith an article and he obliges with a story about *beisbol*, the country's favourite sport. He curls in the lower bunk, poring over the daily newspaper, and includes the latest scores: Managua 7, Rivas 5; Leon 8, Granada 13. Juliet thinks these details are irrelevant. Her own piece describes the three-toed sloth that hangs from a branch in a tree across the street and never appears to move. The sloth may or may not be three-toed — Juliet is unable to count for certain — but she labels it as such, and draws a picture with arrows: greyish brownish fur, closed eyes, long claws. The result is discouraging: her pictures never turn out the way she plans them in her head, though she's frequently pleased with what she writes — sometimes privately amazed, hardly believing the words came from her own head.

Maybe Juliet will be a writer.

She composes and sends a series of letters to the authors of her favourite books, requesting advice. Almost all neglect to reply — several are apparently dead — but within a month a huge cardboard box arrives on their porch in Managua, the delivery itself a miracle, given the city's absurdist system of street addresses (theirs includes the directions "two blocks north of where the little tree used to be"). Encyclopedia Brown's publishers have responded with charitable force: Juliet and Keith rip open the package to discover a generous collection of paperbacks. But the author's letter looks suspiciously mimeographed. Though Juliet reads it carefully, she can discover no clues to How to Be a Writer. If there is a secret formula, the author of Encyclopedia Brown is not sharing.

She will have to figure it out on her own.

She has another letter to write. It has just occurred to her that she can, that letters travel to places otherwise impenetrable, and there are things that he needs to know, which she can tell him.

She will write to Ronald Reagan.

She feels the weight of this letter's importance, and begins with a rough draft. Her mother corrects it, and Juliet copies this version onto a clean sheet of paper, folds it twice, and slides it into an envelope. The letter exits the country with a departing delegation from Pennsylvania, who will post it upon entering the United States.

Dear Ronald Reagan, the letter begins. *You should come to Nicaragua and see what is happening here.*

Juliet believes that in his busyness a visit is something Ronald Reagan has been overlooking, and all he needs is an invitation — hers. She imagines Ronald Reagan walking down this very street where the supposed three-toed sloth hangs, and seeing the children. She senses that the children are of particular importance. They will crowd around him and talk to him, they will explain, and he will stop paying for the Contras to fight.

She spends some weeks in eager anticipation, either of a letter or a visit.

Gradually Juliet thinks of the letter less and less, though it is more a matter of the idea losing its immediacy than of Juliet losing hope. She continues to wait, in pleasant and secret expectation. Even many years later, after Juliet is grown, even many years later, after Ronald Reagan has died, she finds herself in odd moments waiting, and she thinks: I am waiting for his letter.

This is her special gift and curse: the ability to have faith without evidence, to see vividly what isn't there and what will never be.

Here is Ronald Reagan in his Oval Office in his White House. Though Juliet knows otherwise, the White House is a little cottage set in an emerald garden. Inside, the cottage is filled from end to end with one huge, egg-shaped wooden desk that dwarfs the President, who sits behind it impatiently, rummaging through heaps of letters and answering a big black phone.

His fingers linger on a crumpled envelope. The return address has caught his eye — who could be writing to him from Managua, Nicaragua? *Zzzzpt*, the gold-handled letter opener slides under the flap. *Dear Ronald Reagan*, he reads, in a child's printing (Juliet has failed all attempts to learn proper handwriting). Not even halfway through the letter, Ronald Reagan is daubing his eyes. His heart is heavy. He continues.

The children. He has not considered them. He has not considered how some of them are being killed by his very own freedom fighters. How they lack for food sometimes, because of the war. How they are scared of his warplanes flying overhead, booming as they crash through the sound barrier. How the children at school, Juliet and Keith too, scatter and freeze when they hear that crushing noise, how everyone shouts that the Americans have come, that they've dropped the first bomb — the one everyone is waiting for — on Managua.

Of course, Juliet writes, *it wasn't a bomb after all. We are happy you haven't dropped any bombs yet. The bomb shelters are holes in the ground, and only the children will be allowed in. I don't know what we're supposed to eat in there*, Juliet writes.

Nobody here has done anything to you, she finishes. *You should come and see and then you will know.*

And Ronald Reagan, in his Oval Office, holds her letter in his age-spotted fingers, bends his head, and weeps. He is so thoroughly overcome that he must put his head in his arms on the desk, and tears flow down his wrist and smear Juliet's words.

He is quiet like this for a long time, thinking about the children, remembering his own, but most importantly, his thoughts turn with curiosity and compassion towards this particular and extraordinary child, this *Juliet*, who lives in Managua, Nicaragua. He is thinking that he must invite this girl to come and visit him at the White House. He will order a special meal, discovering in advance Juliet's favourite foods (mashed potatoes mixed with green peas, and chicken gravy), and there will be a fancy ball, and Juliet must dress up in a puffy skirt and twirl on the dance floor, and newspaper people will come and take pictures of her and print these pictures in their newspapers, and Juliet will answer questions like *What is it really like in Nicaragua?* and *How does an eleven-year-old girl like you manage to change the President's mind?*

Juliet will answer that it wasn't hard: she just wrote him a letter. She just wrote and told him what was really happening.

Ronald Reagan lifts his head. His face is wet in its creases, his eyes red and swollen. He is already thinking of a plan. He will stop the airplanes. He will stop the freedom fighters. He will stop the war. He will go to Nicaragua. He will see the children. He will save them.

But first, he thinks, I must write back to Juliet.

WHAT HOWARD HUGHES
LEFT BEHIND

Every day on their way to and from school, the Friesen children pass a white graveyard. It tilts on a hill. Each cross is white. The mausoleums are white. The dust is white, because the rainy season has dried up and the landscape is reverting steadily away from greens and floral hues to bleached browns and greys. It makes Juliet wonder: is the world always brown and grey and white under the surface, or is it the opposite, a world of colour hidden under the surface, just a few rains away?

Is there always a world in reverse beneath the surface, waiting to be revealed?

In the graveyard, visitors leave behind plastic flowers. These, and a scattering of toys and dolls, offer the only colour, garish but appealing against all the white.

It is a graveyard for children.

"What's the age limit?" Keith asks, but their mother does not know. What constitutes childhood in a country where a thirteen-year-old like the cook's daughter, Marta, can get pregnant and prepare calmly for motherhood, and sixteen-year-olds, male and female alike, are conscripted from their classrooms en masse and driven to the *campo* to help with the nation's coffee harvest, dangerous work on steep slopes under threat of guerrilla attack?

The children sit in the car with Gloria and watch a truck leave from outside their own school, overflowing with teenagers who sing songs of the revolution, laughing, shouting, waving black and red flags.

"How would I feel as a mother?" Gloria asks. "I would not send you. I would lay down my body."

Juliet believes her and is oppressed by this fervour, which seems both excessive and pointless: her mother would lay down her body and the truck would drive over it. The children would be taken, the sacrifice worse than worthless; it would serve only to steal her from them entirely.

At home Gloria puts a pot of beans on high and they boil over and burn and the stink fills the house. She tosses the mess against the back fence.

Juliet and Keith watch her from above. They have shinnied up the tallest banana tree to get onto the flat roof of their house. They search for treasure and they find: the white bones of a bird, its jagged curving claws; bent nails; misshapen stones; artifacts that they pretend tell the story of a long-lost roof-dwelling civilization. They arrange their collection on undulating zinc near the courtyard's opening, working in agreeable silence.

They can look down on Emmanuel peeing onto the concrete. They have seen a rat walk right out of the drainpipe and into their house. And they hear conversations — they do not think of it as eavesdropping — and by this, they position themselves in time and space, in a reality that is marked by constant change. The Roots of Justice never stays the same; it exists as a stream of volunteers and delegations perpetually coming and going, their arrivals and departures fraught with intensity.

It feels to Juliet that she will know these people forever — how could she not? — and then they are gone.

Andrew doesn't renew his term.

"Don't call it burnout." He hugs Gloria goodbye, her arms piled with wrung wet clothes she will hang on the line in the backyard.

Gloria says, "There's nothing else like this," but there is. It's really very commonplace. It's called war, and on the ground, running, its risks are mundane and it is only and ever about circumstance, and people circling within circumstance.

Their mother is back with more clothes, dry, crumpled, needing to be ironed.

"The blowhard's never even been to Nica and he presumes to tell me —"

"It wasn't just one complaint, Bram."

"Don't invent a conspiracy, Gloria. We stay on. No question."

"If they'll keep you."

"Oh, they'll keep me."

"If we want to stay."

Juliet and Keith look at each other. They want to stay.

They are waiting for their mother. She is late.

She is almost always late, which gives them time to spend

their coins on treats from vendors who wait outside the school gates, but today she is so late that the vendors have packed up and most of the other children are gone, except for those few who have nowhere immediately to go and who loiter restlessly.

Juliet and Keith pass the time by imagining her coming for them on their usual route: "She's turning the corner in Las Piedrecitas. She's coming down the hill. She's at the stop sign by the Palacio Nacional. She's passing the little park. She's going around the big tree. She's close to the Seminaria Bauptista. She's coming around the corner, and if we look up we're going to see her . . . right now . . . right now . . ."

"Nope."

"Okay, so she's backing out of the driveway, and she's going past the guesthouse, past Dr. Romano's, past the three-toed sloth and . . ."

Today is special. Today their mother is taking them to the Hotel Intercontinental to celebrate Keith's ninth birthday, and maybe their father will come too. Their mother hopes.

Keith actually turned nine three weeks ago. It wasn't forgotten exactly, just lost in a shitstorm. (Their mother's phrase; they hate it when she swears. Bad words sound uglier coming from her mouth than from the mouths of other adults.) The children aren't privy to the details, but lying awake in their beds, they smell thick cigarette smoke. Scuttling to the bathroom in what feels like the middle of the night, they see their mother and father pacing the porch.

Juliet witnesses an opaque scene between her father and one of the outgoing volunteers, a woman named Bess with hair shaved close around her head and a wide body tented under colourful cloth. On the street outside their house, Bess weeps; in Juliet's mind, this hysteria connects to Gloria's shitstorm.

Bess is saying goodbye, and the presence of a child is incidental. She is angry. She says to Bram, "I forgive you."

Bram sighs and watches her climb into the waiting minibus with the others who are leaving the country. The driver starts, then stops suddenly, and Bess leaps out and runs back to Bram, and hugs him with awkward fierceness that he does not seem to know how to receive.

"I forgive you too," he says.

"Fuck you," says Bess, and returns to the minibus looking much happier.

Bram looks at Juliet, who looks at him. He shakes his head and attempts no explanation. "I tried," he tells Juliet. It might become his motto.

A delegation of fifty lay pastors from across the United States arrives almost immediately. Keith turns nine. The delegation brings with it no packages from home, and therefore no birthday gifts. Keith has to make do with a brief announcement and a stocky emergency candle stuck into a plate of *gallo pinto* at an orientation meal attended by fifty strangers, who join in singing him Happy Birthday.

Gloria determines that this is not enough. She promises to give him something special, and there is no place more special in Managua than the Hotel Intercontinental. The Hotel Intercontinental is an oasis in the desert of Managua, louche and spectacular amidst the wreckage of the former downtown. It rises in the shape of a concrete pyramid and offers a pool, and a daily brunch buffet that serves a shambling contingent of foreigners: stringers covering the war from this side of the mirrored bar; men sporting Eastern European moustaches; well-meaning Canadians and Japanese; missionaries; drifters; spies.

The children have been once before, when board members of the Roots of Justice visited from Washington and footed the bill. The hotel accepts only American dollars, and its buffet is spread with American food. Juliet and Keith give up imagining their mother on her way to pick them up, and imagine instead what they will eat: waffles and ice cream and macaroni and cheese and Jell-O squares and pink grapefruit juice and tapioca pudding.

Still their mother does not come.

"We could walk to the hotel." (They can see the building, stabbing the clear sky, from the curb where they sit.)

"We're supposed to wait here."

"What if she's not coming?"

"She's coming."

"What if she forgot?"

A taxicab screeches to a stop before them and Gloria leaps out. She wears sunglasses and a long dress that tangles around her ankles and exposes her shoulders and collarbone. "Get in! Get in!"

"What took you so long?"

"Where's the car?"

"Where's Dad?"

There is a sound Gloria makes when she is not in the mood for discussion. It begins in her throat and pitches through clenched teeth and open lips. It is neither groan nor sigh nor grunt, but all combined, an expression of disgust, pain, and deep irritation that only a fool would prod and disturb.

"I have dollars, I have bathing suits, I have your little brother, and as long as the buffet is still open for business, we are going to celebrate this goddamned birthday."

Luxury is air conditioning, macaroni and cheese splattered with ketchup, coagulated fingers of burnt breakfast sausage, french toast with brown syrup, and Juliet is greedy for all of it. She eats diligently through rubbery pasta and smears of sweet sauce. Keith joins her on the velvety banquette. Above his swim trunks he has a boxer's square torso; there is a bruise under his eye that nobody knows how he got. It makes him look tough.

They hear their mother's laugh soar above them, as if swinging from the elegant chandelier overhead. In unison they turn towards a commotion at the buffet. It is a shock to recognize Isobel's brothers, Dirk and Jonathan, piling their plates high with sticky desserts. Isobel stands as far from her brothers as possible.

Gloria flutters her fingers, face bright with excitement, voice carrying across the cushioned room: "Children — Juliet, Keith — you'll never believe who's here in Managua, staying right in this very hotel!"

Juliet hesitates, half stands. Isobel chooses a skewer of grapes and pineapple chunks and comes towards them, placing a grape between her lips and pulling it off. She sits on the bench opposite.

"It's been ages," she says.

"Hi." Juliet feels shy. It is only in seeing Isobel that she comprehends the depths of her loneliness, at school and at home, with only her brothers for company. But she can't say *I missed you.*

The grown-ups congregate around the children's booth, and Heinrich pretends to address Juliet and Keith. "We are here for a conference."

"Oh, but you should have called, you should have told us." Gloria looks at Isobel, as if Isobel has been mildly neglectful.

Clara says to Gloria, "We know how busy you are."

Gloria turns to Clara: "But this is such a happy coincidence!"

"We are enjoying the sun." Clara's expression does not change as she nods and takes her leave, through the swinging glass door into the patio's heat.

"Of course you will join us by the pool." Heinrich bows to the children. He is holding two fancy cocktails, and he grins at Gloria, broadly. "One of these must be for you. I don't know what I was thinking when I ordered."

Gloria places Keith's folded glasses on the small metal table beside her dilapidated plastic lounge chair and he cannonballs into debris-littered water, joining Dirk and Jonathan in their rowdy play. Juliet turns somersaults, brushing her hands on the pool's pebbled blue bottom, but Isobel ignores everyone and floats and gazes dreamily at potted palm leaves sagging overhead.

She pulls her top half out of the water and rests with elbows on hot ceramic tile, and Juliet joins her, mimicking the posture.

"Did you see that boy?" Isobel whispers.

"What?"

"That boy with no shirt, like, sitting by himself?"

Juliet points, "Who — him?"

"Oh my God, I can't believe you did that! Oh my God, Juliet!"

The boy under consideration is not a boy, in Juliet's estimation, but a man, grown, nursing a moustache into fruition, smoking a cigarette. If he notices any of them, it is Gloria, unselfconsciously rubbing oil into her brown shoulders and arms and thighs, slapping it under the straps of her worn black bathing suit. Clara reclines beneath an umbrella, long limbs sheltered by flowing white cotton, reading a paperback novel with a picture on the cover that looks like a photograph but is actually a painting: a fiery sky, a castle, a woman with hair blown wild and upper bosom heaving, a man sweeping her somewhat resistant body towards his naked chest.

"Rubbish," she tells the girls.

Both women sip out of the fancy glasses brought to them by Heinrich, suck on cut fruit swimming in peach-coloured liquid.

"Did you know that Howard Hughes once lived in this hotel?" Heinrich begins.

"I didn't know that." Gloria turns her face, shades her eyes. Emmanuel kneels on her belly and gnaws a triangle of grilled cheese sandwich from the buffet. Crumbs spatter her chest, the bones visible and pronounced.

"Who is Howard Hughes?" Juliet kicks underwater, hair drying beneath the fierce sun.

Heinrich's story goes like this: First, you have to know that Howard Hughes was an immensely wealthy, eccentric

American inventor — and that eccentric means strange or peculiar, some might say crazy.

"Like you, Heinrich," suggests Clara, never lifting her eyes off the page.

In 1972, just before Christmas Eve, a powerful earthquake struck the city of Managua, killing ten thousand people in an instant. Cars bounced in the street like basketballs. But the Hotel Intercontinental stood firm. That same day, at the tip of the hotel's undamaged top, a helicopter mysteriously landed and took off, ferrying away Howard Hughes, who, unbeknownst to the world, had been living in a warren of penthouse suites, completely naked, surrounded by boxes of tissues.

"And you won't believe what Howard Hughes left behind." Heinrich stands bareheaded, relaxed on the balls of his feet.

"I can't imagine," says Gloria. "What did he leave behind?"

"Please," says Clara. "You don't want to know. Heinrich, spare us."

"But it's the best part." Because what Howard Hughes left behind was room upon room filled with neatly labelled and organized bottles of his own urine.

"Why?" Juliet asks.

"He was afraid of germs," says Clara sternly, as if they all might learn a lesson. "He had a compulsive disorder. And he was addicted to drugs."

Less than two years after the earthquake, Heinrich tells them, Howard Hughes was dead, a disfigured, rotten-bodied version of his original self, and all his inexplicable behaviour died with him. This is where Heinrich's story ends.

"Why?" Juliet asks again.

"Why what?" Gloria says impatiently.

"I don't get it."

"There is nothing to get." Clara is kind. "It is a story, that's all. It doesn't mean anything."

Juliet thinks a story should always mean something.

Isobel wrenches herself out of the water, and Juliet follows, flat on her belly across gloriously scorching tile. Clara dries and combs her daughter's hair before allowing the girls to return to the air-conditioned dining room.

"He saw us — I swear to God," Isobel whispers. She has nipples that have begun to swell into breasts, that push out triangles of bikini fabric, and Juliet is flattered to be included — "He saw *us*" — despite her humble one-piece, ragged in the behind. "Oh my God, he's coming in, too. He's following us. Don't look, don't look."

Juliet studiously obeys, but Isobel cannot help herself. "I am totally going to kiss that guy," she tells Juliet. He is too far away to hear, ordering himself an umbrella-accented cocktail at the bar.

"When?" Juliet asks, to stop herself from asking, Why?

"How should I know?" Isobel is practical.

Juliet is hungry again but Isobel is not, so Juliet sits alone, damp bathing suit soaking into the furry fabric of her chair. She gnaws the edges of a flap of pink ham ribboned with white fat, stabbed onto her fork, twirling it slowly. She is only dimly aware that this behaviour is rude, and she carries the impression, from her mother, that it doesn't matter anyway.

People disappear and reappear in this hotel.

The bathrooms are furnished with benches, ornate mirrors,

and shag carpeting. Juliet pulls her bathing suit right down and sits naked upon the toilet seat. Slowly she counts backwards from ten. The toilet paper is thick, not pink and nubbed. Yanked back up, the suit snags damply on skin.

Warm water pours out of the golden tap.

The bathroom echoes silence, but for a breath, a sigh: in the mirror, Juliet spies feet exposed under a locked stall door — two pairs, one bare and one shod in black hard shoes. She freezes, hands dripping. Her panic is nonsensical, radiating from an unmoving, lodged danger, and her heart returns to thumping, crashing, as she runs away.

Juliet stares, shivering, around the busy dining room. Her brother sits owlishly by a window, burnished in sunlight dimmed by dusty glass. She cannot see any of the grown-ups from here, or Isobel, but she isn't looking for clues or explanations. She isn't looking for anything. She is a sponge, absorbing information, holding it, sinking, unable to do anything with it.

It seems that she lives in an unknowable world, on this side of a great divide; on the other side are the grown-ups, who know everything, who hold the answers to the gigantic questions that plague her: How do you know you're in love? How can you be sure about God? What if you're wrong? But she doesn't really want to cross that divide. She doesn't really want to know, for sure, that they don't know either. Someone needs to know. Someone needs to be sure.

Juliet scoops herself a sloppy bowl of chocolate pudding. Sitting across from Keith, she devours the pudding. He sighs, but he can't eat today. He does not know why. He looks at his plate of food and feels hunger, but he cannot swallow even one bite.

Heinrich slaps by them. Juliet looks, but she isn't certain: was it a pair of shoes she saw in that stall, or could it have been sandals paired with black socks like those Heinrich wears, white hairs on his legs tufting out above elasticized cuffs?

Gloria waves from the other side of the window. One arm twists behind her back to hide the burning cigarette. She is close to the glass, looking for and finding them, waving to Juliet and Keith, mouth wide, high cheekbones bright.

Juliet licks insipid chocolate off her wrist.

Isobel slides onto the bench beside her. "Don't tell," she whispers.

Juliet shifts her a glance. "Okay."

"He gave me his room number." Isobel sits in triumph.

Behind her mother, Juliet sees Emmanuel jump silently into the pool, the splash of water displaced by his body, his hands raised, disappearing. But he can't swim. Behind her mother, Juliet sees Clara leap, then emerge. Her mother turns slowly, too slowly. Clara's white dress sucks against her skin and Emmanuel's dark head is a blotch against her breast, as they bob together in the water, laughing and laughing.

It seems only natural that Heinrich and Clara will invite Gloria and the children to spend more time with them. Juliet does not question why her mother lets them skip school, why she packs their bathing suits and towels and hats and a basket of fruit and a knife, why they wait by the gate with such excitement for Heinrich and Clara to arrive in their pickup truck, for Heinrich to lean out his window and slap the metal door with his open palm: *"Vamos a la playa!"*

"*Caliente el sol,*" sings Gloria in reply.

Lake Xiloa is a volcanic lagoon near the city, with a beach of startling black sand. They have visited it several times in the company of volunteers, and once, before Christmas, with Bram. The waters have no bottom and are believed to be haunted, layer upon layer of sunless depths through which to fall. Festooning the beach are huts with picnic tables, their supports sunk into concrete under palm-leafed roofs. The water lapping the black sand is buoyant and soft with nutrients and salts soaked out of volcanic rock.

There are paddleboats for rent, but Clara hates boats: she hates water. Today's book cover is indigo-skied, stars over a midnight lake, a woman in pale, flowing nightwear, a man with a riding whip.

"But who will come with me?" Heinrich wonders.

"Oh," says Gloria. "I suppose . . . but we can't take Emmanuel."

"Isobel will look after him," says Clara. "Isobel hates boats too."

"Mom!"

"You're better off where I can see you," says Clara. "Your father might throw you overboard."

Heinrich sighs.

"Subject closed," says Clara. "Enjoy your tour."

There are no lifejackets.

The other side of the lagoon is darkly treed and looks near enough to touch. It seems they could be there and back in time for lunch. Sitting side by side, relaxed in bucket seats, Heinrich and Gloria pedal cheerily, and the children — Juliet, Keith, Dirk, and Jonathan — sprawl across the flat back section and dangle their feet into warm water. But no matter that the beach from which they've set sail grows smaller and smaller, no matter the churning pedals, they never seem to advance.

The trees on the other side are anonymous, merged into a singular, unyielding mass.

"Strange," says Heinrich.

It is as if they are under a spell: everything moves and no progress is made. Flickering shimmers dance on the water's surface, but there is nothing to see. No fish. Sunlight penetrates the upper layer of green water, but beneath is cold and obscured, dead. Juliet could sit for hours and stare, as if into a burning fire, mesmerized.

Slowly, stealthily, waves rise and beat at them, lap, lap, lapping with liquid tongues at the boat's sides, licking higher, oozing across the pale pink deck.

Heinrich's sons beg to swim.

"Forget it," he says.

The boat heaves and plunges, temporarily weightless, awash. Juliet believes it is unsinkable. She also believes that taxis and buses never crash, that every movie that makes it to the theatre must be objectively good, and that her own hands clasped in a certain special formation across her waist will act as effectively as a seatbelt in a moment of emergency.

"Should we turn around?" Gloria's sunglasses are suddenly incongruous.

Heinrich heaves on the rudder, and the boat shudders. Out here, in the middle of the lake, the weather is different, changed. When did it change? Black clouds gather. The wind flings spray onto their exposed bodies and chills the skin; goosebumps rise, a strange, forgotten feeling in this perpetually hot country.

"Turn around," says Gloria.

"I am trying," Heinrich says in a low voice. "Can you pedal any harder?"

Fear brushes Juliet, but washes away in a moment. She thinks about Dirk's hand, quite near her own. She thinks about touching it, by accident. They are turning. They float in silence, a pink speck of life upon spreading, quiet black. *Ca-chunk-ca-chunk* splash the puny paddles beneath.

Juliet sees that Heinrich's hand rests atop Gloria's on the rudder. She sees, but does not see, because her mind is elsewhere, distracted, working to sustain belief in this vessel, because her mind loops round and round the same narrow track of internal, necessary reassurance and all other images and sounds are peripheral, taken in through the skin, dimly scratched on the canvas of her mind, to be recalled later like a dream bleached transparent.

"I'm thirsty." Keith's glasses are splotched with droplets of lake water, spits of rain. "When will we get back?"

"I don't know," Heinrich says after a while.

They are making their way towards land, but it is not the beach from which they came.

"We're close now."

"I don't know," Heinrich says again.

Waves nudge them intractably towards a rocky cliff face; at a distance, it looks sheer. Up close, they are lifted and flung whole into a secret space beneath towering stone, hollowed-out watery caves that threaten decapitation.

The boat is thrown like driftwood, grating against invisible rocks, trapped.

"How well do your children swim?" asks Heinrich quietly.

"Oh God." Gloria herself cannot, Juliet knows.

"I have to get into the water and push. These pedals are shit."

"Go," says Gloria.

With one hand slipped behind her neck, he pulls her towards him and kisses her forehead. "I'm so sorry."

No one says anything. Eyes open, bodies still and low. They have crossed into another world, a raw and splayed world that holds them captive. All is very quiet, or very loud — it is impossible to tell, either sensation overwhelming all else, the rest of the world beyond reach or interpretation, removed. Juliet feels the soft green watery depths beckoning. She feels what it would be like to capsize, to be thrown adrift, to struggle and to sink.

Heinrich splashes overboard. He swims strongly, fighting the boat. At times he is pinned to the rock face, straining and ruddy. His lips will explode.

Juliet crunches her knees against her chest and holds on.

In Managua, littering Juliet's shelf and the floor under her bed, is a pile of books she is in the midst of devouring, called "Choose Your Own Adventure."

Grandma Grace sends them from the United States in packages, along with Black Stallion books and the entire Anne of Green Gables series. The Choose Your Own Adventures are intended for Keith, but Juliet's taste is for words in any form, any shape, any combination, and she finds these particularly edible. In each, sections of narrative end with several options. The reader makes her choice, flips through pages to find the corresponding subsequent section, and discovers the consequences. Callous death awaits the wrong choice: an abrupt plunge over a cliff's edge, burial beneath a convenient avalanche. Other choices rescue the characters, but unsatisfactorily, and others yet escort them to the most happy of endings.

Juliet unpeels the books whole, retracing her steps, reading every possible combination. The stories are simple adventures, the choices lacking moral cause and effect. If you follow the path through the pine forest, you die; if you hike through the swamp, you live.

Life is nothing like a Choose Your Own Adventure. Except for when it is, in its randomness: a cancer cell splitting and spreading ruthlessly within the bloodstream; a storm rising on a deadly lake. Except for when it is, in the way the ending changes — in memory, in meaning rather than substance.

"Pray," Gloria commands.

Almost imperceptibly the shoreline is changing. They are beyond the caves. There are fewer rocks, more trees. And then, there is sand, there are huts in the woods, cooking fires burning. Slowly, slowly, Heinrich crawls beside the boat while Gloria pedals and Dirk directs the rudder.

They can see Clara in her fluttering white wrap.

They can hear Emmanuel's wails of grief. At heart, he is closest to knowing what was almost lost, what almost happened out there on the silent lake, because he is closest among them to the state of unbeing. But he has no words, and he won't tell. None of them will, exactly.

There are enough ghosts without inventing ones that might have been.

The real choice, the one that changes this story, is made invisibly.

Gloria staggers onto the beach, following the children, weeping in a way that frightens everyone. Here is Heinrich. He is weak, stationary for this moment, ankles underwater. He looks at the women and children on the black sand. He takes a step. Even then, Juliet knows there is more significance than what can be glimpsed in this instant, on this beach. Choice isn't revelatory. The shock of one charged moment is nothing compared to the languid, haunting reverberations that undulate into a long and unlived future.

Heinrich chooses Clara.

"Why can't I go to the pool tonight?" In the gravel parking lot, Isobel picks up an argument that has chased them all afternoon.

"You know why." Clara's shawl flaps furiously in the deepening breeze.

"It's our last night. Juliet can come with me. She can come back with us and spend the night."

"She cannot," says Clara.

"Please? Pretty please? Pretty please with sugar on top and whipped cream and icing and chocolate sprinkles and —"

"We are saying goodbye, Isobel. This is it."

This. Juliet feels tears well and trickle foolishly through spiky eyelashes, even while the boys run up slurping *bebidas* out of plastic bags, sticky liquid spilling.

"I told you not to buy them anything!"

"We'll swing by your house and drop you off," says Heinrich. He makes it sound like a generous offer. Gloria is unmoving behind her sunglasses.

The grown-ups squeeze into the cab, and all the children, except for Emmanuel, ride crouched and bouncing on the flat metal bed behind.

"I kissed him," Isobel breathes into Juliet's ear. "And that's not all."

The wind carries everything away.

Bram greets them at the gate. He lifts his children over the side of the truck, knowing nothing of this day. Their house waits silently behind the fence.

"Goodbye," everyone sings. Juliet would cry, but the grown-ups are laughing, and laughter is easy, laughter lifts and snares, lifts and lies. All these grown-ups, talking over each other, drowning each other out.

"Our paths will cross again." Heinrich slides his frame behind the wheel of the truck. He says it twice. "We'll meet again."

Juliet believes him. He is certain. He seems to know for sure.

Grown-ups. They think they can change change itself.

Because this story collapses, crushed from beginning to end. Juliet has to steal everything she learns about what happens next. The grown-ups speak of it with a low solemnity that masks horror, shock; but they cannot pour it out.

Because these two families will not meet again. Their paths will never cross.

Here it remains — this story that goes on until Juliet is a middle-aged woman standing in her wintry kitchen holding in her hands a diminished collection of possibilities. Here it is — an indestructible essence that dangles like the blown glass ornament in Juliet's kitchen window: a story from another country, from a time long ago. Inside the glass is a frozen figure. He's hanging by the neck. Who will find him? Who will cut his big blond body down and lay him to rest?

Juliet's questions might wake for eternity, never to find peace. Is this story hers to hold, or even to behold?

No matter: she holds; she beholds; and the mystery is sealed. She cannot alter its insistence that it will be the thing that it is, no matter how horrifying, how unwanted, how inscrutable, how grievous, how — if she catches herself looking at a certain time of day, when the light lowers and shines through it — shockingly beautiful.

AMULETS

ONE

Seven of them are travelling towards the Honduran border over mined roads in a white Jeep . Every spare inch is crammed with supplies: notebooks and pens, a new tape recorder, batteries, water canteens, butane lighters, chloroquine and Bactrim and iodine tablets. Juliet and Keith perch atop luggage behind the back seat, trying not to kick each other. Juliet asks Yuri, who is turned around so he can entertain them, why there is enough room for their bodies but not for their legs.

Yuri says it is because they are upright creatures with lengthy appendages.

Bram sits peacefully beside Josiah, a new volunteer, who is driving and has been since Estelí, where they stopped for lunch at the home of an American nun, Sister Mary Grace. Juliet scooped beans and rice with cold, black-spotted tortillas before running outside to play alone in the shaded dirt.

Sister Mary Grace held Juliet's brother's clammy head, her blue-veined hands stroking his hair. Keith did not resist. Juliet saw him through the open doorway, resting for this moment against Sister Mary Grace's white blouse, his head a dark shadow. The mouldering backyard was surrounded by concrete walls embedded on top with broken beer bottles. From the yard next door erupted the clucking of invisible chickens, a noise Juliet will associate with the hurtling of time, with there not being enough.

"God be with you," said Sister Mary Grace, waving as they pulled away.

The answer to that is *And with you*.

They are in the mountains now, past Ocotál's hallucinogenic pine forests, and climbing. It is the dry season and the surrounding hills are pale, chalky. The road twists and snakes, and when a Russian-made truck speeds past from the opposite direction, the Jeep's tires leave the gravel. In the back, with the luggage, Juliet shrieks with glee as she is flung into the air.

"I feel sick," says Keith.

"Bram, he's going to be sick!"

A shortlist of things to fear: the hills opening up, automatic weaponry, macho posturing, stepping on a mine, thrown into the air, engulfed in flame, ambush. What Juliet fears: snakes. She huddles in the truck with Emmanuel, who is sprawled in sweaty sleep on the middle bench seat. Gloria supports Keith beside the rear tire, the sound of his struggle, his fight against his body, wrenching in the absence of the bruising wind. The others urinate into a field of bleached grass. The air is heavy, inert. Insects rasp.

Juliet does not see the men with guns, sees instead her dad and Josiah and Yuri raise their hands above their heads. A skinny dog circles, sniffs at whatever came out of Keith, and Gloria almost screams, rises, dragging Keith with her, her shoulder blades bashing the truck's dusty frame.

Juliet sees them now, one older and one younger. They carry machine guns, AK-47s, which everyone here calls *ah-kahs*. They might be a father and his son, the boy wearing ragged fatigues, ammunition across his shoulder like a pageant sash; he is not much older than Juliet herself. His father's incongruous dress shirt is almost transparent, yellow under the armpits, hanging over a pair of black belted pants. He peers through the back window, into Juliet's eyes, and she sees a deep brown poke of blood mottling the white of his left one, the hair above his lip silver spikes trapped in folds of skin. He ignores her, so calm that no line in his face changes shape.

"What can we do for you?" calls Bram.

"*Americanos.*"

"We're going to Jalapa," says Bram.

"So go." The man waves the hand that holds a cigarette.

Slowly Bram returns his arms to his sides. "What's happening? Do you have information?"

"Ah, you are Americans. You'll be fine."

"Is it the Contra?"

The man shrugs.

"The Frente?"

But there is no telling what the man knows.

Doors slam. No one bothers with seatbelts. Josiah pulls on the steering wheel and the Jeep's tires spin, spitting gravel. Juliet looks back at the father and son standing in the road, watching them go.

"Easy," Bram says to Josiah. "If you need a break, take a break."

Josiah does not want a break; he wants a cigarette. Yuri lights one for him, and one for Gloria too. With the windows open, smoke and dirt stream through the vehicle like a river that tastes in a fine grit on Juliet's tongue, inside her cheeks.

"Have you ever seen a sky so white?" Gloria's hand quivers as she lifts the cigarette to her mouth.

"Uh-oh," says Bram.

A pickup truck blocks the road. The Jeep fishtails to a stop on stones. Stillness. Dust choking, drifting slowly downhill.

"Which side are they on?" Gloria holds the cigarette, unfinished, but does not draw.

"Not ours."

"Everybody out!" The leader stands in the truck bed. His men are lean, dressed in jungle fatigues in varying stages of decay; boys, really.

The teenager who guards them cannot stop talking, words crashing against words like kite string unravelling into the sky, laughter, flashing teeth, excitement, hysteria. The others eviscerate the Jeep, packages and packs ripped open, Juliet's own bag dumped. One of the boys steps onto her baby blanket.

"No!"

Time blinks, stalls. But the leader bends, flicks the blanket to the teenager, who offers it to Juliet. He grins. "For you."

Gloria uses the blanket to wipe Emmanuel's howling face; woken prematurely from his nap, he is not happy.

"Trouble's come looking for you." The leader sweeps his gun at them, addresses Bram, who stands in reply: "We're going to Jalapa."

"You should go home instead."

Bram is silent.

"She's a nice truck. How does she run?"

"We are going to Jalapa."

"Ah, my friends, it's going to be a long walk."

"Give him the keys," says Gloria in English, rising. Reflexively, one of the boys trains his gun on her.

Bram steps between them. "Take what you want."

"Ah, thank you, thank you." The leader reaches for Bram's hand and shakes it as if he is concluding a pleasant business deal, slaps his shoulder.

Their guard marches the family and Yuri and Josiah away from the road into leafless brush, pushing deeper and deeper into the lush mountain desert. Small plants can be seen growing everywhere, tough, pale scraps of life clinging, rooted beneath the dust, waiting for sustenance. Hanging on.

Is this it? It does not occur to Juliet that it might be. She is thirsty, her mother has given Emmanuel her special blanket, and every winking shadow is snake-shaped.

The teenager stops. "Wait here." He pats Juliet's head roughly, like an older brother might, before backing away, gun pointed at them, then turning and running.

They hear the Jeep's engine turning over. Dust from its exit, and the pickup's, floats down to them.

"I can't believe it," says Josiah. He's excited. "I can't fucking believe it. Contras. Right here."

"They're operating pretty deep for the Contra," says Bram.

"Holy shit," says Josiah.

"Watch the language."

"I'm sorry. Fuck."

Bram wraps his arm around Gloria's shoulder, the palm of his hand cradling her cheek, pulling her head gently against his body. She resists.

"We quit," she is crying. "We quit this job. We quit this country. We are going home. Do you hear me, Bram? We are done."

And Bram says: "Have faith, Gloria."

In the middle of the road are tire tracks, boot prints.

"They took my baseball glove," says Keith.

Bram lifts him, protesting, to kiss the top of his head. They begin walking, slowly, following the road north and east.

"Wait."

They all hear it: the rumble of a struggling engine in pursuit. Juliet instinctively scrambles away, but Bram calls her back. If the advancing vehicle is populated with enemies, so are the hills surrounding, and if Juliet's dad believed only in that, he would never have come to this country in the first place, would never have put his family into a Jeep and driven these roads. The fact that Juliet and Keith and Emmanuel are here, in this landscape, in this moment, is proof that the worst can be changed into something else.

They all hear what Gloria is muttering under her breath, as if it were being said by someone else: *I give them back to you,*

Lord, I give them back to you, I release them, Lord, they're yours, take them.

A colourless Lada brakes on loose gravel — peeled-off roof, doughnut tires, and holes where once belonged head-lights and windows.

"Get in." His white dress shirt flows loosely around thin arms; his gun, and his son, nowhere in sight. *"Americanos."*

Yuri balances Keith and Juliet, one on each knee, beside Gloria and Emmanuel in the back seat.

"Your lap or mine?" says Josiah to Bram after a pause, and laughter pours like medicine down their throats. Juliet can feel herself breathing again. She tugs the blanket from Emmanuel and sinks her hands into its softness, wrapping her wrists like a fur muff. Emmanuel hits her and grabs.

"I don't want to leave," she tells her mother. "I don't want to go home."

"Give the blanket to Emmanuel, Juliet. Now."

Afternoon shrinks to twilight as the ancient engine broaches corners and guts its way into a valley and out again, where await them plots of *jocote* trees and orange groves and cool pines barely visible in the raw blackness of night. The driver refuses their invitation to stay the night, but not a few of the American dollars Bram has kept hidden in the lining of his boot. Yuri's pocket flashlight illuminates the rutted main street of downtown Jalapa.

Juliet steps over a narrow, garbage-strewn concrete chan-nel that separates the road from a line of attached houses. Charlotte waits in the doorway, electricity off, the cramped room alight with candles. A pot of beans bubbles on her little gas stove over licking tongues of flame, blue and orange.

Charlotte has a hug for each of them, but Bram holds her at arm's length. "This has been a day and a half," he says.

"And Gloria," says Charlotte. Their hair lingers together as their heads touch and part.

"I couldn't let Bram come all by himself," says Gloria. "Could I."

"Pineapple?" offers Charlotte.

Keith and Juliet eat and eat. They gorge themselves until their tongues prickle and burn with the fruit's sweet acid, and then they rinse sticky elbows and chins in the *pila* standing in the tiny courtyard.

Stunted banana trees are growing all around them, right out of the dirt floor, and the shadows of bats pass in and out of the house through the wide opening in the tin roof. It is just the two of them here, spying on the grownups through jungly leaves. She loves her brother — but is this retrospect? They have the capacity to argue over the most insignificant subjects, over who sits where, over who saw what first; they toss magic phrases at each other like amulets, lists of words that have weight only because they've agreed between the two of them that they do: *black ball beats them all, called it, stamped it, red ball, silver ball, no backsies, no cheatsies,* and others she can no longer recall. And there is no one to ask: Do you remember? Can you tell me, do you remember what they meant?

Here they are, still and together in this private interior forest, and she loves him. She loves that it is the two of them, that they have each other for protection, that in the worst of moments she can glance at him and away and know: he knows too. Even if they never talk about it (because they never do). Even so. He knows. He knew.

What it feels like to float unmoored, to be carried on the breeze or blown by hurricane winds, to be given back to God. What it feels like to part suddenly from friends, to live without warning, with terminal uncertainty, to know everything in an instant will change. What it feels like to be called, to let go of the self, a feeling of running amidst an epic rainstorm, drenched and amazed, shot far beyond the boundaries of what is proper and expected.

Maybe this is what it feels like to be a boy with a gun. Maybe.

Think of the things these two could say to each other, here, under green-veined leaves. But it seems they never say the things that could be said, and it seems that is okay too, because what could these two say to each other that would fit more perfectly than a line of words strung together by magic, a spell that binds them, brother and sister, in this house lit by flame, in this town under siege, near the border of a country that is not theirs and never will be, and which they do not claim?

Here they are. Let them be.

TWO

Of all the songs sung by the Roots of Justice volunteers, the one Juliet loves most asks, "Where have all the flowers gone?"

Each verse follows a repetitive pattern, carrying forward until the song curves around to end at its own beginning, illuminating it so that the meaning changes, she sees differently, she understands where all the flowers are growing in the first place — in a graveyard, beneath which soldiers lie. The delicious shiver as the guitar strums into its final surprise of *Gone to flowers, every one.*

Why does this song so affect her? It is composed of only a few spare lines, but it needs nothing more to build a cumulative picture so vivid, so elemental, of the double forces of creation and destruction. What are flowers, if not for plucking? What is youth, if not for abandon? What are seasons, if not for turning? What are soldiers, if not for war?

But war is never mentioned in the song.

How can the most important part be left out and the song still say everything that needs saying? But it does.

Juliet is going to tell a story. She knows the rules, the five W's, five sister witches who must be beguiled into gathering and pouring out their tinctures and their powders, lest the story emerge from the pot deformed, unbreathing, lest it bubble until it is burnt away, stillborn. Magic. It's as good as anything for explaining why one tale comes out for good and another does not. Effort, though a fine starting place, is not the half of it.

This story emerges in a dark barroom; they serve underage, and she thinks she is in love with the boy who listens to it. This is a theme. She will give it to the ones she loves, and she will love the ones who listen. It grows with her. It fills journals: a black hardcover with blank pages meant for sketches;

another, a gift, leather-bound; several flimsy drugstore note-books. It ages. It is stamped into three passports. Years separate it from itself, decades. It is a silent argument, a dream she waits to have again, an album of photographs never taken.

Who? Juliet. What? Going away. Where? To Nicaragua. When? When she was still a child, aged ten. Why? Yes, why? Because she went. Because it happened (didn't it?). Because it happened (not like this).

There is no time to waste: Juliet knows this. A test has found something in her brother's blood, a disruption, a word that can be spoken only in a whisper, and only when there is no way to avoid saying it altogether. The more it is said, the more it multiplies — that is what it seems to Juliet. *Cancer, cancer,* spreading on the tongue, filling the cheeks, spilling into the air, mutating and deadly; but Juliet is a child and *deadly* does not mean to her in childhood what it will mean to her when she grows up. Neither does *cancer*; both glittering, but without consequence. When she is a child, the words are separate from her, crusted like jewels inside stone, cannot be dug out and admired and feared.

She knows enough to be afraid.

She does not know enough not to be just a little bit thrilled. Maybe she never will.

Juliet and Keith perch on duffel bags, wearing, for once, clean clothes. Juliet's shoes have been purchased for this occasion at the American store, where imported goods can be bought with dollars. She already regrets her choice: their electric blue, their lack of laces, which she so admired on the shelf, look ridiculous in the murky sunshine that pours through hot, dirty windows.

Bram hugs Gloria and speaks into her hair. She is weeping.

Juliet looks at Keith, who is looking at the floor.

Out the windows are coconut palms and broken concrete and trucks painted military green and soldiers smoking cigarettes. Will Juliet ever see anything like this again?

But she must.

Call me, call me as soon as you — *Bram* — and I'll come as soon as I — call — please, forgive me, what choice do we — you never — we haven't — this isn't, is it? The end?

Emmanuel sleeps slumped in the seat between Keith and Juliet. The airplane is half empty, the largest plane on which Juliet has ever flown, expansive, enormous, and plush. The stewardesses offer the children colouring books and crayons and any kind of pop or juice they might desire, but Keith will only take a small sip and shake his head, no thank you.

Gloria has disappeared. At first Juliet thinks she has gone to the bathroom, but she is gone for so long that cannot be it, no, and then Juliet begins to hear, so slowly, creeping into her eardrums, a muffled wailing from the rear of the plane, a keening that rises and goes on and on, and she begins to know, horribly, that this is her mother.

This is the sound of her mother breaking into little pieces.

Juliet stands, like a sleepwalker. Keith's eyes are closed, weary.

Juliet sways. Suspended in thin air, she floats along the carpeted aisle until she comes upon this small disturbance, these women in blue skirts and jackets pinning to the seat this crumbled, echoing body: her mother's. Her mother's head rocks from side to side on orange fabric, hair mashed and wild, in one hand a lit cigarette that is burnt almost to her knuckle, in the other a glass of white wine, which the stewardess is whispering to her to lift, to drink, to swallow. And the plane floods with consequences, the plane careers the sky with all that will happen, all that may, all that is being left behind, and all that refuses to be.

Juliet can't see out these windows. It isn't dark yet, but she cannot see. The plane is over water, but she cannot see. She can't see the blue and green earth turning below her, pulling her towards the endings that await.

Keep it like this. Float. Suspend.

Drink, drink, you'll feel better.

My son has cancer.

He'll be fine, says the stewardess. You have to believe.

Tell me, asks Juliet, what could you hold in your hands to prevent anything bad from happening ever? What could you wear around your neck, what could you eat or drink, to what god could you pray, what could you burn, what could you promise? And if you knew, would you?

The story begins like this. The story begins: Juliet is telling her story.

PART TWO

DISRUPTION

APARTMENT NUMBER THREE

Oma Friesen's first name is Elizabeth.

In the New Testament, Elizabeth has grown to old age unable to bear a child; she is visited by her young relative Mary, who has been told by an angel that she will bear the son of God, and at this news, in Elizabeth's belly, a baby leaps for joy. Both will bear sons: fruit given to women who believe that nothing is impossible with God.

If Oma Friesen were named for the biblical Elizabeth she cannot know, and she wonders, because she has come to believe that a name is a fortune, a gift from parent to child. But the question had not arisen in her before her parents died, a year apart, each of a brain hemorrhage. Oma Friesen was seventeen — and nobody's oma — when her father went to bed with a vicious headache and did not rise again, and eighteen when her mother's coffin nestled into the ground beside her father's. And though she was not alone in the world, her sisters were grown and married with small children, and she was free to do what most young women of her era could not: she escaped.

"Where did you go?"

She went to West Germany, which was then a nation impoverished and defeated after the Second World War, to the village of Bad Dürkheim, where she worked for a Christian agency that housed, clothed, fed, and instructed forty children chosen from those families most desperate in the surrounding villages and towns. The children were not orphans, but Oma Friesen, herself an orphan, believed their situation was more pathetic. These were children abandoned not by fate but by those who should love them most, sent away out of raw necessity, the ruthlessness of desperation.

The agency's focus was the children's moral instruction. Oma Friesen thought little of that but kept her opinions to herself. Already she was the woman she would become: compassionate, but practical.

Now she is no longer young. Her only son, Juliet's father, is long grown. For many years she lived by herself. During those years she established small and particular routines, which she continues to follow though she is no longer alone. Juliet and her family, all but Bram, have come to stay; they have nowhere else to go.

Every day, even on Saturdays and Sundays, Oma Friesen dresses in clothes that look the same: off-white elastic-waisted pants creased down the centre of each leg, a flowing flowered top, and running shoes. She sits at her table and eats an English muffin drizzled with honey and drinks a cup of black, unsweetened tea, and just before eight, she leaves the apartment to ride the bus downtown, where, on a shabby, quiet street, in a rambling brick house that has been converted into a shelter, she counsels girls who are troubled by unwanted fruit.

Oma Friesen used to manage a home for unwed mothers — girls who had been sent from away to birth their babies in secret, adopt them out, and return to their families unscathed — but such homes have gone out of fashion. The new shelter is for girls who have been hurt or abandoned, who are angry and suffer addictions, and who long to keep their babies.

It is Oma Friesen's job to listen to the girl, and to ask the girl to listen for the baby leaping with joy inside her womb.

When she tucks Juliet in, as she does on nights when Gloria stays at the hospital with Keith, she does not linger or ask to hear Juliet's prayers, as Grandma Grace would. She says, "Goodnight, child," and she turns out the light, whether or not Juliet has marked her spot in her book. It comforts Juliet to hear her in the hallway in her rocking chair, knitting needles clicking in the near dark.

Oma Friesen's apartment has five rooms: the bedroom shared by Juliet and Emmanuel (he falls asleep with the light on when he's not staying at the hospital too); the bedroom Gloria shares with Keith, which was Oma Friesen's before they arrived last month; the living room, where Oma Friesen now sleeps on the pullout sofa; the bathroom; and the kitchen, which, though cramped with five around the table, is spacious enough to eat in. The hallway is a thin slit down the centre of the apartment to which the other rooms cling; it begins at the front door and ends at a window, high in the wall, that receives the eastern morning light. A lone spider fern hangs in the window and the rocker sits beneath, strewn with shed fronds. In a hidden compartment in the embroidered footstool, Oma Friesen stores her knitting supplies. This is not a play area.

Oma Friesen's apartment is in the basement of a red brick building that stands back from a moderately busy street in a small city in Canada, a foreign country to which Juliet has only recently been told she also belongs. Three storeys tall, not including the basement, the building is a narrow structure that houses one separate unit on each floor. In the front yard, two maple trees flourish in spring bloom. The building backs onto a creek, which Juliet has not been expressly forbidden to explore, and to which she retreats when she is sent outside to play. It is shallow, and on its steep, slick banks garbage gathers in the spines of weeds.

Juliet has never seen another child at the creek.

No one from school walks down this street. She has been placed in the sixth grade. In her classroom the children are being taught their first words of French, but the children in the other sixth-grade classroom have been learning French since grade one, and the divide between the two groups is visible in their clothes and shoes, and the colour of their skin. The children in the other classroom are white, hair brushed sleek and tidy, their clothes branded with alligators, their shoes with shiny pennies.

Juliet knows that fortune is on her side. She has no alligators, no pennies, and her hair is braided, infrequently, by Oma Friesen into two long plaits that as the week passes fray into a halo of loose strands. At recess she wanders the muddy playground with a girl who wears white jeans and thick glasses, and another who must cover her hair with a headscarf, even for gym class, and whose parents do not let her listen to the Bible story their teacher reads every morning; instead she stands in the hallway with the melting boots until it is over.

Both of Juliet's friends come by bus and carry their lunches; they eat sitting in the foyer outside the front office with the other children who do not walk home for lunch.

Except, the girls are not exactly friends; they are agents of mutual protection.

Juliet walks home for lunch. On days when Keith is at the hospital, Oma Friesen leaves a sandwich wrapped in a washed milk bag in the fridge, and an apple, and Juliet pours herself a glass of milk. The apartment is empty, silent but for the breath of its own shifting weight.

On days when Keith is not at the hospital, Juliet's mother is here to heat up a can of soup for their lunch. Between treatments Keith goes to school too, but it is much worse for him than for Juliet; if she is the latecomer, he is the freakish stranger, his appearances rare, his skull hidden under a baseball cap, dark spots like bruises beneath his eyes. He is not entirely bald: he refuses to be parted from the sparse bleached strands that remain and float like spider's silk around his naked skull. The boy who sits behind him knocks his hat off. Keith puts it back on. The boy knocks it off. The teacher makes Keith stand at the front of the class, without his hat, and tells everyone that Keith has cancer.

Then they call him cancerboy.

Juliet hates them with an anger that has no expression. She wishes Keith could stay home on days when he is not at the hospital. She wishes she could stay home with him. They would play in the creek, away from the mockery of Canadian children, who care too much about too many things Juliet and Keith know nothing about: television programs, movie stars, punk rock bands and boy bands, fashion, hockey, ringette.

Oma Friesen does not own a television, or even a record player. There is neither time nor money to waste at the movie theatre (Oma calls it a waste). The mall is a very long bus ride away, and there are perfectly decent clothes to be found at the second-hand store. Hockey is a violent sport that rewards angry men and boys. Ringette is an unsolved feminine mystery.

The books Juliet chooses from the school library are various. She reads as if famished, every spare minute, even on the walk to and from school, her focus on the page; underneath the spread words her feet move in a blur along the sidewalk.

At suppertime Oma Friesen asks Juliet to put down the book and join them, but Juliet is far away. Quietly, firmly, Oma Friesen lifts the words from Juliet's fingers. Juliet blinks back to these strange underground rooms, where she finds herself seated at Oma Friesen's laminated tabletop, a paper napkin in her lap, faced with another bowl of bland slop served out of the orange and brown Crockpot: beans, hamburger, barley, macaroni, canned tomatoes, more or less. The tableau remains the same: her dad is not here.

"Do you know the story of Romeo and Juliet?" Oma Friesen asks Juliet.

Gloria says, "She wasn't named for that. I just liked the name Juliet, that's all." Washed out and past pale, Gloria's dirty turtleneck smells strongly of underarm sweat. Keith is resting on the double bed he shares with his mother. They are waiting for the sound of him waking, retching. Gloria will snap alert, as if shocked by an electrical current, to run to him.

Oma Friesen says, "More tea, Gloria?" and Gloria stares at her. "Oh. Yes."

Oma Friesen pours. "I tell the girls at the shelter, the name you choose will be a gift to your child, so choose with care. I had such lofty intentions for my poor infant boy. Abraham — prophet, patriarch. What a burden, and no one could stop me. But he went ahead and made his name his own. Maybe that was the gift I gave him: to rise above."

Oma Friesen offers her thoughts in little stabs, an awkward dance performed without a partner; Gloria remains silent. Oma Friesen does not sigh when she reaches the end. She waits with unreasonable expectation for someone to care; she will wait without malice and with hope, generously.

Juliet says to her mother, "Can I take horse lessons?"

Gloria says, "No."

"It's not fair."

Gloria says, "What is?"

Oma Friesen takes Juliet's hand and squeezes it. She smiles warmly, her eyes bright with sudden tears, and she says, "Juliet, you will love passionately: that is your parents' gift to you."

Gloria says, "It's just a pretty name, that's all."

"It is that. Like yours, Gloria."

"I was named for a song, I think." Gloria has waited to speak until the thread is nearly gone; considering. She hums to herself. Juliet frowns, reminded of something she'd forgotten had been lost: her mother making music.

Her mother stops. She looks at Oma Friesen. "It could be a curse, too, not a gift. Doomed to star-crossed love. But I didn't name her for that."

Juliet reads *The Secret Garden* and *A Little Princess*, which feature characters torn out of one life and tossed into another: fairy-tale endings that leave her sobbing. She dances through the Emily books and thinks Anne slightly inferior.

But she also devours books she cannot possibly understand; she is at an age — eleven and a half — that does not object to partial comprehension. Books that confuse and mystify appear to hold important information just out of reach. She stumbles upon Canadian literature: a stack of paperbacks beside her mother's bed. Juliet reads *The Diviners*, which she cannot make sense of, especially the parts to do with sex, and *Surfacing*, crammed with vivid images that fail to cohere in her brain; nevertheless, she finishes both, moved by a sense of being on the edge of discovery. She reads a book called *Lives of Girls and Women*, but it frightens her in a way she cannot explain, were there anyone here to tell. As she reads the stories a terrible feeling swells in her: that as she grows older she is tumbling forward and down, faster and faster, out of control.

She has never spent this much time alone.

Unsupervised, she is expected to sit at Oma Friesen's kitchen table to eat, to read, and to do her homework. After school she may help herself to a cookie, baked and then frozen in vast healthful batches by Oma Friesen, and if weather and time permit, she may go outside to play.

But Juliet does something else instead, something she knows she should not.

She opens doors and walks right in.

The calendar that hangs above the black telephone in the living room has changed from wildflowers in bloom to a field of fluorescent canola: May to June. Juliet examines it. The days on the calendar are marked: *treatment, treatment, treatment, home.* But one day is circled in black, at the end of the month, and the word inside reads *Bram.*

"Is my dad coming?" Juliet asks Oma Friesen.

"Maybe." Her grandmother wields the honey spoon like an artist, drizzling delicate floral designs or labyrinthine animal shapes onto the pocked surface of the toasted English muffin.

The phone rings, and Juliet scrambles: "Hello?" She knows it is her father by his silence. The pause of long distance prefaces everything he says. His words have to travel along hundreds of miles of wire stretched between his mouth and her ear.

Bram's work continues: he is in Costa Rica, lecturing at a seminary; he is flying to give a talk in Miami; he will return to Nicaragua to arrange for a group of three hundred protesters to travel to the Honduran border; there has been a kidnapping. He cannot come to them.

But he says to Juliet, "Don't worry. I will get there soon."

Gloria drags herself from the bedroom — the sickroom — squeezing shut at her neck a robe of pale lilac — Oma Friesen's. "Pass me the phone, I need to talk to him." The sickroom has developed its own weather: grey fogs that descend and hover, humid fevers that shine the ceiling, bone-chilling winds that wail between walls.

Gloria says, "I will not discuss this when we have no privacy." She says, "I'm not angry, I'm exhausted. I'm a shell of myself. If you could only see me."

"Do you have news?" she says. "I do love you."

"I do love you," she says, "but I can't talk to you."

To the world at large and the room in general, Oma Friesen declares, as she often does, "To everything there is a season."

The clock over the sink points its short hand just shy of a quarter past, and its long hand centimetres beyond the number twelve. It is Wednesday, the twelfth of June. Juliet, a girl in her twelfth year of life, sits at her grandmother's table, alone. Before her is a glass of milk and half a soggy tuna salad sandwich prepared with sweet pickle relish on bought white bread.

Juliet stands. Standing, she swallows the milk and wipes the skin above her upper lip with her turned wrist. She wears blue jeans, a white short-sleeved shirt that buttons up the front, and a green corduroy vest with a pocket over each hip. Into the right pocket she places the remaining half of her tuna sandwich.

She is filled with something that is not courage; it is not determination; it is not sadness or questioning or the desire to err. It is the perfect calm of a girl who knows what she is about to attempt and who is being pulled onward by the inevitable. It is the perfect calm of a girl who neither guesses the consequences nor suspects that there will be any.

The front door to Oma Friesen's apartment opens onto a stairwell that leads to the front entryway. On the other side of the stairwell is a cavelike laundry room shared by all the tenants. The washer and dryer are not being used right now, but when they are, their thump and whirr can be heard dimly inside Oma Friesen's apartment.

The smooth plastic railing beside the stairs slides under Juliet's hand.

She thinks, *Oma Friesen, what a big house you have.*

At street level, noon light pours through tall windows and heats the small foyer. Juliet steps directly up to the closed door marked with a brass number one. She tries the handle, hot under her palm, and it turns. The door is open. The threshold beckons. The girl steps silently across it and into otherness.

She pushes the door shut behind herself. She is in a room darkened by a blind drawn down over a square window that would otherwise gaze onto the street. An aura of illuminated dust motes marks its outline.

The girl feels her way past heavy lumps of furniture to the kitchen, where a plate of bread crusts rests on the counter. Everything in the room is grey, lit dimly by a rectangle of glass high in the wall above the cupboards. A cat leaps on silent, padded paws to the gold-flecked Formica, startling the girl, but only for a moment.

"Hello," says the girl. The sound of her own voice, alive in the still air, claims this place.

Boldly she presses her fingers over the bones of the cat's pulsing skull, flattening its ears. The cat is telling the girl exactly what it wants, its soft body beneath her hand seeking pressure. The warmth of its interior motor hums as the cat noses her sweater, bats at her pocket; it finds what's hidden. It wants the sandwich. The girl is happy to share. She feeds the cat ripped portions off of her fingers, its rough tongue scratching her as if into a new life, another body, one that feels one with this shrouded world.

When the sandwich is gone, the cat leaps to the floor, darts out of the room, and disappears. The girl cannot find it in any of the darkened rooms, though she can hear the patient sound of the animal retching, coughing, disgorging itself of the sandwich. The sound of this act, taking place somewhere nearby but out of sight, is so familiar that it does not disgust or surprise her.

She says, "I have to go now but I'll come back."

The foyer's brightness stuns Juliet: overexposure painted by dilated pupils. She stands outside apartment number one, its door closed, and breathes deeply and with contentment. There is no hesitation as she continues up the stairs to the second floor, to the door marked with the number two. Again the handle yields.

The girl expects no less.

This room is dazzling and barren. Light rushes through the thick maple leaves outside the window, throwing shadows that move across the green shag carpeting that makes a wall-to-wall appearance on every floor. There is nothing here but a television with a monstrous antenna balanced precariously atop a red milk crate. Elsewhere a mattress lies in the centre of a room, a sleeping bag crumpled upon it. The fridge is packed with sticky bottles of condiments and two cases of diet soda. Behind the bathroom mirror are brown bottles of pills.

Nothing living is kept on purpose in apartment number two. No plants, no fish, no animals, and even in the spider's web wafting across the corner of the bedroom window, no spider to be seen.

The girl says, "Hello? Hello? Hello?" making an echo of her voice, and she says, "Goodbye, goodbye, goodbye," not certain whether she will return. She feels no great desire to discover more than can be seen in apartment number two.

There is one more elbow of staircase, the yellow handrail slippery under Juliet's palm, crumbs of dirt crammed into the angles of the steps. But the door to apartment number three is locked. The handle gives ever so slightly in either direction, and she rattles it with perplexity, almost shock, that this last secret is closed to her. Surely this is not what is meant to happen. The door must open. The girl must discover what is hidden behind it.

Juliet walks to school through a heat wave, dressed in brown boys' shorts and a red T-shirt, purchased on her behalf and without her approval by Oma Friesen at Oma Friesen's favourite thrift shop. Oma Friesen buys all her clothes, linens, and household accessories second-hand. When the items were presented to Juliet, they smelled of rotting threads, decrepit attics, and damp cellars permeated by decay. Even freshly washed and dried, the smell clings, a reminder that Juliet does not belong to these clothes and these clothes do not belong to her. But this makes sense to Juliet: nothing in this country is hers; everything is strange, almost like home but off-kilter.

In Canada, the month of June is spent indoors in stifling classrooms whose windows are cracked open yet do not breathe. Juliet is certain these days are wasted — she learns nothing new, nothing of consequence or even of interest. It seems to be expected and accepted, a wilting of intentions built deliberately into the system: to be done with something in Canada, one must be more than done, one must be extinguished. The teachers give up teaching and fill the hours with "fun" activities: crafts, skits in French (*Bonjour, Papa, comment ça va? Ça va bien, merci, et tu? Ça va bien, merci!*), board games, Xeroxed sheets of math problems, National Film Board films, extended recesses.

There is a new development on the playground at the end of this grade six year. The sultry heat brings it on, and it appears, fully formed, at the far end of the school grounds, where the yard dips down, hidden, into a stand of scrubby sumac: "Dare." The game is only for the popular; this excludes Juliet, who is drawn with her fellow outcasts to the site as if to the scene of an accident. The girls who participate, most of them from the other classroom, perform tasks with a mixture of protest and obeisance to the rules: they close their eyes and kiss a boy; when they open their eyes, no one will tell who it was. "Dare" is almost entirely about danger: kissing, touching, showing, saying words that are not allowed; between the boys it is sometimes about fighting or wrestling or taunts.

The game progresses over several recesses as the school year struggles towards its bludgeoned end. The day is particularly hot. The children should be swimming in northern lakes or lounging on concrete beside community pools; instead they gather under the slim shade of the sumacs, frantic with enforced boredom. Under the circumstances, anything might happen, anything to slice the day wide open.

Lazily, a girl in crisp white shorts and a sky-blue polo shirt turns to Juliet and says, "I dare your friend to take off her Paki scarf."

Juliet does not reply. She has assumed herself invisible, and is at once amazed and appalled to discover that she has been seen and observed.

Juliet's friend shrugs, refuses. Her name is Nabihah, and she is accustomed to people, even teachers, claiming they cannot remember how to pronounce correctly such strange syllables. She tells Juliet, when Juliet asks, that her name means nothing here in Canada; it means only *different*.

Nabihah will not fall for the girl's trick, the appearance of inclusion.

"Okay, then I dare her" — pointing — "to take off her glasses."

"So?" Juliet's bespectacled friend throws her chin back like she's taking a blow. Juliet realizes how little she knows about this girl, Mary Ellen, who is removed twice weekly from school to attend mysterious counselling appointments arranged by her mother, who is not her birth mother or her stepmother or even her adopted mother — she is a foster mother. The foster mother, who is Catholic, gave her the name; in the time Mary Ellen calls *before*, her name was Crystal.

"So what? That's all? That's a stupid dare. I take my glasses off all the time."

Silently Juliet telegraphs *danger*, but Mary Ellen is slipping the frames over her ears. One of the boys, slight and blond, removes the glasses from her hand, which opens to let him. Mary Ellen's eyes blink rapidly, shrunken in a face that looks undrawn, exposed. "I did it. See? Now give them back."

"Make us," says the dare's originator.

Juliet recognizes that it is her duty as a friend to say something. But if she does they will turn on her, their instincts tuned to weakness and fear, and she is not brave in this new country. She is not courageous. She is not herself at all, the self she left behind in Nicaragua, the self who followed fisher boys into a seaside cave, who ate shark.

She is not like her brother, who is at least as brave as he ever was, who shrugs off *cancerboy*, who says, with honest curiosity, "What do they know?"

Because she knows what the Canadian children know: they know how to torture. They are looking for something simple: proof of their own power. They want tears and the humiliation of begging; their contentment depends upon it, and they will not be deterred. The scene will proceed as written. But Nabihah, tiny, her black eyes like polished stones, steps forward; Nabihah says, "Stop." And what seemed inevitable suddenly is not.

Juliet imagines that Nabihah's hidden hair is cropped short around her head.

They don't say *Why should we?* They don't say *Paki*.

They don't like Nabihah and they don't know her name, but the surprise of her certainty commands respect. Juliet feels the distance between herself and Nabihah expanding; she thinks, despairingly, We will never be friends.

The blond boy throws the glasses into the dirt at their feet. One arm is twisted and no longer sits properly on Mary Ellen's ear. She's gone crooked.

"My mom is going to kill me, she's going to kill me, she's going to kill me."

The way she says this makes Juliet think it might be true.

The danger, for the unwanted, cannot be quantified. It lodges inside the body and the mind, poison seeping from a secret wound. *I am not wanted*, the rejected child says to herself; she finds it entirely possible to believe that she is unwanted because of some want within, and thus the want within is invented, and recurs, replicates itself as voraciously as a cancerous cell.

She hears his voice all the way from the foyer, instant recognition that pops like a bubble in her brain. Blindly, possessed of a desperate joy she has not previously known, Juliet throws off her backpack and tears down the stairs and past the laundry room (where a woman in black is folding silky items on top of the dryer), sprinting into Oma Friesen's apartment, darting along the hallway, looking in every room until she finds her father, and flings herself into his arms.

He lifts her like a toy and squeezes her against his chest. "My girl, you've grown so long and tall. How can this be?"

She is too overwhelmed to reply.

It isn't until she is set back down that the room slides into focus — the sickroom, air dank with expelled mucous — and the people gathered in it — her entire family, and her oma, all of them, all together, here, in another country.

For a moment no one says anything. No one can. Then Keith begins to cough, and Bram, who is unaccustomed to seeing his pain, bends at his son's side and tries to hold him, to soothe him, placing his big hands on Keith's head the way Juliet's fingers stroke the cat in apartment number one.

"I'm not leaving," Bram says (no one has asked).

The girl's heart jams her throat with its throbbing. She stands frozen, one hand flat against the closed apartment door with the cat twisting around her ankle, rubbing its naked, deep ear into the bones of her bare foot. There are noises in the foyer. She's lingered too long, but her opportunities have grown scant now that her father is here to stay.

Her needs are bold, demanding. She has found patches of white fur on her clothes or caught in the pale hairs on the backs of her arms, evidence that is proof of her daring, proof that she is known elsewhere. That she knows things no one else knows, or knows she knows.

She knows that a single woman lives in apartment number one, older than her own mother but not as old as her grandmother, and she has seen the woman, in pressed pants, snapping towels in the laundry room and folding each with symmetrical precision. The woman's short, fluffed hair is a brash shade of red, and she has told the girl, in passing, "My hair used to be exactly the colour of yours." (This is something grown-ups say often to the girl, or a variation on the theme — my daughter's hair was just like yours; my grandson's hair is just like yours; I always hoped for a child with hair like yours.)

The girl presses her cheek to the door. She has no escape route. The foyer door does not slam immediately; she imagines it propped open as bags drop heavily to the floor. Voices. The girl relaxes fractionally, her spine compressing: the noise belongs to her parents, not to the woman in apartment number one.

Her parents have come into the building talking, stuck in a conversation they do not wish to end though they have arrived at their destination. The girl slumps to pet the cat. Her parents cannot know that their voices, in the foyer, carry as if amplified into every apartment. If they knew they would stop themselves, if they could. But perhaps they could not.

"I don't believe it," says the mother. "I just don't. Why did you wait so long to tell me, if you knew?"

"There wasn't a funeral or any kind of announcement."

The voice of a small child breaks in, whining, and the mother says, "You are a big boy and I'm not going to carry you."

The father says, "I didn't realize you would be so —"

"I can only think of the children. I can't stop thinking of them."

The father says, "It closes a chapter — that's how I see it."

"The hell it does, the hell it does, my God. This has nothing to do with you!"

"I could tell you the same thing."

"Why did he do it? Was there a note?"

"This is a minor incident in another country that happened to a family we hardly knew. Put it into perspective."

"Stupid man," says the mother. (The mother is not allowed to use that word, thinks the girl.)

There is the sound of a small scuffle, footsteps, the child's incoherent protests disappearing down the stairs, followed by silence. The girl takes a huge breath and opens the door, understanding too late that she has made a mistake: the foyer is not empty. Outside apartment number one, the mother sits on the bottom step, surrounded by plastic bags of groceries.

Silently, with the minutest of movements, the girl pulls the door shut behind her. An appealing thought alights: that her mother cannot see her, that she is invisible to the world, that the act of entering and exiting these other apartments is literally transformative.

She is the liminal girl.

Gloria's eyes are puffed and red. Her lips are half open. She rises slowly to standing.

She and Juliet face each other with something that resembles astonishment but may be simple unfamiliarity. Juliet thinks, She's always with Keith. She's never with me.

"What on earth, Juliet? What —"

"What were you and Dad talking about? Who's dead?"

Gloria shakes her head, attempting to focus her eyes, but she cannot. "Oh, Juliet, I don't know. I don't know what to tell you." And Juliet suddenly loses her breath, gasps, though the thought she has formed makes no sense: *Keith is dead.* She cannot say the words out loud because it will make them true.

Gloria does not recognize Juliet's fright. Oblivious, she takes her time, arriving slowly at words as she seems to weigh what should be said or left unsaid. "Juliet, it's Heinrich. Do you remember Heinrich and Clara, and your friend Isobel?" As if Juliet might already have forgotten them, as if coming to Canada might have excised vast landscapes of memory.

"Mom, what's happening? What is it?"

"Heinrich is . . . he passed away. I don't know anything more."

But she does, and Juliet knows it. Juliet is breathing again. She is angry. "Why did he die? Was it . . ." — Juliet struggles to form the word — "cancer?"

Gloria says, "Oh no, no, no, not that, nothing like that."

But her mother knows something she isn't saying. Juliet pushes. "Then why is he dead?"

Gloria's gaze drifts far away. Finally she says, "Maybe he died of sadness. I would almost believe it."

Returning up the stairs to retrieve the remaining bags of groceries, Bram snorts.

"She didn't love him," Gloria says to him. "You wouldn't have known that. He was raising those children practically alone. It was a lonely life."

"The girl is the one who found him," says Bram.

"Hush! Hush!" Gloria throws her hands over Juliet's ears.

"Juliet." Bram peels back Gloria's fingers. "Where did you come from?"

Juliet looks at Gloria, who returns her gaze blankly. It is as if Juliet has walked into her mother's dream. Her mother has no idea what either of them are doing in this dream, which is possibly a nightmare, nor how they arrived here, nor what they are to do next. That is how far away her mother is, that is how far apart the two of them stand.

You can die of sadness? thinks Juliet; the idea encrusts a soft centre of pure terror.

Juliet wants something. She decides it is a horse.

At suppertime she announces her intention to have a horse, and Bram latches on: "A farm!" he says, and turns to Gloria with unexpected excitement; maybe this is love, thinks Juliet.

"Remember our farm?" Bram is speaking of a place that does not exist, and never did, except in their collective imaginations.

"We should look in this neighbourhood," says Gloria, refusing to acknowledge their shared imaginary past, refusing to play along. "The children are already settled into school."

"I hate school," says Juliet.

"But your friends . . ." Gloria waves a hand, manufacturing for Juliet scads of birthday-party invitations and sleepovers.

"Country air is so healthy for children," says Oma Friesen, to which Gloria does not respond, and Juliet thinks, It is settled, just like that. Oma Friesen has spoken. Oma Friesen does not want or need her grandchildren to live in her neighbourhood. She approves of horses and open skies, and of love. As she proclaims, so it will be.

After supper Bram lifts Emmanuel onto his shoulders, ducks the low doorways, and strolls to the convenience store to purchase a local newspaper: farms listed for sale or rent. Gloria and Keith resume a card game at the table; Keith is between treatments, building up his white blood cell count so the doctors can knock it down again. Oma Friesen manages the washing up; in this task, she actively discourages help.

Juliet slips out. Tomorrow is the last day of school. She will not say *Au revoir*; she will say, *Adieu — goodbye forever*.

She cannot visit apartments one or two at this hour; their tenants are sure to be home. But the door to apartment number three is locked; it is always locked. The girl sits with her back against it, her ear on the scratched metal, listening, but hears nothing. She thinks, Maybe no one lives here. Maybe it is empty. Or maybe it is not: it could be filled with anything, with a dead body, with squirrels and birds, with ghosts.

It is very warm on the third floor: a perfect place for ghosts, who, the girl imagines, carry a chill and crave warmth.

When the door swings open, she falls backwards, sprawling into the apartment. Her mouth opens to scream, but she has been quiet for too long, and her throat produces only the tiniest squeak.

"What in the . . ." A man frowns down at her. She turns her eyes to his boots: heavy yellow leather, stained and oily, rubber bottoms grooved like tire treads.

"I'm sorry," she breathes.

"You must be the kid who screams half the day and wakes me up," says the man.

"That's not me." She raises herself on bent wrists. "That's my little brother."

"I work nights. I don't like little brothers."

"We're moving," she says. "We're going to live in the country."

He sees her furtive glance as she tries to take in the dimly lit room: tidy, but dull. "I'm headed to my shift, but I happen to be early. Make yourself at home, look around." He is closing the door, and she moves her feet to let him.

"You're cute," he says. "Cute kid."

The girl stands. She cannot remember anything about herself that relates to the way he is looking at her: a look that is mildly admiring, curious. She stares back at him as if paralyzed, seeing him for the first time above the boots and the rolled blue jean cuffs. He is not a man she would instinctively trust. He is old, but only to an eleven-year-old, to whom even teenagers are old; perhaps in his mid-twenties. His hair is long and thin, pulled into a ponytail, dark blond — what her mother would call "dishwater" — and his eyes are a very pale blue, striking but uncanny, eyes that belong on a husky dog. He is a small man and he has hair on his face, rough stubble, and an earring in either ear: tiny gold crucifixes.

He says, "Don't be scared. What's your name?"

The girl hunches her shoulders, works her mouth, mumbling as if she's lost something, as if her name has been stolen from her.

"Why are you whispering? Don't be scared. Are you scared?" He walks away from her into the middle of the room and spreads his arms wide. "Not gonna touch ya."

A framed poster of a howling wolf hangs on the wall over a black velvet sofa, and on another wall is a bucking bronco. He sees the girl glance at the bronco. "Do you like horses? I like horses."

Way down below, someone enters the building, and displaced wind rattles the door of apartment number three, behind which the girl stands, near enough to put out her hand and touch the handle.

"Don't go yet."

The girl hears her father's voice talking to her little brother, but only briefly, as he barrels down the basement stairs; gone. *Adieu.*

"I'll pour you a pop. Do you like Pepsi?"

The girl shakes her head but he thinks she means yes, and he brings her a glass, no ice. The girl says, "Thank you." He waits until she's drunk half.

"I gotta go before I'm late," he says. "My name's Steven. You never asked. It's polite to ask. You still never told me yours." He takes the glass and shakes her hand, which is damp from condensation.

The girl blurts, "Can I look around? Can I just . . . look?"

He laughs. He still has her by the hand. "What are you looking for?"

But she cannot shape it for him; even if she could, she would not. What gets kept in the attic of the mind, symbols sorted and boxed, imaginary and antique? Different from the mouldering memories stuffed into the basement, which are frightening, and lurk. The attic is what could be; the attic window the view from which a life, and its potential, might be glimpsed, spread out below, in miniature.

She pulls free her hand.

"After you," says the man. She pushes away his name.

He follows her from room to room, pointing out where he's going to fix or improve things: a missing light bulb, a bare wall, no shower curtain around the tub.

He stands aside in the narrow hallway so she can pass without brushing against his body as they return to the main room. The girl goes to the window and moves the dark shade. She was mistaken. There is her father with her little brother, playing in the front yard, not gone inside. They are collecting dandelions, twigs.

The girl feels the stranger behind her, the extra heat of his proximity, seeing what she's seeing.

"Better go, kid," he says, lightly brushing the braids off her shoulders. "And don't come back." She feels his breath as he bends over her, warm in the part along the middle of her scalp. Warm, and scented of peppermint. She hears the crunch between his teeth of a hard candy, the crinkling of a cellophane wrapper dropped to the floor. The carpet is the same in this apartment as in all the others. Her feet are bare. Its fibres are rough.

He does not touch his lips to her skin. His fingers on her neck raise tiny hairs, stroking along her shoulders, down her arms, bare beyond the T-shirt sleeves, to her hands, which he grasps, fingers softly tucked onto her palms, thumbs rubbing her knuckles and tendons.

He is holding his breath. He is gentle. She feels, just at this moment, needed. She is necessary. She is rare. She is wanted.

Down below, her father lifts his gaze, as if he's looking straight up and at her. She sees his mouth make the shape of her name: *Juliet*.

She is named. It could be an accusation. It could be rescue.

The apartment is stifling, its openings closed tightly against all outside noise and light.

He senses the change in her, the fear, and drops her hands.

"Get out of here," he says, whispered, tight. "Please."

She doesn't look at him, and she runs, skittering, away and down the stairs, tearing to the front door and out into bright evening.

In the yard, in the green uncut grass, Bram is glad to see her. He flaps the newspaper: "What do you think of this one, Juliet? Hobby farm, ten acres, pond." (The translation for listings of this sort, generally, will prove to be: *Land pocked with rocks and scrub brush no good for crops, house in suspect condition and with worse plumbing, built carelessly close to a swamp that fills up during spring runoff and floods the cellar.*)

"Uh-huh." Juliet bends to rip handfuls of grass, smelling its crushed fresh blood.

He is coming. Juliet won't look. He pushes open the front door and clumps his heavy boots along the concrete walk, swinging a silver lunch pail with his name written on it in black marker. A truck idles at the curb: his ride, waiting.

As he passes them, Bram greets him politely, "Hello," and the man surprises them all: he steps onto the grass and extends his hand, coming to meet them. "Steven," he says. "We must be neighbours."

"Bram," says Bram. "We're here temporarily, staying with my mother."

"Nice to meetcha, Graham," says Steven.

"Bram," says Bram.

"Graham," repeats Steven. He can't help himself; he is occupied with ignoring Juliet. His glance at her is sneaky; he smiles — Juliet recognizes that he is trying to suppress the impulse — and he winks. But Juliet, kneeling, folds her arms across her chest, one, two: Stop.

"That's a real pretty girl ya got," says Steven. "You'd be smart to keep an eye on that one."

Bram shifts his weight, frowns at Juliet, who is examining the dirt. She feels like smearing herself in dirt; and she feels powerful.

Bram drops Steven's hand, gazes at his own, looking for a mark, a legible sign.

"Good luck," says Steven, a phrase that means nothing within the context of this exchange. Grown-ups say things like this all the time: platitudes that do not apply, and other grown-ups accept the nothingness at the heart of what is being said, as if nonsense spoken out loud is always and ever more acceptable than silence.

He steps into the waiting truck, slams the door, and is driven away.

"What do you have to say, Juliet?" Bram eyes her.

She flushes; she's been caught doing something wrong, but not the thing that she thought was wrong. Something else — unexpected and accidental. Something that will make her father mournful and disappointed, that has the potential to diminish her worth, and that she cannot avoid. She cannot avoid growing out of girlhood and into the tempting lushness of woman.

But Bram doesn't suspect the depths of the change to come, and has already forgotten the stranger. "What say we go tell your mother about this place."

Like a magician, Juliet seals off the door to apartment number three; she won't climb those steps again. This is where she'll keep him, upstairs, silent, locked in: predator, guardian, seer, lost soul, stranger, danger, innocent, alone. This is where he will loiter, waiting in perpetuity as the walls grow thicker and dust settles like another coat of fur on the wolf and the bronco, and the blind rips, its fibres disintegrating in relentless sunlight, waiting, waiting, for the door she's forgotten exists to fall open.

He has a message he's been waiting all this time to tell her. He knows she is a balm.

She needs him too. Once, he had a name.

FLIGHT

Under the dying pear tree, Juliet has a prophetic vision. It is not her first.

Her first, according to her mother's telling, occurred when Juliet was two years old and Grandpa Harold was in the hospital, close to death. He'd been knocked unconscious while visiting a worksite, struck on the head by a falling beam; he hadn't been wearing a helmet. Gloria was pacing the apartment, tears streaming down her face, praying. Little Juliet woke from her nap calling, "Mama! Mama!" When Gloria came running with the new baby — Keith — asleep in her arms, she found Juliet perched on the top railing of her crib. Was she surprised to find Juliet there? She was not; Juliet was Gloria's first child and she assumed all of her children would be just as nimble — (it pleases Juliet that her mother was wrong) — walking at nine months, drawing gasps of concern from fellow mothers at the playground. "Do you know your baby is climbing that ladder?"

When Gloria came running and found Juliet atop her crib

railing, hammering on the windowpane, what shocked her were the words coming out of her toddler's lips. Juliet was shouting, "Grandpa! Grandpa!" (only it sounded like *Dampa! Dampa!*) Could it possibly be? The window overlooked a back alley crowded with rickety wooden staircases, dirty, damp, narrow stucco buildings blocking the skyline.

"What do you see?" Gloria asked, because she could see nothing.

"That man," said Juliet. "Grandpa!" She was not capable of further articulation.

Gloria's next thought was: My father is dead. He is visiting Juliet to say goodbye; I can't see him because I refuse to believe that my father could die. Then the telephone rang; this is Gloria's story. The telephone rang, waking the baby, and over his cries Gloria heard her mother's voice, in another city, another country: Gloria's father had woken out of his coma. He would survive.

That's when Gloria understood what Juliet had been telling her: the man Juliet had seen was Jesus, come to tell Juliet that Grandpa Harold was saved. At that time in Gloria's life, Jesus was a real, living being who entered into the world at will to intercede; that may not be how Gloria sees Jesus now, but Juliet can only guess, because Gloria no longer talks about Jesus or miracles, or even prayer. Her restlessness knows no bounds; her distraction is complete. She has given up hairbrushing and makeup and wears the same pair of blue jeans day after day, belted tightly to keep them from falling off her hips: she scarcely eats. Juliet has inherited the makeup — what little of it there is — gifts sent by Aunt Caroline in Georgia: black mascara that promises to lengthen and curl lashes; bright red lipstick, slick and wet; a compact of blue and silver eyeshadow; pale pink rouge to be applied with a brush, which is lost, so Juliet, who is fourteen, uses a Q-tip, peering into the mirror. Making herself look like someone else, someone older, someone less transparent, tended like the side of a house, freshly painted.

Juliet believes in miracles.

She cherishes her mother's story. It gilds Juliet as visionary, special, and in her mind the story is enriched with detail, memories sought out and sourced from the rush of slippery images that arrive just before sleep. Juliet believes she can remember her smaller, sturdier self balanced on the crib rail, the wet windowpane against her hand. She believes in the existence of the man in the alley, shimmering, his feet bare in the cold rain, his white robes flowing around his body. If this is not a memory, what is? He walks hand in hand with Grandpa Harold, towards Juliet, looking up at her. The two men stop. They speak quietly to one another. When they turn to walk away, Grandpa Harold is gone, and only the other man walks — or rather, floats — slowly down the alley towards the ribbon of street far away. She watches him go.

She waits for him to come again. But no matter how she conjures him, he does not come. Years pass. There is no urgency, until suddenly there is; until there is a crisis. Someone else is dying.

Unfamiliar cars creep up the long laneway, past the front field, where Juliet's neglected pony has eaten all but the newest slivers of grass. The house fills with distant relatives — cousins of Juliet's dad bearing canned-soup casseroles and Jell-O salads studded with grated carrot and half-moons of celery. Jobs are suspended: Oma Friesen sleeps on the couch and washes the dishes; Juliet's dad no longer rises early on mornings or weekends, and his colleagues at the Peace and Justice Initiative come to visit with their spouses, sitting for hours praying, practising the laying on of hands.

But her mother does not sing.

They thought he would live. That is the worst of it. They thought that after three years of treatment his blood cells had fought themselves safe. He was *in remission*. It was over — the periodic spells of her mother driving her brother to stay at the hospital, interspersed with periodic spells of normalcy: the weeks between treatment when her brother would be safe at home, drawing cartoons, learning how to play the guitar, skipping his homework and barely passing tests at school, never having to do the dishes (unlike Juliet — totally not fair).

Declared cured, he was free to play bruising games: soccer and football. He even had to help with the dishes. His hair grew back, as thick and as black as it was before.

Late August is too hot, the whine of bugs in the grasses rising and falling like madness. Fan heads groan on windowsills. Juliet stays out of the house. Keith is in there, surrounded. Juliet knows the vocabulary. She knows *out of remission*. He was in remission. Now he is out of remission. It sounds almost holy. Grandpa Harold and Grandma Grace were missionaries long ago, when Gloria was a child and before Grandpa Harold made his fortune as a contractor. Being in remission is like being sent, as a missionary is sent, back again into the world: *Go, you are called, you have a purpose.* Out of remission: *Come home, whether or not you've completed your work; you're done.*

There is one pear tree on their whole farm, and it is dying. This is where Juliet sits.

In early spring the tree burst out for three days in fragrant white blooms; but whole branches failed to come into leaf, and they scratch, black and bare, against the sheer, rich sky. Cross-legged, Juliet faces the row of ragged pines that separate their several acres from a field of green, whispering corn, which belongs to the neighbour.

It is not a comfortable place to sit. All around the pear tree spreads a mess of tangles and brambles and weeds, interrupted by frost-tossed stones. Juliet's bare legs are scratched and she swats at insects that swarm and scuttle and alight. Into her spine, dull bark imprints its muted pattern. If Juliet turns her gaze to the right, she can see, past the stand of poisonous black walnut trees, the sprawling vegetable garden: the sum total of her parents' truce this spring, flourishing with offerings despite neglect. The cabbages are worm-eaten, the summer squash run rampant, fallen tomatoes rot in the dirt.

The garage is to her left. It is the oldest structure on the property, a log cabin built by the lowland Scots who settled this land in the middle of the nineteenth century — long, long ago, or not so very long ago, depending on how Juliet thinks about it.

Behind the garage rests the crumbled ruin of a smithy. The original settler was a blacksmith, though his workshop was abandoned around the turn of the century. Juliet and Keith have marked out with footprints the shape of the original hut, and have unearthed treasure in the rubble: rusty nails and iron spikes and curved, blunt tool heads, wooden handles rotted off; the iron frame of a bellows. They arranged their discoveries on the flat remains of the rough kiln and posted a cardboard sign at the end of the lane, which failed to tempt even one visitor: MUSEUM! A BARGAIN AT ONLY ~~25~~ 10 CENTS!

That wasn't even two months ago. Not so very long ago, or a long, long time ago, depending on how Juliet thinks about it.

The house behind her is alive. She senses it as a breathing, altered presence, its thick stone walls stretched outwards by the pressure of what it must contain. It will stop breathing when he stops breathing. Juliet's chin drops to her chest and she stares at her fingers, curling open in her lap.

The past is like a dream. It feels too long ago to affect her, yet she gazes upon it as on a marvel, drifting into the familiar tropical geography that cups her body like a carved stone shelter. Nicaragua. She has learned that the name of that country does not mean to her what it means to other people. Canadians, if they have heard of it, find the word difficult to pronounce. If they have heard of it, they think of war or poor people, of grinding bad luck. It is not, yet, a country to which a tourist would travel for pleasure, unlike other tropical countries in the hemisphere. It is not a vacation destination; it is a disaster.

But when Juliet thinks or says the word out loud, she is overwhelmed by a sensation of deep satisfaction.

It is not that she wants to go back. She cannot imagine going back. It is that she holds Nicaragua as a secret, as mysterious and significant as a chamber of her own heart. Like other secrets she will come to hold, it cannot be talked about in any ordinary way; it will out in its own time.

———

"Juliet! Juliet!" a woman's voice calls from the covered porch that runs along three sides of the square house. Juliet does not answer. It is not her mother's voice, or her Oma's. She turns fractionally so as not to disturb the trance she may or may not be caught in, and she sees a woman named Kay coming towards her. "Kay as in the letter."

"Juliet, it's lunchtime. We're spreading out a picnic on the front lawn."

Juliet blinks and turns deliberately away.

"It will be lovely," says Kay, panting. She answers the phone at the Peace and Justice Initiative; she files papers and makes photocopies. During the school year she allowed Juliet to sit in her twirly chair and play receptionist after school, though she also said, "If you were my daughter you wouldn't be out in public wearing that much makeup." Kay has no daughters, no sons, no children of her own. She is a single woman. A single woman is dangerously unattached; she is on the lookout, or the warpath, or her high horse, according to Gloria, so *watch out.*

Juliet attends a private school in the city, paid for by Grandma Grace and Grandpa Harold, who also settled the down payment on this house and paid for airline tickets to fly Juliet's family to North Carolina last winter, for a holiday at their cottage to celebrate the end of Keith's treatment.

At last Keith could swim underwater again: the doctor had yanked out his Broviac, a tube inserted under the skin of his chest into which the killing medicine was pumped. The whole family came to the hospital to watch its removal. Keith sat on a lowered bed and the doctor demonstrated how he would pull on the catheter.

"Will it hurt?"

"Yes, but then it will be out."

After that, Keith visited every room to say goodbye to every kid. Juliet admired and feared the way her brother talked to the sick kids, his ease with their weakness. She felt nothing but shamed panic, as if she'd been caught peeking: the wan bodies resting with eyes towards open doors, looking for someone to come, gazing without the energy to rise up and escape; the squeezed rooms, barren despite clots of teddy bears and silver foil balloons. She would have given anything never to go back. Anything except this.

The nurses wept to witness their escape.

Juliet sees her family — mother, father, brothers, herself — at peace in the humming elevator; Keith clutches his discoloured Broviac tube in a see-through plastic bag like a prize. The nurses wave. The doors close. They fall at high speed, whisked through a hot metal tunnel to the brightly lit main floor, where the children are given permission to choose a sandwich from the automatic cafeteria, each of them sliding a red tray along a rolling track: egg salad on white on a white plate, framed behind glass; chocolate milk; a brownie.

On the highway, four paved lanes cut through buried farmland, and a car guns neck and neck with theirs. The man in the driver's seat gestures and mouths, wild-eyed, at Juliet and Keith. "Dad! He's swearing at us!"

"You cut him off," says Gloria.

"The hell I did!" Bram flourishes his middle finger and revs the station wagon's engine. "Asshole! Take that!" The car swerves, the children scream with delight. It is so unlike their dad.

"Eat my dust!" yells Bram.

Kay would never believe that happened, thinks Juliet. She halfway disbelieves it herself, seeing her dad as he appears at the office: mild, sinking, sucking on a cough candy, hands laced behind his back. "You're a lucky girl. My father thought he could beat sense into his children," Kay told Juliet as Juliet twirled in the chair. And then, musingly, almost to herself, "Then again, I never went out in public looking like a harlot."

Juliet keeps her eyes down as Kay crouches before her in a beige skirt that reveals strained calves and plump knees. Juliet has seen her father drop his hand to rest on these very knees, hairless and sheathed in taupe nylon, for a moment. She has seen these very knees permit the action, perhaps fall open ever so slightly: an invitation.

"Come and eat." Kay reaches for Juliet's shoulder, lands heavily as if balancing herself.

Juliet shrugs free. "You're not my mother."

Kay sways to uncertain standing. Her beige pumps are slightly grass-stained, heels sinking into soft dirt. "Your father is bringing Keith outside. The picnic is all spread out. So much food."

"I'm not hungry," says Juliet.

"Don't come for the food," says Kay. "Come for your brother."

Juliet looks up and sees Kay looking down, her eyes soft with tears. Rage courses through Juliet's bloodstream and bursts behind her eyes. "I'm not coming," she says. Everywhere she looks she sees fakery: an invasion of affectation, outsiders staking their claim, stamping their pity, crying their tears, *helping*.

A picnic?

Keith does not, cannot eat. He looks at food set before him and lifts a spoonful to his mouth, and his tongue wads, his throat closes, he gags. He has told Juliet what it is like to want to eat and to feel his body refuse.

Fury clears a path. It lights the air around Juliet. *Just try to come close, just try.*

Kay surrenders.

Noise from the picnic, which she cannot see, carries over the farmhouse roof to the pear tree, improbable laughter bouncing off the tarpapered garage wall. Juliet keeps her eyes on the row of pines. Something will happen. Something — someone — will come.

She wills the glowing figure to appear before her. She wills him to walk out of the cornfield. He is in there, she knows it, a vision on the verge of emergence, bearing a message she will carry in a dead sprint around the house to the gaping picnickers, but most of all to her family: *He is saved! Keith, you're saved!*

Just to think this thought breaks it. It shatters like glass. And she sees through the possibility to the cornfield, to the pines, to the restless summer sky. She sees herself sitting bone upright and alone.

The word *saved* has no meaning. It is empty and fantastical, in this context worthless. It implies rescue. It implies the light-ning strike of a saviour, and that is not what real saving would look like. If Keith were really saved, he would simply and surely continue to live. His lungs would pull and push air; his heart would beat steady and strong; he would rise and walk on his own; he would taste food and swallow it down without thinking twice; his pain would be from a knee scraped, fall-ing off a bicycle, or a wrist broken, falling out of a tree. He would live, as Juliet lives, with the luxury of ample time, the comfortable belief that there is more and more and more of it, that it flows like water, that there is always tomorrow.

But this is not a vision. The vision is coming.

Juliet hears it before she can see it: a dull drone.

Her heart will crash out of her body. A motorized forma-tion is speeding across the sky, casting shadows ahead of it-self: nine winged machines aligned nose to tail and tip to tip. Juliet spirals inside a memory that has no shape or sound or sense; it exists as pure physical response, a switch flipped in the depths of the mind. Her body thinks it knows the mean-ing of this approach: death and darkness, human-made fear, bombs released and tumbling in slow motion towards the earth, landing like fire, shrapnel, chemical eruption. The other Nicaragua.

Juliet cannot move. She is paralyzed in the place where her body will be found, afterwards, silently.

The glinting planes have come so close. They are upon the little farm. They shift like airborne dancers on the stage of sky. They pass over the barn and the house, and the noise for a moment squeezes out all else, and just as suddenly it departs, fades. Juliet stares through bare branches, heart opening and closing like a hand making and unmaking a fist, and she watches them go. She hears the others running into the lane to see what they can see.

She thinks, This is my sign.

But she does not know what it means. The effort required to manufacture symmetry: is it a kind of beautiful violence? The machines mimic birds, but they are not birds. They are armour protecting a fragile human body within. No bird could fly with such precision, requiring such careful planning, such practice. That is not how the bird flies. That is not what concerns the bird.

She cannot hold her thoughts. She does not have the depth or the capacity to contain their expression. She thinks instead: They were gone so fast. I wish I could have looked at them longer.

Everyone else is milling around the lane, talking about the planes.

Nobody comes to get her. She unwinds to standing. There they are: she can see them all. She sees Keith in her father's arms, and his legs dangle, skinny and weakened. He would never consent to being held and carried if he were strong enough to walk on his own. She sees her father, collapsing inside himself like a gigantic balloon deflating; all of his bulk is caught around his waist. She sees her mother, unkempt, mildly hysterical, laughing wildly. She sees her little brother Emmanuel ducking away from Kay, who is forever trying to pet him, to hug or to kiss him, to press his cheek. She won't give up, and he turns and kicks stones at her, purposely.

Look at them. They form nothing. Their dance is not engineered.

Juliet isn't angry, not at all.

The house stands square, emptied of its people. Except for the face. It is watching Juliet from an upstairs window — her own bedroom window. Juliet stops like she's been shot, shades her eyes against stark midday sun. It is a child's face, a young child's. She knows the spindly strands of flyaway hair and the bare chest and the sagging diaper. She knows the pudgy baby palms pressed to the window's pane, and she sees the child's entire body, the feet balanced on top of a crib rail. She feels the rail pressing, as if against her own soles.

She thinks, There's no crib in my bedroom.

Oh!

She is alone. No one else can see what she is seeing. It is up to her after all. She raises her hand, palm flat as if against glass. The past stands still, stands forever in the window, and love rises without bidding, will not be swallowed, emerges full-throated like a song.

Juliet is running in a dead sprint across the grass and over the stones towards him, towards her living brother. She does not know what she will do when she gets to him. Or maybe she does. It does not matter. She is flying with the ease of a bird.

THE FOUR CORNERS
OF A HOUSE

She thinks, I love them all the same, I do. A mother does.

She has forgotten where she is, her mouth moving silently, her frozen gaze set upon the pear tree, black and fruitless in this season of harvest. A figure passes before her eyes, an interruption, and she stares, shocked to see that there is a girl walking through her dining room. The girl balances on one wrist an open book, a bowl of cereal in the other hand.

She thinks, Who is this? As if her living child were more than a stranger: frightening, spectral. *Daughter.* She thinks, I do not know her; she rushes further and further from me.

An explosion of expelled breath breaks her panic, and she turns, blinking rapidly.

"Watch me?" The boy looks up. The round wooden table, now too large for the family, is peopled with Lego figures: commanders and captains and masters and warriors. Every scenario imagined by the boy is a battle. His being is sharpened like his imaginary weapons, his sabres of light, his swords and spears. He hurts her.

Thought is slow, drags itself forward. She repeats in her mind, I love them all the same. A mother does. But she cannot remember why she is telling herself something so obvious, and so impossible.

Between her hands is a mug of coffee gone cold, a film of milk soured on the muddy surface.

She thinks, Two are left, as if the children were stones deposited by a retreating glacier, their hard surfaces evidence of what was once here: a family entire, whole. I have these two, she thinks, almost frantic. They need me. A mother knows. And she pursues the girl — wait, wait — and presses her into a hug, sloshing the cup of coffee on the floor outside the bathroom, jostling the cereal bowl.

The girl shrinks, stares darkly as if assaulted.

I love you, she says to the girl. She can smell her own rank breath, a thirsty air.

I know, the girl says, though she might as well be spitting.

She sets the cup of coffee on top of the piano and bends to wipe the spill with the corner of her bathrobe. It takes her exactly this long to forget that she has been holding something and has set it down. Will the coffee cup be found today, or tomorrow, or in a week? Will her husband find it or will she, or will it be discovered only when it is knocked to the floor by a passing elbow, and the screaming will begin — her own. She will not be able to spare herself the release.

Every emotion is filled to the brim, quick to spill and to die: hunger is not mere hunger, it is starvation; anger flies beyond frustration, it is rage; sensations possess her and as suddenly evaporate, burn off, and silence follows. Blankness shrouds her like a fog in which she can find nothing, not even herself, in which there is no warning.

The girl is gone. You see, she thinks, they hold themselves apart from me. It is not just her imagination.

In the kitchen she touches her face, her hair, she slides her hands down the front of her body. Her feet are cold despite the woolly men's socks she wears against the dull autumn chill that creeps under doors and insinuates itself at window's edge. She sees the coffee pot bubbling on its flat black burner. She opens the creaking cupboard and removes a mug. She pours herself a cup of coffee and dresses it with milk from the fridge, sugar from the bowl.

She takes a sip. She swallows.

She tastes nothing until the taste becomes residue, bitter, persistent, a reminder of the original sip that yet bears no resemblance to the creamy sweetness she knows it must have been.

At the long mirror over the row of sinks, girls apply eyeshadow, lipstick, powder, mascara. Their tools and compacts leave tracks of colour and black on white porcelain. The floor is littered with ripped paper towels. They don't turn off the taps. They release strands of pulled hair from their fingertips to float on the air like their words.

She sits on the toilet behind the locked stall door. She has heard her name.

She has heard: *dead*.

Does the girl who speaks know that she is trapped here, listening; does the girl who speaks think she will be afraid to stand or to flush?

She hears the stall door open; its slam echoes against the

painted concrete wall. She hears her own voice pitched high, spiny, an insect's phosphorescent whine. She is saying, All of you will be dead. All of you will die and then you will stop talking and someone else will talk about you being dead.

Someone says, Hey, we're just . . . like, sorry, we didn't . . . Someone hugs her.

She freezes stiff, arms hanging, furious, humiliated, goaded into giving them what they've wanted all along: a reaction, a secret pulled out of her like an essential organ. She knows something they do not. They want it too, but only for the purpose of diminishing it to the point of elimination.

Look at this mess. Look at what these girls leave behind for someone else to clean up: their sticky threads of hair, their crumpled paper towels, their spilled powders and handheld mirrors and the lids of lost lipsticks.

Yet when they exit into the noisy hall beyond, look at them: immaculate, condensed, instantly legible.

By comparison, she is a scrawl in the mirror. A pimple rages on one cheekbone; she has picked at it for days, and her attempt to cover it glares like putty over a throbbing wound. Blood-red nail polish is chipped where her teeth have been. The only part of herself she admires is not of her: the hoops that swing like trapeze artists from her earlobes.

The bell rings straight through her skin to her heart, rattling its chambers.

She bends and scrubs her face under the cold tap, dirty water running through her praying hands and down her wrists, running, running.

He can see his own breath. The walls are not insulated, the room heated by a portable electric grate. They have done little to change or improve their square stone farmhouse, bought more than three years ago, and paint peels from the low ceiling, darkened by water marks. The walls are dirty and of a violent turquoise that does not belong to this century. Who, now, would choose to paint the walls of an office this colour, even if such paint could be found? Today's colours are neutral and bland, clean, comforting: he thought it would be nice to do the whole house over in something called taupe. His wife refused. She said, You might as well slap porridge on the walls. They argued.

He has forgotten what argument feels like. He has forgotten irritation.

Now she would let him paint the walls any colour at all; the argument is over. It is not that he has won and she has lost. It is not that he has persuaded her and she has acquiesced. It is that she no longer cares. No, he thinks, it is much graver than that. She has forgotten how to fight. She has forgotten that she ever cared. She has forgotten all of them; him most especially.

His desk is spread with books.

The books are open. He wills his eyes to gaze upon the words, his mouth to shape them. He thinks, and immediately regrets the thought, This is an opportunity that you cannot squander.

He has always intended, secretly, to finish what he started long ago, before children, when he was a young man with hair on top of his head.

Now he may. A gift.

A gift? Low discomfort rises from his belly like a belch. How can he pin onto the body of his son even the least good?

His wife would say, You feel nothing. You are dead.

He cannot disagree. He presses the tips of his fingers together, urgently, as if by this gesture he might will himself to feel. He is wearing black gloves with cut-off fingertips. He lifts the palms to his cheeks and rubs. Thinly woven wool catches on bristles.

The computer on which he works glows green; the letters of the unfinished dissertation glow brighter green. The room quivers: darkest, vilest green.

He thinks, I hate this colour. I'm keeping it.

He says, This guy is the master, this guy is the commander. He says, Boom, exploding bombs away! He says, Fire on it, fire on it, commander, the bad guy is coming, the dragon. He says, Attack, attack. He says, Commander, we need you, do you read, do you read. Commander! Destroy! Destroy! He says, This guy, this one, where is his weapon?

He checks the floor under the chair.

There it is.

She blames her husband. He is the one who stopped praying; when there was still hope, he quit. He confessed it to her. Naked with rage, she beat his bent forearms. How dare you, how dare you? There are churches full of strangers praying for our son — and you've given up asking?

She blames him, but she thinks, He is not to blame. Who has such powers? What difference would one prayer make, or a hundred, or the prostrations of thousands?

She is kneeling now, by their marriage bed, her cheek against the quilt, eyes staring at a blurred pattern in which many triangles come together to make the four corners of a house. The memory of her own prayer eats at her. She sees herself kneeling at the end of another bed — her child's — palms stiff against the metal frame, murmuring, Whatever you want, God, he's yours, he's yours.

I didn't mean it, God, she thinks. He was mine! I thought it was a test. I thought you would command otherwise: untie the boy, douse the flames, cast the knife from my hand. He would rise up, puzzled and bewildered. He would forgive me. We would walk down the mountain together. He would live.

Who does she blame? There is no one but herself.

She is invisible in the school hallways. Even teachers avert their eyes. She eats her lunch in the library and stares at the row of shadowy pines. She hides behind her hair.

Do they expect her to go on crying?

She will not.

Do they think she is rawer than they are, that the least slight, the least scrape will harm her further?

They are wrong. She is tough as hide. You could cut her but she would not flinch. You could throw at her any name, any false rumour, and she would stand still and steady as a rooted tree. You could push against her and she would not move.

She sits and stares at the pines, and her eyes wash with sudden water.

She can't stay here. She can't go home.

She walks out the back doors, onto the crunching soccer field, eyes forward. No one stops her.

She pushes through pruned shrubbery, over curving sidewalks, across backyards of dead grass, the suburban maze of houses empty in daytime, dark but for strings of light winking on Christmas trees. She sees herself as shadow sketched on their windows. Behind glass, the houses are tombs for soft furniture. Their cupboards shelter more food than any family could consume. Warm and dark, they forgive her for anything.

She returns to school in time to meet her father. Hunched over the wheel, glassy-eyed, he glances at her. How was your day? Good?

He mutters under his breath something she cannot hear, could not even if she were paying attention, the clacking of discrete words like beads on a string.

He prays.

He invokes the name of God. But he does not stop at a single utterance. The god on whom he calls has many names, names not to be called lightly. He has not learned all of them and he hopes God will forgive his ignorance. The names move through him like water, washing his lungs. Each name connects to an exhalation. The names roll smoothly, as if they are waiting at all times to be spoken, eternally offered to anyone in need.

He says: Jehovah. Father. Mother Earth. He says Mother Earth with the same weight and necessity that he says Allah, Jesu, Holy Spirit. He says: Shiva. Mary. Buddha. Saint Brigid. Saint Francis. He says: God. He says: Love.

When she sees his lips moving, she looks away. It is too late to take her by the hand, to confess this prayer. It's shot beyond fear or habit. Each of them is filled with shame in the presence of the other. There was never, he thinks, an excess of kindness between us. Now, he thinks, I could be kind, but I do not know what kindness would mean to her.

In the alien dark, eyes open, he rolls away from her pitched and sleeping form and looks at the window, where shadows are moving, the last snow of the season is blowing. He says: God. God. God.

He senses where this is leading, though he cannot let himself grasp the possibility. He is being led into the turquoise room, shuffling; his mouth will shape the words, letters will form on the screen, and he will discover space for work that does not consume. He will find himself   not yet, not yet, but some day, not even so very far away — saying Thank you.

He cannot bear the thought.

He eats paste. He pinches at quiet time. He markers in blue on his face. He refuses to hold a pencil. He colours the ants purple and yellow when his teacher reminds him that ants are red or black only. His winter scene has sunflowers. He pretends he cannot read even the simplest words. Enfolded in the teacher's arms, he shatters. He weeps into her shoulder until the fabric is soaked. He says, I want my mom.

The woman in the office telephones.

Finally his mother arrives. He smells her before he sees her, an upper layer of freshly sprayed blue perfume and underneath a sweeter smell that he trusts, that smells like the black mould growing on the underside of his mattress at home. She breathes it out as she takes him into her arms, and he melts against her.

He isn't crying anymore. She strokes his back and his wet forehead.

She says, He's just tired. He needs to rest.

The teacher nods. Take him home. Of course.

At home, in the yard, the ground is thawing, muddy. She makes him a snack and sets it on the porch on a plate: a hard-boiled egg. He is digging a hole into chilly earth through pale yellow grass and early green fronds. He licks dirt off his thumb. He gathers pinecones and piles them into the hole, and rotted black walnuts — a separate hole. He considers the peeled egg.

He buries it too.

She has a duty to care; she is a mother.

She creeps to her daughter's bedside, kneels and waits for her eyes to adjust to the grey light. The girl's face is relaxed, like that of a much younger child. She can see the infant in her, the rashy cheeks, the toddler who could not sing in tune, the seven-year-old bossing a playmate — No one will want to be your friend if you play like that! — the gangly, downy-limbed older child who could run like the wind, away, away. How she envied her daughter's weightless, leaping stride.

She folds her hands in prayer and bends to the girl's thrown arm, crooked at the elbow, touches her forehead to the open palm and whispers, *I love you.*

Yet when she raises her head, she shivers. It is as if the girl, by the necessary act of breathing in and out, is collapsing through a translucent membrane into the world of flesh and blood. Here, in this room, in her prayer, in her hands, she grasps instead the presence of the son who is gone. He cannot breathe in a world of flesh and blood. He will gasp like a fish out of water; he will die.

She thinks, He is dead.

She thinks, I will not survive this.

It takes all her focus to hold him. If she lets herself hold the living, he will vanish completely. A mother would not let her child vanish. No.

She sits in her bedroom before the mirror. She picks at her hair with a wide-toothed comb meant to enhance rather than frizz her new curls. The curls have been imposed onto the strands by means of a chemical that burned her scalp and watered her eyes.

She leans forward, elbows on the vanity's glass top. Into one ear she stabs a silver spike, the length of her smallest fingernail, and fastens it at the back of the lobe with a tiny screw. She repeats the process on the other side and inclines her head to examine the results, turning first to the right, then to the left.

The vanity came recently from her Oma, who has moved into a smaller apartment, her father lugging the leavings from the rear of a borrowed pickup truck across the icy porch and into their house. His office received a heavy easy chair with a leg rest that springs open. He is probably sleeping there now. In their cupboards are Oma's dishes, edged in gold, that her mother refuses to use except for company — and they never have company.

The vanity is old and was made by her Opa, who died so long ago that no one remembers him, not even his only child, her father. Her Oma does not speak of him. It is as if he never existed. But the table is proof that he lived, that he worked with his hands using scraps of wood, that he designed and cut and sanded and painted an object that could be handed down to his granddaughter.

Now she has gone and scissored photographs and placed them under the glass, to make it her own. Her mother screamed, How dare you cut him apart, it's like cutting him out of our lives, we can never replace those pictures! What point explaining? She deliberately chose from the album a photograph that was blurry; yes, she cut off his head, arranged it in a comical fashion with her own cut-off head, and her mother's and her father's and her little brother's. The heads perch like pears on a tree cut from a magazine. There are other photographs too, on top of other landscape scenes. Her pony, the dog, cats, swimming in a sunset sky. There is an old photograph she knows not to cut, taken on a beach when they were all so small. So long ago: wasn't it a dream?

Already, the glass pins down distant, lost colours. The girl in the mirror hurtles beyond reach. Staring, she wills herself onward. She says, I will be beautiful, as if beauty were a mask to be chosen, as if its appearance could be commanded; as if it will serve her, and not the other way round.

A knock on the door.

But she doesn't turn, she doesn't say Come in. She is fifteen years old. She is wearing acid-washed jeans and a sweatshirt cut and frayed by her own design at the arms and waist and neck. It is six degrees outside and the sky is pouring cold spring rain. It is six degrees and a storm rattles the window of her room, droplets pelting against glass.

The hoops in her ears are made of blue ceramic and curve almost to her exposed collarbones, heavy. Every movement animates them. She is aware, even without looking in the mirror, of their unnatural presence.

The knock again. Her mother: What are you doing?

Nothing.

May I come in?

No.

Please?

She turns, hoops swinging and softly kissing her neck. She does not recognize her own voice; she is not squeezing her face into this shape, muscles twitching, nostrils curling, the hiss of sound, the taste of hatred. *Get out!*

He opens the windows but neglects to drag the heavy screens up from the basement. Let it in, he thinks. He opens the windows to the smell of a rural spring, of manure spread upon the fields, and of cut grass, and mud.

He sits in his mother's easy chair and releases the handle. The leg rest leaps into position, lifting and cradling him, and he is relaxed, and he sleeps, lightly. His dreams are of this moment: they incorporate the rattle of a neighbour's tractor, the crunch of a child's bicycle tires in the gravel lane, the meow of a cat.

He wakes as easily as he's slept, as if a gentle hand is parting curtains of translucent fabric before his eyes, easing him from one space to another, showing him how little difference there is between here and there: You belong in both places. One is as real as the other.

In his dream the son was riding the bicycle.

In his dream the cat was become the son. The cat turned to look at him, but only a glance, disinterested, the way a cat's ear twitches towards an unexpected sound. The sound that drew the cat's attention was his own voice, groaning, and that is what woke him.

He sees a cat. He recognizes it: the female tabby, originator of all the cats on this farm, the matron, the elder. The cat has come through the open window; she walks across his keyboard and letters leap nonsensically onto the green screen. For a moment he panics: what if some crucial thought he will never think again has been erased? And then he relaxes. He thinks, If I can't remember it, it couldn't have been that important.

He says, instinctively, *tsh-tsh* to chase away the cat, and claps his hands. And she obeys, trotting out the open window and loping down the porch roof, tail stuck straight up into the air. It is only when he sees the cat preparing to leap to a branch that he remembers the crux of the dream, a memory like unearthed lace, full of holes, disintegrating even as he grabs for it.

His son. His son has been in the room.

He is paralyzed in his chair into a position that mimics relaxation, and death. Behind him the door is shut. In the chill breeze his face is wet. He thinks of the names of God, but he does not say them.

He thinks of how he has moved away from the names of God, or how they have moved away from him. He thinks, So. That was temporary too. Now I know.

He finds a nest of kittens. The mother does not hiss and spit at him but rolls to one side, as if to show them off, her nipples in two fat rows along her belly. The kittens are blind and he touches the head of one, black with orange markings, like its mother. He can feel its skull, and through the bones of the skull, thin as eggshell, he feels the beat of its heart, racing. He goes all along the litter and touches each kitten on the head. The mother cat seems pleased, and he thinks, She wants me to.

Last of all, he touches the mother cat on her head, and she pushes into his fingers, purring.

He has not forgotten the kitten that he drowned last summer. They think he has forgotten. His mother said he was too little to understand; but he understood. When he looks at the kittens, he remembers what it felt like to lift the little body and to dip it into the bucket of water. It scratched his wrist when he lifted it out. He wanted to wash it. It had yellow crust around its eyes, and its fur had gotten wet and dusty and had dried into matted points along its spine. He did not know it would die.

He remembers his sister sobbing, and his mother and his father too.

No, he thinks. That was something else. That was another time.

The barn hums with the sound of insects hidden everywhere. He stands and scratches a mosquito bite on his ankle.

There is a square hole in the floor through which he has climbed up into the mow. He kneels at the top of the ladder and makes quiet noises. He throws clumps of straw: bombs exploding. He swings down the ladder, talking under his breath. He is not the commander, he is not the dragon, he is not the bad guy. He is himself, in the middle of a battle.

She takes an interest in the beans growing in the garden. She puts up several dozen quarts using her mother's recipe; in fact, she does not use a recipe, so familiar is she with the method and means, lodged into her being during teenage summers spent working in a hot kitchen.

The beans are snapped and cleaned and packed vertically into jars with salt and bacon and hot water, and cooked in the massive black canner into a dull green oblivion. When opened and heated and served with butter, they will taste not like summer but like the memory of summer — as if by alchemy, turned to comfort. Anyone could enjoy these beans, even the elderly with no teeth or, if speaking of the toothless, even the very young.

She thinks, Who do we know without teeth? And then, Who do we know, anymore? Who would we invite to our table, to share in this imaginary meal?

A stain of sweat rises on the fabric of her T-shirt, under her breasts. She is wearing a tied kerchief to keep her hair out of the cooking. The windows fog with steam. She sees her reflection in the side of an aluminum bowl filled with beans that need cleaning. She guesses her age in the distortion of metal: Less than four decades, more than three. She feels off balance thinking such a confused thought, even playfully. She mutters: Thirty-six. She yells for her daughter, Come and help, young lady!

I am not a young lady, I am an old girl. A joke they used to share.

She snorts.

The girl stands on the counter, and one by one she hands her cooled jars. The girl lines them up in jewelled rows.

Next, she says, tomatoes. And in between, peaches. And right about now, pickles: dill, and bread-and-butter, and sweet relish. Any vegetable can be finely chopped and tossed into sweet relish: cabbage, cucumber, zucchini, the vegetables that spread and produce out of all proportion to one's desire to eat them.

While they work, they talk. She talks. She says, Slice them thin, like this. She says, Could you run to the garden for more dill? She says, My grandmother loved pickles. She used to make a dozen different kinds. They didn't make salsa in those days. They didn't even know what it was — ethnic food. Oregano was an ethnic food. They used celery as a flavouring, not to eat. They canned something called chili sauce, but I never liked it; I won't bother. It's sweet, not spicy. We should look up a recipe for salsa, something spicy. We should go to the library.

She falls asleep perfectly exhausted, with burns on her inner arms and cuts on her hands that sting when they come into contact with anything acidic — vinegar, tomato juice. The deepest cut is on the left palm, between thumb and forefinger.

Later, she thinks, I already knew. I knew exactly what I was doing.

But later it is easy to imagine certitude; is not everything that happens, she thinks, inevitable? Proven by the simple fact of its happening?

They fill the cupboards and the freezer. They fill August and September. The girl looks at her with eyes that neither charge nor accuse nor deny. She tries to mirror in return this gaze, but she cannot. What is it to love? If it is to know, she feels certain that she loves her daughter in a child's apron, in her bare feet on the counter, with her loose brushed hair and purple eyeshadow; but if it is to give in return, in kind, she cannot. Her love stops here. Her love bashes against a wall behind her own eyes and does not advance any further.

Her love is ruthless. I already knew, she thinks, later. I knew I would leave them.

She writes the advertisement and calls the newspaper office and reads it out. She sends a cheque from her own bank account to pay for two printed lines in the classified section. She remembers when an advertisement like this would have stirred her fantasies. She smiles and dismisses her younger self. Her younger self never practised driving stick shift under the guidance of an older boy who had his licence. Her younger self never grinned sideways and pulled to a stop on a country road and climbed into the back seat and saw the stars through the side window, past the head of a boy who is kissing her neck and leaving his mark.

Pony for sale. White gelding, 14 hands, approximately 10 years old. Trained English and Western. Gentle with children.

On the day when the new owner arrives to load the pony into the trailer, she sits on his bare broad back and pats his shoulder while he nibbles grass in their front yard, near the porch. She has never before ridden him across the yard, up to the porch. His hooves dig into soft dirt, leaving grooves, but her mother does not seem to notice.

It's time, her mother says. You're ready.

Of course I am, she thinks, irritated.

He spooks at the truck's rumble, and she slides off and grabs his faded halter. The new owner operates a riding stable. She wears tall black boots. She is brisk, running her hands down his legs, checking that they are clean. She opens her palm under his whiskered muzzle and surprises him with an offering of grain. Now he will go anywhere with this stranger, who leads him into the empty trailer and ties his head under a bag of hay. His hooves clatter in dismay as they pull away down the lane.

She worries about the broken taillight. She thinks, That wasn't a real goodbye. It happened so fast. I thought there would be more time. Prone on her bed, face down, she cries, but her tears are scant and she soon pushes herself upright.

I am different now, she thinks, gazing into the mirror. She is curiously satisfied with what she sees. The vanity is cleared of its tubes and powders; only the most essential remain. Her hair has outgrown its false curls and falls long and sleek to her emergent breasts. Mirror, mirror on the wall, who's the fairest of them all?

Entranced, she believes she has arrived at an answer, and the answer is beauty, surely and truly, scraped down and unadorned.

At a moment like this, in this body, who could think of anything else?

Wake up, wake up, it's been a year.

He is surprised by how little remains to be completed. He is surprised by how easily the task is done. The footnotes and endnotes require the most effort, but the work is deeply satisfying, like lingering over dessert, accepting a second helping, a glass of sweet liqueur. He thinks, It is easier to end than to begin, but recognizes that proof stands against the theory: his own children stand against it. Think of how easily each was begun, almost as if he'd had nothing to do with it.

He watched his wife change and grow, he rubbed her swollen feet and pretended not to mind the extra fat she carried under her jaw, though he'd married her for her lines. By the third pregnancy he knew with confidence that the lines would return and he would have her back again.

She was the one who rose at night to feed each baby, by breast. He slept soundly. She consulted other women: remedies for teething pain and diaper rash and fussy palates. She ground table food to a pulp and trained them to use the toilet and dealt with knotted hair and scraped elbows and tears. She wiped almost all of the tears, on her wrists, her palms, on her shirtsleeves, her belly.

That is what baffles him most. She sees an end, with the children, with him. He cannot see it. The children will be with them forever, alive or dead. The children will be with them until they themselves are dead, and then they will be with the children, and with the grandchildren and the great-grandchildren, even if forgotten — a chin might turn up, the lines of her jaw, that flaming red hair their daughter pulled from him, who pulled it from some unknown ances- tor — and forever and ever and ever they will belong to each other. There is no escaping the fate of their connection.

He means the children but he means her too. There is no escaping the fate of his connection to her, and hers to him, even if it is only through their offspring.

Ah, she says, you understand me better than you think. How could I be afraid to go when we will always be together?

Don't do this. Please.

She says, They will adjust to the change. They will adjust better than you.

He says, A narcissist will say anything to prove she is right.

No, he does not say it. Can someone who rises at three o'clock in the morning, night after night after night, to lift a sweating, squalling infant to her breast, to feed and com- fort and soothe, be considered a narcissist? He is not a doctor of psychology. He is a doctor (pending) of twentieth-century American history, with a specialty in the covert influence of the American government in the larger Americas, during but not confined to the Cold War period.

He is thinking of growing back his beard. The stubble comes in grey. He is standing in the bathroom cupping his chin and right cheek in his hand when he hears her crying in their bedroom. The bathroom has two doors: one opens to the main room and the other to their bedroom. He slips through this one, and he holds her, and she lets him.

He does not touch his cheek to hers: the stubble would scratch her skin.

He is tall and she is small, contracted, a bird against his chest, crying: It's been a year already, it's already been a year.

This is not a supper like other suppers. This one is special. His mother says it is special the way a birthday supper is special, "because it marks an occasion," except no one is having a birthday. "It marks an occasion," she says, and her voice is hard, not soft. "He gets no more birthdays, so we'll remember this day instead. For him."

The day that his brother died. One year ago.

Nobody ate anything, one year ago. He remembers choking on a piece of toast, his grandma whacking him on the back. He remembers the house filling up with people and the platters of ham and lasagnes, and even though nobody was eating anything, it was almost jolly. All that food. All those people. He remembers trying to trick himself into thinking it was a party.

But not today. Today no tricks could work. They are alone, just the family. Just his mother, his father, his big sister, the dog. And one chair for his brother, set with an empty plate and spoon and fork and knife and napkin and a glass filled with homemade grape juice. Who poured the juice? What does it mean? Does it mean someone thinks his dead brother might come back to drink it tonight?

That is the kind of thought he tries very hard not to think, blinking fast to push it away; and the fear. The chair is directly across from him and he can't help looking at it. He is relieved when no one puts food on the empty plate, a relief that is almost too big, that spreads his arms wide and knocks over his own glass of juice.

But no one yells. They leave the juice to soak into the red tablecloth, and his mother pours him more from a glass jar, in silence.

He is not hungry. He remembers what it feels like to be hungry, and he tries, because his brother isn't here to be hungry, to eat.

There are canned green beans, his favourite, and pork chops topped with stewed apricots, which he scrapes off and dumps onto the placemat, and a salad made of yellow rice with olives and green peppers and a salty cheese, none of which he swallows. He takes one bite because his mother tells him he must. And spits it into his hand and the dog eats it.

He wonders, Would the dog like stewed apricots? The dog would.

For dessert she has made pie, two kinds, his brother's favourites. There was an argument this morning: his mother thinks pumpkin was his brother's favourite, and his father, who does not usually have an opinion on the subject of food, is certain it was apple. There was never such a fight. The screaming. She cleared a cupboard of a whole stack of dishes and did not sweep up.

His father swept up the smashed gold rims and white shards. He did not like seeing his father cry. He went to his sister's room and she sighed, but let him sit on her bed and listen to the music she was playing on her boom box. But when he hummed along, she said to him: Go away. You are making fun of something that means something to me. And he said: Uh-uh. And she said: Then stop humming. So he stopped.

So they eat two kinds of pie. He finds his appetite. Two pies are better than one. There is ice cream for the apple and whipped cream for the pumpkin.

They are each supposed to say something "for the occasion." It is supposed to be something about the brother, who died one year ago in the back room, in their parents' bed, and who has not come back tonight to drink his glass of grape juice. Not yet. Not ever. Maybe. He blinks and blinks.

It is his turn. He looks at his plate. He says, I don't remember. He is telling a lie. How could he forget?

He remembers that he did not want to sit in the bathtub after his brother had taken a bath because he was afraid; it was not even *What if I get sick too?* He was afraid in a way he didn't understand. Afraid to get close. Afraid to see the thing that was happening to his brother, the way he was hollowing out. He did not want to touch his brother, or touch anything touched by his brother, careful to watch which cup his mother used to serve his brother a drink, and memorizing it so he would not drink from the same cup by accident.

He looks at his mother. She says, It's okay. You were so little.

They will always tell him this, always. He will accept it without correcting them or revealing that he was bigger than they knew, and smaller.

His mother offers him another piece of pie, and he says yes. She says, Which kind?

And that is it. That is where the story stops and he begins to cry.

JULIET WEARS BLACK

Juliet wears black.

She accessorizes with a draped orange silk scarf and orange feathered earrings, but her choice, purchased at a thrift store, is no accident. She does not think she is being angry or rebellious. But her mother thinks so. Her mother says, Ah, wedding as funeral. I see. Kissing Juliet twice over, on each cheek, as if she's become European rather than merely relocated to the West Coast.

Hello, Juliet, picture of elegance, says her newly minted stepfather, Jesse, drawing her into an embrace as if he has not heard Gloria's words; and perhaps he has not. It is some relief to Juliet that her stepfather does not remind her, in any way, of her father. Her mother might have gone down a checklist, so perfectly opposite are the two men. Jesse is small, compact, a marathoner who smokes weed and uses words like *chill* and *babe* without irony. Does Juliet like him? The question is impertinent and irrelevant, and the answer is she doesn't not like him. It is just that he is a stranger; his customs and habits are strange to her.

She can, however, say with certainty that she does not like his children. She is satisfied that the feeling is mutual. The girl is her own age, nineteen, and the boy is two years older, and they were raised mostly by their mother, who is also here.

Why let a little divorce get in the way of a big friendship?

The mother, who does remind Juliet of her own, at least in physical type — slender, dark-haired, fine-boned, though with unnaturally large breasts — used that line in her toast at last night's rehearsal dinner, an informal event in the open-air restaurant at the top of the beach, towards which Juliet and Emmanuel are walking now, away from the short receiving line in the sand. Juliet and Emmanuel pass the photographer, who squats on her heels, the better to frame the newlyweds as the tide swells romantically towards her mother's bare feet, and her stepfather's. His toes are hairless. Juliet wishes she did not know that.

It has been an "intimate" ceremony.

Why rehearse at all, when we're all basically in the wedding? Juliet asked Emmanuel. But at age ten he rolls with any expectation; he does not question. Last night they shared a beach hut with the stepsister and stepbrother — Gloria's arrangement. Gloria had imagined for them a night of riotous card games and fraternal bonding: this is what Juliet assumes. Instead they waited to take turns in the bathroom, and the stepsister complained that the shower was outside and exposed, and the stepbrother asked, curiously and perhaps with some pity, So you used to live here? Emmanuel said, I was just a baby. And Juliet said, Yeah, we used to live *here*, with sarcastic emphasis, as if the stepbrother had meant this very hut on this very beach. There are three bedrooms in the hut, and Juliet volunteered to share with Emmanuel. She was glad to, even though her brother got up twice before midnight to go to the bathroom, looking for chances to use his new flashlight.

It goes without saying — or it does to anyone who knows the situation — that their father is not here. It goes without saying — does it? — that he has had nothing to say on the subject. Nothing at all. He arranged for their visas. He arranged for the legal papers necessary for a minor to travel to another country without a legal guardian present. He drove them to the airport. He said, Have fun.

Yeah, right, Juliet replied. She said this on his behalf, for him. She did not think he particularly wanted her to, but he was being left behind. She had to give him something.

Actually, she thought she would: have fun. She was prepared to appear symbolically morose and resentful and to wear black, but she meant to have fun.

The ceremony is brief.

Her contribution is a poem, not composed by her, and chosen by her mother, the sentiment and phrasing not to Juliet's taste at all. She attempts to read with sincerity, but who can hear her in the gathering wind? She pronounces the last line with a hesitant upswing in tone that reveals — if anyone can catch it — an emotion she would rather keep private: the question mark of loneliness, the question mark of home. She looks to her mother, whose smile is strained and false, like that of someone who has only been pretending to listen and who is thinking of something else, and her mother nods, as if to say, You did your best, now back to your seat, dear.

Emmanuel and the stepbrother light a torch together to symbolize unity; a candle would not survive the breeze.

The stepsister performs a dance. Costumed in a white body-suit, she manipulates a broad white scarf that whips in the rising wind off the ocean, to stunning effect. Juliet can see that the dance is beautiful, and genuine. She can admit it. She can compare it to her own offering and shrink just a little on the inside, but she knows she could not have offered more. It isn't in her.

She is not in a generous mood over this marriage.

She limps with Emmanuel to the lit-up restaurant, where tables have been arranged in the room in which they gathered yesterday evening. She taps her heeled shoes on a wooden post to clean them of sand before entering the restaurant, an unnecessary formality. She has chosen shoes that she will never wear again, vicious spikes that dig holes in the beach, straps that threaten to cripple her, pressure that makes her head ache. Worst of all — and she thinks she knew this would be the case — the shoes are utterly out of place. The restaurant is naturally casual and of the beach, and many guests, following the example of the bridal pair, have removed their footwear. On principle Juliet refuses, though she cannot actually locate a defensible principle.

Because I don't want to. Because I don't have to.

Two guitarists dressed like gauchos strum folk songs in the corner. Juliet hobbles to the bar. Her brother climbs onto a stool. One Coke with ice, one Coke with rum.

The stepbrother greets them, hesitates, chooses the stool next to Emmanuel. Juliet notes the hesitation, thinks, He didn't want to do that, he is just being polite.

The stepbrother waves to the bartender, who is also the owner, a fit Belgian whose wife has soft white hair and works all day in a turquoise bathing suit that does not disguise her accumulation around the middle, her blue-veined legs. For this occasion she hurries around the room lighting short candles in glass vases, a sarong tied around her hips.

Nice wedding, the stepbrother says.

You don't have to sit with us, she says.

The stepbrother's stillness is too sudden, too silent, his chin tucked; he swallows. A chill spreads in Juliet's stomach, then lower, to her pelvis. The stepbrother meets her gaze, nods politely and excuses himself.

I'm a terrible person, says Juliet, but Emmanuel says, No, you're not.

He asks the bartender for a deck of cards. Go Fish?

You can't play Go Fish with two people, says Juliet.

Ask them. Emmanuel points to the stepbrother, who stands with the stepsister.

They're busy, says Juliet.

The stepbrother and stepsister are talking to an older relative or family friend — their relative or friend, not Juliet's — and they are saying things like Thank you, yes, it was a lovely ceremony wasn't it, we're so glad Dad's happy. The relative looks at Juliet and smiles as if to say, I know who you are, and returns to the conversation. Now, thinks Juliet, she's saying, Oh, but how is it for the other children, are they happy too? They don't look it, do they? All alone. And Gloria's family, were they not able to come? The stepsister is rolling her eyes. Gloria *never* talks about her family, it's kind of weird. But the stepbrother is defending them. Her sister is here, she flew in from Georgia. No one else had a passport, and it was short notice, and . . .

Juliet is sorry. She telegraphs *sorry* with her eyes, but in matters psychic her talent is reception, not transmission.

Emmanuel has laid out a game of solitaire. Juliet finishes the first rum and Coke and orders another; her feet throb a little less, resting on the bars of the stool, soothed by the early gentle massage of alcohol. Juliet points to a move that Emmanuel has missed, red queen on black king. She thinks, I'm going to drink until I'm gone; but she modifies the thought. No. I'm going to drink until I'm having fun, for real.

She sees Aunt Caroline coming for them. And how's your dad doing? is the first thing Aunt Caroline thinks to say, busy and bursting with sympathy.

He's not here, so I don't know, says Juliet.

I've tried to get in touch over the years; I've written letters; I've tried to tell him, You're still a part of our family . . . Aunt Caroline continues in this vein: her hopefulness, her forgiveness, her wish to be reunited, and Juliet nods and swills the second rum and Coke. Juliet knows better than to try to say something of substance in return, something obvious and true like He doesn't want to be your friend, and he's not part of your family. She is amazed at how adults insist on telling you things you don't want to know. No, it's worse than that: adults insist on unburdening themselves on you, as if your young, healthy shoulders could carry more, as if you could bear their troubled thoughts and desires across closed borders and turn their selfish whimsies into offerings and make peace.

I am not an ambassador, Juliet thinks. She envies Emmanuel his oblivion, but then she thinks, No, that is not fair; he's lost more than I have. His childhood gnawed by departures.

Uh-huh, uh-huh, she says, clinking the ice in the bottom of her glass. No longer listening to Aunt Caroline's individual words, Juliet is smiling, inclining her head, murmuring false sympathy, and nearly misses the change in tone, the leap from one subject to another that requires her attention and reply.

Is that your real hair? Aunt Caroline asks.

Real hair? thinks Juliet.

The colour, the curl, says Aunt Caroline. It's just so beautiful, I thought it couldn't possibly be your real hair.

Oh, it's very unreal hair, says Juliet.

Tsk, tsk, says Aunt Caroline. Juliet is certain those are her precise words.

It's my hair, Juliet sighs, turning to the bartender, but he is busy with another guest at the far side of the counter. It's all my own, she says, returning to Aunt Caroline. Nothing else, no chemicals, no nothing. I don't even brush it, she says. It's basically hair gone wild, feral hair, hair returning to its natural state.

She is like this: get her talking, drag her out of her silent regard, and she won't stop until she's said ever so slightly too much. She can see it in her aunt's eyes — pity — Poor Juliet, just like her mother.

Not like my mother, thinks Juliet, not so, not true. Example (a), the shoes. Example (b); but she shakes her head. Example (b)? Example (b): everything else about me.

Her mother has chosen not to sing during the ceremony. She said, I would be too nervous. I can't perform at my own wedding. It's not all about me.

Parse the words: are any of them truthful, or would each sentence make better sense read in a mirror? Gloria is not a nervous woman, she has an icy reserve, a chill that permits her freedom to pursue, to leave, to choose at will, with control. She thrives on performance: it's the blood that feeds her. Oh, and finally, if a wedding is not about the bride, who is it about? The groom? Sure, he's here, he's shown up, he's dressed in the light embroidered *guayabera* the bride has chosen for him, and he's happy to repeat some sincerely maudlin words invoking eternal bliss; but it's not about him. He knows it. Nor is it about the friends or the larger family; least of all is it about the children.

It is all about Gloria.

I get another chance to be a bride! was how she told Juliet. *Spare me.* Juliet did not say it out loud.

It is curious to observe, when parsing Gloria, that her chill, the premeditation of her actions, does not prevent her from saying the wrong thing at the wrong time. She has a gift for making people uncomfortable. She has a gift for tracking to the edge, holding someone by the hand and pulling him or her over with her. People like it — some people. People who don't mind being led on an adventure on someone else's terms. People who don't mind taking the blame.

It is safe to say that Gloria was not always so precise, so definitive. When Juliet was a child, her mother was someone not softer, not more soothing, but messier, prone to anger broken by spells of drifting distance. She would wipe her child's face after a meal with a wet washcloth as if she were wiping an inanimate and slightly disgusting object, performing a duty with impatience, without passion or sympathy. And then without warning she would want to hug her child, the child's bones creaking under her fearsome insistence. Age has sharpened her lines. She is no longer muddy around the edges, but crisp, crackling with energy. Witness her onstage.

Tonight everyone will get to.

Gloria did not perform during the ceremony but she has written a song for her new husband, to be debuted during the appetizers.

I'm hungry, Emmanuel says.

I have to pee, says Juliet. Watch my drink?

To get to the bathrooms, Juliet must stagger in her daggered heels out behind the restaurant, away from the beach, where two rooms, one for men and one for women, are contained within one flat-roofed concrete structure. The path is poorly lit by light spilling from the kitchen door, propped open and flaring with the clatter of pots and knives and a voice singing out of tune in Spanish.

She thinks she hears the sound of a chicken protesting — that it's being killed for their suppers?

In the mirror, beneath unflattering fluorescent tubes, her scarf is askew, her mouth relaxed. A good sign? She is not sure.

She eases a foot out of one shoe and places it, quivering, on the cool, gritty floor. Mistake, she thinks. Dammit. Only a disciplined masochist could force the suffering foot back into the shoe. She pauses for a moment, one hip tilted higher than the other, considering, taking this thought in.

She makes a decision. She believes herself to be a person of discipline, though she has done little to prove it in her nineteen years on this earth; but she is not a masochist. Therefore the other shoe comes off. She bends and picks both up by their heels. Her chest sighs out, *ahhhh*, involuntarily, and she smiles.

Okay, Mom, I'll go barefoot. You win.

Her mother's voice in Juliet's head: It's not a competition. And don't you feel so much better? Isn't this wonderful?

The appetizers are circulating, and Emmanuel holds two skewers of grilled sausage pieces mixed with shrimp. She drops the shoes under her stool and says, One of those for me?

No. Get your own.

Aw, c'mon. Share?

Get your own. They're mine. I'm hungry.

Fine. She feels good. She stands and wanders after the Belgian woman. From up close, she is surprised to see the muscles in the woman's upper arm as she balances the tray. The woman looks as though she could swing from vines in a jungle, sarong flowing.

Juliet takes a moment to choose from among the skewers of meat and shrimp arranged on a greasy banana leaf. She says, I'm vegetarian, but . . . and steps back from the tray directly onto a foot, bare heel intimately squashing bare toes. So sorry!

Oh, says the stepsister. But the *oh* does not refer to the treading of her toes, because the stepsister continues, So you're that kind of vegetarian.

Well, no, says Juliet. I mean, I'm a real vegetarian, it's just — I'm vegan, says the stepsister. She is still wearing the white bodysuit, paired now with a white wraparound skirt. She's slender as a sylph.

I think I knew that, says Juliet. With her teeth Juliet slides a round of sausage off the skewer. She chews, thoughtfully, and then with passion. She says, This sausage has to be home-made, it's literally the best thing ever. She corrects herself: I don't mean *literally* literally. You know what I mean.

The stepsister, a scarlet wrap flung light as air around her shoulders, looks towards the ocean, which glints like a perfect postcard under the fast-falling sun. We hardly know each other really, do we, she says.

Do you think that we should? says Juliet. Should we spend more time together? Is that what stepsisters do?

It's hardly practical, is it, says the stepsister. We live so far away.

Will your dad be disappointed if we don't . . . get to know each other?

My dad, says the stepsister, already thinks we get along fabulously. He thought we got along fabulously before we'd even met, and he'll think we get along fabulously even if we never speak to each other again.

Ah, says Juliet, as if she might use the information for something; she can't think what.

We might not like each other anyway, says the stepsister.

Juliet chews another round of sausage. She says, I actually really like you right now. I don't know why.

How much have you had to drink? says the stepsister.

Ha, says Juliet.

They smile quietly, privately, surprised. In a moment they will turn away, walk away. It is not that they can think of nothing more to say to each other; it is that they recognize the risk of investigating further, even superficially, of testing the limits of their mutual interest. Juliet thinks, Small talk is big talk floating on the surface, buoyant as one of Emmanuel's balsa model airplanes. She thinks, What is this? This is the debris of small talk; more serious, a little plane wreck among the waves, and everyone climbs out wearing life jackets; everyone survives.

At the bar, Emmanuel is playing cards with the stepbrother.

Juliet begins a smile but does not complete it.

The stepbrother glances up but appears engrossed. Do you have any fours? he says.

You can't play Go Fish with two people, says Juliet.

Yes you can, says Emmanuel.

No you can't.

Can.

Can't.

What do you call this?

Boring, says Juliet.

You don't mean that, says the stepbrother. She tries to read his tone: Plain old reproachful? Jokingly reproachful?

Needlingly reproachful?

We don't really know each other, do we, she says, repeating his sister's words.

We will, he says.

Oh God, says Juliet as the speaker system — portable amp and tinny microphone — crackles to life. Her mother's voice whispers, seductively amplified, Testing, testing . . . Welcome everyone, welcome here, to this wonderful country I wish I could call home again, to Nicaragua. *¡Nicaraguita!*

The guests applaud tentatively, uncertain: is she testing or toasting? Dammit, Mother, this is just like you, thinks Juliet.

Please, could I have another? Juliet says to the bartender. The owner, busy with wires and plugs, has been replaced behind the counter by a young man with his shirt unbuttoned to the breeze, lean, *guapo. Muy guapo*, she thinks.

¿Ron y Coca? He indicates her empty glass.

Sí, por favor.

You speak Spanish, says the stepbrother.

Not really.

How long did you live here?

A year and a half or so. I was just a kid.

Is it the same?

She laughs, not a nice laugh: she can't help herself. No, she says. Sorry, no, I don't mean . . . I can't even compare. I didn't see much on the bus from the airport. It's a different government. It was nothing like this, okay? It was nothing like *this*. She points at the polished wooden bar.

Ask him, if you really want to know, she says, pointing with her chin at the bartender.

I don't speak Spanish, says the stepbrother.

Me neither. Juliet smiles at the boy behind the bar, and he smiles in return, examining her in a way that she understands and for which she is grateful. She feels her body expanding under the boy's gaze — not that she is growing larger, but that the muscles are loosening, making space between the ribs; the hip joints relax, the spine straightens, the chest rises. She looks down and makes an unnecessary adjustment to her skirt, arranging it across her thighs, looks back up and receives the drink he is waiting to slide across to her, so that their fingers will meet.

Gracias.

De nada, señorita.

What is her mother saying? She wills herself to not take in the words, to let them wash over her, pure sensation. The sound of her mother's voice is gentle and insistent as the tide. Not too warm and not too cold, she strikes a perfect balance; she lulls them into thinking she is saying something worth listening to, but Juliet refuses to hear it.

I'm glad she likes my dad so much, says the stepbrother. Juliet has to look him directly in the eyes to determine: is he serious, or is that a joke? He meets her eyes: he is serious.

I'm glad you're glad, she says.

I like your dad too, says Emmanuel. He's going to take me kayaking.

Cool, says the stepbrother. Cool. He took me on this one trip, we kayaked in the ocean; there were whales.

Really? Emmanuel is impressed.

Gloria opens her song, stops. She is accompanying herself on acoustic guitar, and there is some fuss over the placement of the microphone. She begins again. The room stills. Juliet stares into her sweet brown drink, rocks the glass to move the fissured ice, tapping softly beneath the sound of her mother's voice.

She does not, contrary to her expectations, hate this song. It's not bad, really; really, it's quite good; really, it's good. It is. The quality is not in the words — her mother's songwriting tends towards repeated phrases of limited originality — but in the melody, as it always is, and the unexpected rhythmic turns; and the voice, most of all.

She really can sing, Juliet thinks.

She has never gotten comfortable with this situation: being an audience for her mother, being in an audience, with an audience for whom her mother is performing. No. She rephrases the thought: her mother performs for herself only, and the audience is an afterthought, though a necessary one.

Afterthought, aftermath. Things her mother does not think about. Or does she? If she does, she seems untouched by reflection, she is not hindered: she makes herself free and unconcerned.

Why Nicaragua? It was not the first thing she said to her mother when her mother broke the news, plans in place, ring on finger, accommodations booked. I know it's soon, but why wait? I'm not getting younger.

No, the first thing Juliet said was, Please don't have a wedding. Get married by all means, enjoy being married again, whatever, but please, please, please, do not have a wedding. Do not make us come.

But it's already booked! Don't think of it as a wedding, think of it as a holiday on the beach.

Does Dad know?

Of course.

You told Dad before you told us.

He had to know. I needed to check your schedules to make sure nothing would conflict.

And then Juliet said, Why Nicaragua? Why not anywhere else? Anywhere?

But Nicaragua is the perfect place, said Gloria. I want to share it with Jesse.

You are going to wreck my Nicaragua. But Juliet stopped herself. She could do that. She could stop herself. It was proof she was not like her mother. See, Aunt Caroline? Not like my mother.

She has tears in her eyes. By gazing into the drink and not at her mother, she has allowed herself to let go, to ease into the song's ending, its unwavering high note held softly but tenaciously. The note does not drop down or fall off the way your ear anticipates, but holds, diminishing by increments until you can hear it no longer, though you imagine you are hearing it still.

There is no assigned seating around tables, no formality surrounding the food. Heaping platters are placed buffet-style in the middle of the room, the smells of freshly grilled meat and wood smoke floating on the ocean breeze. The guests, sunburnt, dehydrated, crowd in famished anticipation.

Oh, wasn't it beautiful, beautiful? Jesse's former wife and current best-friend-forever bumps hips with Juliet, sabotages her into an embrace. And that song . . . I just melted.

Juliet holds an empty plate over her breasts like a shield.

Mostly she can find things to say, whether she wants to or not; in desperate situations she will say out loud whatever fool thing enters her mind, but she searches her mind, and it is empty, empty . . . check: still empty.

Beautiful. Just like you. What a stunning family you all make all together. The photographs will be divine. The woman holds Juliet by the shoulders and pushes her away to arms' length, the better to assess the truth of her proclamation.

Still nothing. Juliet works her mouth into a semblance of a smile.

Ah, the woman says, squeezing Juliet to her bosom, where Juliet's knuckles, clutched around the plate, are dug into the woman's trembling flesh by pure force. Juliet is oddly relieved: this woman is not in the least like her own mother, less substantial, wobblier. Juliet thinks, This woman would say anything to stay friends with an enemy, she would dissemble. Her own mother could not be bothered — there is that.

The woman smells of coconut suntan lotion and rum. I'm switching drinks, thinks Juliet.

The woman lifts her hands to run them through her own, platinum hair. Oh, this breeze, this glorious breeze. Juliet puts between them a platter of thick french fries cooked in beef fat. Pushing, hurrying, reaching over outstretched arms — Oh, excuse me, so sorry — Juliet heaps her plate: schnitzel of chicken, mussels, tomatoes stuffed with shrimp. When the woman turns, her lips forming a new thought, Juliet has escaped all the way to the condiments at the far end of the table. Juliet tilts her plate and mouths to the woman, *yum-yum*.

Your sister is going to starve, says Juliet. The three of them have chosen to eat at the bar.

I hear there are waffles for dessert, says the stepbrother. She can eat those.

Waffles aren't vegan. Waffles have eggs and milk.

Really?

Totally making it up. I literally have no idea, says Juliet. My dad does all the cooking. He's pretty good at it, if you like butter and melted cheese. Not *literally* literally, she adds, then stops and asks: Or is it literally literally?

What's your dad like?

Well, he's not here, says Juliet.

The stepbrother blinks.

And you'll never meet him. So it doesn't matter, Juliet finishes up.

Why would I never meet him?

Why would he want to meet you? Juliet glares over the top of Emmanuel's head. It irritates her to have to state the obvious. She shakes her head in disgust.

¿Uno más? says the bartending boy, reaching to clear her glass. Another one?

No, gracias. Quiero algo . . . She wants to switch poisons but she cannot think of another drink.

¿Vino? ¿Cerveza? She shakes her head. Not wine, not beer. *¿Jugo de fruta?* he suggests. Fruit juice.

His selection is limited. Rum is, after all, a specialty of this country, the fermented clear juices of sugarcane. She gives up. It will just have to be. *Ron,* she says, *con cualquier cosa.* Rum with whatever. Let him choose.

Con ron. He nods. She has no idea what drink will appear.

It sounds like you do speak Spanish, says the stepbrother. And I'm sorry about your dad. It's nothing to me, I mean. But I'm sorry. If he's unhappy.

That's not what I said.

Bring the damn drink, she thinks. She does not mean to sound upset. She thinks, I am not upset. Upset is not the word that explains what I am. Unhappy is wrong, too. I am, I am . . . She looks at the half-eaten food on her plate and pushes it towards her brother — Do you want some? — but he shakes his head. How much does he hear and absorb? She thinks of him as a baby, but when she was his age — When she was his age, she was here, not *here* here, but here in this country.

She thinks, He knows more than I think he knows.

Juliet, I'm sorry, says the stepbrother. I keep saying the wrong thing.

She sinks a little, breathless, to be named by him. She meets his eyes. She shrugs. I don't know what to say, she says. The bartender slides an oversized wineglass across the counter, decorated with a paper umbrella stuck into a chunk of pineapple that floats in an orange sea. He says, I hope you like it, pretty one — but not in English. She translates it in her head. It sounds better in Spanish. She smiles for him, a real smile, relieved to give and to receive on such simple terms.

Juliet? says the stepbrother. Now that he has begun saying her name, she thinks, he wants to say it again. She has to stop him saying it.

Your dad seems like a good person, she says, and regrets the words immediately. Could she have gone with more of a cliché, a conflicted cliché at that, a flimsy impression? *Seems.* Mom is happy, she says. Anyone can see that.

Maybe we should talk about something else, says the stepbrother.

Why aren't you sitting with your family, all the relatives that came? Why aren't you sitting with your sister?

He laughs, and she likes his laugh: it is shy. He says, Because I'd rather sit with you.

And that is when she thinks, *Uh-oh*.

She looks at the bartender to remind herself that he is there; she reassures herself that if she needs something, she can ask the bartender. The bartender, she thinks, and he smiles as if he's heard.

Because she likes him. Shit. Not the bartender, of course, though she likes him too. No. The stepbrother.

She is afraid to look at him, as if she's gone transparent.

She says, Excuse me, and slides off the stool, carrying her drink. She's lost her scarf, her shoes. She should walk to her mother's table. This would be a good moment, between the mains and dessert, when the gauchos are strumming and the restaurant swells with sound and laughter. There is a pause, a rare unspoiled chance, and she should use it.

But instead she skirts the room, steps into sand, towards the ocean. It is dark now, and outside their electrified haven the night is deeply black. The stars look like spilled salt. She walks towards the sound of water.

She thinks, I think he likes me too.

She thinks, I feel a little bit sick. Her feet meet water sooner than she expects. The tide has come in. She drinks the glass dry, the umbrella poking her cheek. No one comes for her. No one follows.

She thinks, So maybe he doesn't like me.

She chooses a roundabout route to the bathrooms, picking her way in the shadows, holding the empty glass and hoping not to step on anything sharp, or alive.

Aunt Caroline is washing her hands at the sink. Juliet sets the glass on the counter and without a word chooses an empty stall and shuts and locks the door.

Now, how many drinks is that, Juliet? says Aunt Caroline. Are you keeping track? You don't want to be sick in the morning or do anything foolish. When I was married to my first husband — that is, my only husband — I used to go out with his friends, and the wives would say, Drink, drink, Caroline, you have to, and like a sheep I would do it, *baa, baa*, I would drink with them, but I never liked it, I never really liked it, it was only that they told me to and so I did. Of course, I was weak when I was married to him. I did whatever anyone told me, and it wasn't until later, until afterward, that I realized I don't like to drink. I certainly don't like to be drunk. And, Juliet, I don't even like the taste of alcohol!

Fruit juice, Aunt Caroline says. Fruit juice, a little soda water, some ice.

You should think about it, Juliet. Think about your choices. Think about what you are doing to that beautiful young body of yours. Juliet? Are you okay in there? Juliet?

Juliet is fine. In all senses of the word, the senses she wishes to apply, she is *fuh-hine*. She says, I'm just taking a crap, Aunt Caroline.

Oh for God's sake, says Aunt Caroline with genuine disgust. You are just like your mother.

Am I? thinks Juliet, who is not taking a crap. She waits for a while. Finally she says, Aunt Caroline? Thinking she might have quietly gone.

I'm still here, says her aunt in a singsongy voice. I'm waiting for you, Juliet.

Oh for God's sake yourself, says Juliet, and stands and flushes.

I just want to give you a hug, says Aunt Caroline.

Let me wash my hands. Juliet takes her time, lathering and rinsing and elaborately drying, using one of the folded cloth towels set in a basket on the counter.

This can't be easy for you, says Aunt Caroline as the hug begins, progresses, continues, elaborates. You and Emmanuel have been such good children, such good children. Juliet waits for it to be over. She waits for Aunt Caroline to spill her feelings as projected onto Juliet; Juliet will let them bounce like marbles onto the floor. Aunt Caroline never had children; she is saying this even as Juliet is thinking it. You and Emmanuel are like my children. Keith too. Keith was mine, too.

Juliet peeks to see what she imagines: the shape they make in the mirror, their posture humorous and sad. She wonders what Aunt Caroline wants in return. If Juliet knew, would she offer it? She does not think so. Adults always want something. Most often it is absolution and not forgiveness, it is reassurance and not questioning. Adults want confirmation of what they believe about themselves; they don't want to be shown evidence otherwise, even while they insist on going around telling children: you're wrong, and I know better.

Juliet thinks, Well, I'm an adult now. I'm not like that.

Aunt Caroline sighs, goes to a stall for toilet paper, blows noisily.

She says, No more alcohol for you tonight, Juliet.

Juliet smiles.

I mean it!

I know, says Juliet. She waits for Aunt Caroline to leave, thinking an exit might never be accomplished were it not for the entrance of cousins from the other side, three girls older than Emmanuel and younger than Juliet, giddy with sugar and with staying up past bedtime. Aunt Caroline shakes her head, beetles together her eyebrows in a warning sign, a reminder, and takes her leave.

Juliet exhales. She has forgotten, temporarily, the source of an underlying sensation of thrill and dread. She leans her hip against the counter with arms folded and lets the idea of him — the stepbrother — wash into her consciousness again, slowly, like a drug administered by mouth.

In open air — the shock of oxygen — she stumbles with giddiness to the pool side of the restaurant, which is fenced, the gate shut after dark; scratches her bare arm on something and almost falls.

Oh. Jesus. They are kissing, they are against the fence, away from the light, going at each other like, like, like a simile she doesn't want to pursue. Euphemisms glide through her mind like ice dancers in inappropriate costumes. Is that a nipple, a butt cheek, I see before me? Doing the nasty, says a rich announcer voice in her head, deep and male.

Hey, she says. Hey, Mom. Hey, Jesse. She says it as much to stop the imaginary announcer's voice as to call out to them, to interrupt.

Oh, I didn't see you there, Juliet. I was just, we were just. Her mother laughs, panting. The two of them are fully clothed but unwilling to disentangle themselves. It is quite dark, but Juliet knows for certain that her stepfather's hand is squeezing her mother's breast.

I just wanted to say congratulations, says Juliet.

Oh, honey, oh, baby, that is so sweet. Her mother rubs her own cheek as if she is wiping away sudden tears. Oh, that is just . . . With pellucid excitement she flutters her hands, calling for Juliet.

Group hug, says Jesse and throws his arms wide.

There is nothing to do but submit. And it's nice, Juliet lets herself think, it's nice to be held. She thinks, I like this guy, he's fine. Fuh-hine. She thinks, The difference between my mother and everyone else is that she goes ahead and does what makes her happy. Damn the world, damn the rest of us. I don't hate her for it.

Hey, says Jesse, you're an old soul. She's an old soul, Gloria, I can see that. Takes after her mother.

Are you keeping an eye on Emmanuel? asks her mother, perhaps the first time she's given him a thought all night. Do you know where he is?

I'll check, says Juliet. She is done with the embrace, finished, embrace completed, and her mother is done too. It is only Jesse who would hang in a while longer, for who knows how long, waiting to see what might happen, surfing the good vibrations long after the tide has turned.

I like him, she thinks, but he's a flake.

The owner is behind the bar, near the back entrance, drying glasses with a white towel.

Where's the other one? Juliet asks. She says, He made me this perfect drink, rum with fruit juice and fruit, and —

Kitchen, says the owner, scrutinizing her. She blushes. He blends her drink in a cocktail shaker and pours it over ice, smooth as silk. No umbrella, no floating pineapple.

From where she stands, leaning elbows on polished wood, she can see her brother working his way through a waffle as if he's performing a chore that requires deep deliberation. His eyelids are heavy. Though near him, the stepsister and stepbrother have turned away. The stepsister touches her throat in laughter. Juliet thinks, They are speaking in code, that is how well they know each other. The shorthand Juliet shares with Emmanuel is limited by the difference in their ages, by the things that she remembers and he does not; they have grown up in two different families.

Juliet's family had a mother and a father, and three children, and dismay and uncertainty were held at bay by a series of sudden moves, dangerous leaps that carried them ahead of disaster, just out of reach.

Emmanuel's family has a mother who lives apart, and a dead brother, and dismay and uncertainty are held in their father's hand, and he is afraid to show them. Intuiting their father's fear is more frightening than anything he could reveal, any unearthed body or living ghost.

Her mind feels heavy; it weighs down her skull, tilts her off balance as she swallows a sip of liquid. This drink, she thinks, is better than the last. She nods appreciation to the owner, who is watching. She can't walk over there to her brother. She can't invite conversation, or comparison. She thinks, I envy them.

She has forgotten why she likes her stepbrother, if indeed she does. When she looks at the nape of his neck from this distance, exposed and clean like a schoolboy's, she feels nothing. She is staring at a stranger's neck.

Emmanuel has seen her. He lifts one hand, bending back the wrist in a weak wave. She smiles but does not go to him. He does not seem to expect her to. She thinks, Who will tuck him into bed?

Juliet finds the boy, the bartender, behind the kitchen, leaning against the restaurant's wall, smoking a cigarette that he extinguishes underfoot as soon as he sees her coming for him. He is wearing rubber sandals, cheap and thin, the kind someone in Canada might reserve for use in the change room of a fitness centre.

There is no escaping where we're from, she thinks, feeling rather hopeless, losing her courage.

But he is thinking something else. He removes the drink from her hand, sets it beside the doorway, and inclines his head, inviting her to walk with him some little distance, beyond the light. She trusts his mental map of the landscape; he's done this before. His palm alights on the curve of her lower back, slides around her hip to the front and pulls her against him. It is such tangled relief to be touched. This exchange is something she knows and understands and does not fear: the give and take between two people meeting in silence. She turns to him and her hands are beneath his open shirt, his heart a separate animal under her ear.

They might go on like this, they might fall to their knees, sink into the sand, carrying each other towards expectant and willing danger — imagine the shape of a night that never was, a future that will not be. They might go on like this, but for her mother's amplified voice crackling through the loudspeaker, calling through the darkness, discovering Juliet and urging her return, delivering her to the fate that will be hers, to the self that hinders and drags on her — capable, sturdy, robust — that cannot be altered.

I have to go, she says. My mother.

She is forgetting that he does not speak English.

Mi madre, she says.

His fingers are caught in her hair. It pulls, it hurts just a little to come apart, and she has to use her own fingers to brush through the strands, to release him.

She would reclaim her drink as she passes the open kitchen door, but it has spilled, the glass broken; she steps in it before she realizes. The stepbrother is coming for her. Stop, she says, glass. She stands amidst the mess in her bare feet, and he keeps coming. She looks down at his polished black shoes.

Aren't you hot in those?

He lifts her without asking — Put your hands around my neck — and swings her out of the shards. Setting her down, he says, You've lost an earring.

Flustered, she checks her soles, flicks off a piece of glass that has not cut her. She says, Is this part of the plan? She means Gloria's.

Is there a plan? he says. If he thinks there is not, he's either misunderstood or he doesn't know Gloria well enough yet.

The children — Juliet and Emmanuel and the stepbrother and stepsister — sit cross-legged on red tile before Gloria, separated from her by the microphone stand. She rocks in a chair, her guitar across her lap like a much-loved child, and she says, Once upon a time, this was a lullaby I sang to my three children. I give it to all of you as a gift, to welcome my new children, Anne and Mike, and to remember my lost child, my Keith, and for my own sweet Juliet and Emmanuel.

There is a swallowed sob from the audience. Aunt Caroline, thinks Juliet.

Her mother closes her eyes. Her throat is exposed, and Juliet admires the tanned skin stretched across her fit breastbone, her elegant arms. Her chosen bridal gown is light but not white, a full skirt whirling from the boned bodice, appropriate for a second marriage and a beach wedding. Juliet experiences a shot behind the eyes, a burst of pride at her mother's unexpected accomplishments, her feats of transformation.

The lullaby is an original song, written for this occasion. In the same instant that Juliet knows it, she forgives her mother for the lie, for the created memory of a past that does not exist and never did. Like her mother, she wishes that it did, and she wishes that by wishing alone any of them could make happen what should have happened. She closes her eyes and touches her fingers to the empty earlobe. She thinks, Here is a gift, so take it. She thinks, A gift is a gift: you don't get to choose, whether it be a secret kept, a polite falsehood, a book you've already read, or a sweater that does not fit. You open it, you open your mind, you do not think about how you might use it or whether indeed it is of any use to you. You understand that the giver is giving you what she can, that she is doing her best.

You say, Thank you.

Goodnight, goodnight, what is dark will be light, what is sleep will be wake, tomorrow.

The audience loves it. The audience gobbles this stuff up, sucks it directly into its swollen gullet, its hidden, needy core. As one they bite lips and reach for a hand to squeeze; they shake their heads, eyes bright with tears; they murmur, *Oh.* Everyone needs a good cry once in a while: that is her mother's philosophy. With gentleness like a touch on the head, a blessing, she strums through the final chords and arrives at dropped quietness, bows her head, her flat hippie hair falling across the strings, the picture of idealized modern maternity, though her children — all but Emmanuel — are too old; they do not fit perfectly into the scene.

Applause.

Her mother, lowering her chin in humble gratitude. Her mother, rising to curtsy, laughing, to bow.

A toast! Jesse stands and raises his glass, and the guests search for and lift theirs, though the children continue to sit cross-legged, no drinks in sight. To my new family, he says, choking on the words, unable to squeeze anything else out.

To family! shouts the room, and there follows the clink of glassware, someone tapping a dirty fork on a plate, and then another and another, and it's turning into a wedding, thinks Juliet, as the guests chant, Kiss, kiss, kiss, kiss, kiss.

Awww. The collective sigh of appreciation washes the room and dissolves into laughter. There is a crowd at the bar, and Juliet stands to see that the boy has been called back to serve. He smiles at her crookedly, not embarrassed or regretful, the most straightforward face she's seen all night.

Do you like him, then? asks the stepbrother.

Well, she says, thinking about it. I do.

The stepbrother lowers his mouth towards her ear, says to her shoulder, And do you like me, too?

She shakes back her hair and laughs at him. Don't be stupid.

He won't give up. He waits for her with an open face.

She has not looked closely at him, does not even know the colour of his eyes — blue. She examines him slowly, in the middle of this room, without emotion. His hair is the dusty brown of someone who was a blond baby, cut shorter than she prefers. His left eyebrow is broken by a scar where the hair will not grow. He does not look like the kind of person who would have a tattoo; she sets the question aside to ask later. He is not a tall man; he takes after his father, she thinks, but not in a bad way. She imagines him running long distances, riding a bicycle up a ski hill, surfing. She knows nothing about surfing.

I need to put Emmanuel to bed, she says.

I'll come with you.

They follow the white circle that emanates from Emmanuel's flashlight, and Juliet wishes she were wearing shoes. They walk along the top of the beach, but it is not groomed. Broken shells stab her feet, she catches a toe on a clump of driftwood.

Did you say goodnight to Mom? Juliet thinks to ask only after they arrive at their hut and the stepbrother is unlocking the door with the key attached by a tiny chain to a carved wooden parrot.

Sort of, says Emmanuel, which is good enough for Juliet. Brush your teeth.

But Emmanuel staggers over the threshold like a miniature drunk, head lolling, dazed. He has walked here bravely — Follow me! He is spent. Juliet leads him to their shared room. Do you want to wear pyjamas?

He does not answer her. She removes his sneakers and covers him with a sheet.

But she does not return immediately to the main room, where she knows her stepbrother is waiting. For her. She sits on the edge of her bed and drops her face into her hands, breathing into the cupped space between the palms, the bones of her skull almost legible under her fingertips. What could she read in them? What message? What, other than this discrete moment in a lifetime, this force of the present lifting her from the hips, carrying her deeper into darkness?

Where are you going? Where have you been?

She lifts her face. She stands and glides between these two walls, and like a thief breaks into the spacious expanse of to-night. It has room enough for both of them. It is forgiving and generous and vast.

She meets him. In silence, he takes her hand. In silence, they walk together, outside. They do not pause. They sink, they give way.

A breeze rises, a luscious night wind, and lifts her. She is removed, she is carried away from the picture they are making in the sand. She sees them from above, earthly cut-outs, and she floats higher. Here is the palm-roofed restaurant alight with song and sounds. Here are the people dancing and getting drunk and remembering themselves in their bodies, remembering what they were going to be, when they were young; being young. Here is the beach — no, it is receding: here is the ocean, here are the waves, here she is pulled out, lifted higher. Up here the air undulates like water beneath her outspread arms, her lifted head, her belly and breasts. She is not grand. She is small.

She will be taken from this place and unable to return. She thinks of the things she's said and forgotten to say, in equal measure, equally mistaken.

Her arms stretch, but the struggle is brief; she submits. It is almost out of sight, almost gone from her. What is gone? Oh, she knows now what it is; she's read this story before. It could be named *childhood*; or it could be named *a dream*. She'll never find that beach again. She'll keep trying.

But just now she does not need to. She is here on the beach that is, damp and cool, the beach on which she is lying indented with another, entirely possessed of her body, entirely discovered in this primitive circle of craving and kindness.

Hey, Juliet, he says. Are you okay? Juliet?

He will say her name and say her name, just to taste it.

She thinks, I've never said his. She searches for it in the debris on top of the water. She says, I'm wearing black. Do you think it means something?

Good or bad? he says, and slips the other feathered earring from her ear and steals it into his pocket.

They begin. This was where they began.

GRACE

Juliet lies on the Murphy bed pulled down from the wall, its thin metal legs snapped into position. The room, the entire apartment, is chilled, and she shivers in fetal position under a thin sheet. There is a window along the wall, slatted blinds drawn against the rising early sun, shadows easing, longer and thinner, across the carpeted floor. Everything in here is white. Out there, it is already hot. Out there, Grandma Grace is taking her brisk morning walk along the winding black-top of the retirement village, built on Florida swampland that roils underfoot. Acres of quilted sod, laid out in rectangles, are sinking. Juliet feels herself sinking.

She hears the apartment door open and close. She hears her grandmother's breathing in the hallway, heavy from exertion, her grandmother's knock on the bedroom door: "Breakfast, Juliet?"

Juliet thinks, This was a mistake, coming here, telling. Her errors compound, interest she will never be able to pay. She needs to go home. She cannot answer.

"Juliet. Answer me: cereal or toast?"

But she does not answer. There is a small rush of quiet, the almost silent animal padding of footsteps on wall-to-wall carpet, and Grandma Grace returns. She opens the door with her elbow and walks around the bed to place a tray beside Juliet.

"Eat. It will settle your stomach."

Juliet closes her eyes, and the tears well through her lashes.

"Worse things have happened," Grandma Grace says, and strokes Juliet's cheek. "Worse things will. We will get you through this. Life goes on."

The phone rings, and Juliet's body tenses.

"If it's your mother, I'll tell her you're sleeping," says Grandma Grace.

"What if it's Mike?"

"We'll let it ring through to the machine."

They wait. Several mechanical beeps precede the sound of a voice, coated in static, talking into the empty living room. "Mother? It's Caroline here. Just to say I'm on my way and I'll be there later today. Tell Juliet I love her, and I can stay for as long as you need me."

"Not Aunt Caroline," says Juliet.

"Juliet, I'm going to sit right here until you eat something. You don't know your Aunt Caroline well enough. She's exactly who you need to talk to. She's been through this herself, before it was legal. She will understand."

"I don't want to talk about it."

"You don't have to talk about it."

Juliet nibbles on the toast crust. She feels as though her limbs are coated in heavy fur, dragging her down. The inside of her skull is lined with the same fur, inhibiting coherence.

But her stomach is a prune, a shrivelled, tough wad in her gut that rejects nourishment. Juliet sits up straight and begins to gag.

"Oh, Juliet," Grandma Grace sighs.

Juliet backs out of the sheets and stumbles in her underwear and T-shirt down the hallway to the bathroom, where she shuts and locks the door. The toilet seat is composed of puffy off-white plastic, the water is tinted blue, and when nothing comes up, Juliet closes the lid and sits on its fluffy cover: a lavender mat made of water-resistant synthetic wool. Lit by dim oversized bulbs set in a row above the mirror, every flat surface is clean and empty. The entire apartment is like a sterilized operating room, all the tchotchkes removed to prevent Grandpa Harold from swallowing or hiding them; only last month, after he'd started his day by swallowing his dentures (partials, but still), did Grandma Grace move him into a home for the demented elderly.

Juliet has not yet visited, though Grandma Grace goes every day, to feed him his lunch. Juliet has been taking the opportunity, in her absence, to slide open the screen door and smoke a cigarette on the back stoop. She does not intend to smoke forever. She thinks of it as a hobby picked up in a foreign land, which will be discarded as soon as she returns to normal life.

Seated on the toilet's lid, Juliet swivels her hips and leans towards the mirror. Peering into her own face, she feels nothing. She is at a distance from this freckled, sunburnt, unkempt girl. This girl is not Juliet. This girl is a fragment of the real Juliet, a scrap. The real Juliet waits at home, in another country, for the return of her body.

Grandma Grace knocks on the door. "How are you?"

"Fine."

"Can I come in?"

The door is locked. Juliet does not answer, listening to her grandmother try the handle.

"I wish nobody had to know," says Juliet.

"Nobody will," says Grandma Grace through the shut door. "Now. Juliet. Let me in."

Aunt Caroline arrives bearing scented candles and a box of herbal tea. Her hug is vise-tight and her tears are expected, but that doesn't make either easier to bear. It is evening, and outside the sliding glass doors Juliet sees fog rising off swampland like steam out of a volcano. Grandma Grace has prepared a green salad with cilantro and tomatoes and is boiling water for pasta. Fighting a lethargy that feels fatal, Juliet sets the table.

Aunt Caroline gets right to it. "Does the father know?"

"Hush, hush." Grandma Grace drops three handfuls of spaghetti noodles into the pot. But Aunt Caroline wants an answer.

Juliet sinks into her chair and rests her head on the cool china plate. Aunt Caroline is asking the wrong question. The question should be, Does the man who is not the father know? The man who is the father is irrelevant. She has already forgotten his face; richer with detail is the room they shared: two beds, a green mosquito coil on the windowsill that burned itself orange and ash. They did not share a bed all night, but afterwards moved to separate beds, in silence.

The open window faced the town, not the ocean. In the morning he walked with her up and down streets, searching for something recognizable, a house preserved in her memory from childhood, but the town had been taken over by surfers, foreigners selling smoothies and yoga on the beach.

He spoke to her in English but it was not his first language. He was kind. Without him, she would never have deciphered the bus schedules. She was not bothered by their exchange, though it was of some relief to learn that he lived in a different part of the country. He called her once, at the house in Managua where she was boarding with a mother and her four daughters, but they had nothing to say to each other over the telephone. It had seemed the only consequence of their night together would be the teasing of the four daughters, aged twelve to seventeen, who eavesdropped on the phone call and who knew about her boyfriend in Canada. On Saturdays the sisters huddled in their bedroom around the television and watched *telenovelas* made in Mexico. Juliet slept on her own cot, but the others shared double beds. There was space for little else: the girls stored bales of clothing in black plastic garbage bags under their beds, digging through them at dawn and pressing out the wrinkles with an iron before leaving the house. Juliet also slid her backpack under her cot, but she never ironed. She favoured paisley-patterned cotton skirts that fell in crinkles to the ankle, T-shirts, hiking boots in which she kept her American dollars.

It was a miracle anyone found her attractive. She was appreciative. She was ambivalent. She was without excuse. There had been rum, and a lot of it. That is not an explanation.

"You do know about" — Aunt Caroline's voice hushes — "*condoms*, don't you?"

Juliet lifts her head off the plate. She says, "It's too late for the safe-sex talk."

"You need to get tested. For disease."

"She knows that."

"This pregnancy could be the least of her troubles."

"Caroline," says Grandma Grace, "your tone is not helpful. We do not sit in judgement."

"We should tell your mother." Aunt Caroline turns to Juliet.

Juliet looks to Grandma Grace, who shakes her head and dumps the pasta into a colander in the sink. "I expected more from you, Caroline. You, of all people."

"What do *you* want to do?" Aunt Caroline sinks heavily into the chair opposite Juliet and reaches for her hand. Juliet lets her squeeze away, milking the bones of Juliet's hand as if she might drag out one glistening drop, one tear, one bodily expression of regret.

"I just want it to be done," says Juliet, "and I want to go home."

The telephone rings. Aunt Caroline leaps to answer it. She covers the mouthpiece with one hand and whispers, "It's Michael, Juliet. *The father.*"

Juliet shakes her head. Aunt Caroline nods hers, holding out the receiver. Juliet stands and slides open the glass door, walks into a landscape as foreign as tundra. She walks barefoot through slippery grass that holds her footprints. She imagines quicksand, and crocodiles. She imagines sliding under and disappearing. She walks until the apartment, and the larger block of low stucco building that contains it, is reduced to rectangles of yellow and blue light.

"Well," says Grandma Grace. "I made a mistake. I'm sorry."

Aunt Caroline has gone, leaving the scented candles and the box of tea.

"No," says Juliet.

"When I think of all the mistakes . . ." Grandma Grace's voice trails off.

"Like me, you mean? Like how I was a mistake?"

"That is not what I am talking about."

"An accident, then."

Grandma Grace exhales heavily. With a black pronged utensil she lifts a portion of waving spaghetti fronds and lays them on Juliet's plate.

"I'm not hungry," says Juliet.

"How can a life be a mistake? Or even an accident? And yet."

"Are you trying to talk me out of this?"

"I am talking about being human. The mistakes. We all make them and they pile up, Juliet. You can lie down and let them bury you or you can forgive yourself and be kind. Be kinder."

Juliet watches her grandmother in silence.

"You were meant to come to me, Juliet, and you were meant to tell me first. Your mother, what choice did she have? Your Oma Friesen is a good woman, a crusading woman, but she is hard. Once she got wind of that pregnancy, there were no options."

"A mistake," repeats Juliet.

"You are young. You have your whole life. What *do* you want to do?"

Juliet drops her eyes. I want to pretend this never happened, she thinks.

There is a knock on the door.

Grandma Grace stalks the plush carpet and checks the fisheye peephole. "It's Caroline. I knew it would be. I knew she wouldn't get far."

Grandma Grace unlocks the door, saying over her shoulder, "It's going to be fine, Juliet."

"I'm sorry," begs Aunt Caroline, not bothering to remove her shoes. "I was walking around the parking lot wondering, 'What should I do? What should I do?' I couldn't just get into the car and drive away. I could not. Not when Juliet needs me."

"Caroline?" says Grandma Grace.

"It was the right thing to do. I know it. I went and called Gloria. I did. I thought she should know."

"Caroline."

"She's dropping everything. She's on her way."

There is a silence so piercing it hurts Juliet's head. She will not permit herself to contemplate the tripwire of consequences. She picks up her fork and winds a thread of spaghetti loosely around and around the scraping tines, an ellipsis of noodle that refuses to bind, that she cannot therefore lift to her lips and take in.

Grandma Grace is stamping with fury. "This is my fault," she rages at her night reflection in the sliding glass doors, "for raising such a stupid child."

Aunt Caroline hovers on the threshold.

"Come in and shut the door," snaps Grandma Grace.

Juliet looks from the mother to the daughter and feels pity

for each. They are betrayed by stubborn difference that persists despite age.

Aunt Caroline says, "I am very afraid, Mother. I am so terribly afraid for Juliet's life." She is wearing a light jacket with sleeves that pinch around the fattest portion of her upper arm. Juliet sees that she is shaking, and she is reminded of Gloria, though the two sisters are unalike in taste and manner and form. The fork scratches the plate.

"You are projecting," says Grandma Grace.

"This choice could ruin her life."

"Your life was not ruined."

"I have no children of my own." Aunt Caroline addresses Juliet. "After the operation, my *womb*" — she whispers the word, pauses to eat her lips — "fell barren. If I had my life to live again, I would change just one thing. I would have that baby." She turns to Grandma Grace. "He would have turned twenty-seven in May."

"That baby — that embryo — wasn't a boy," says Grandma Grace. "You don't know that. She doesn't know that."

"He visits my dreams," Aunt Caroline tells Juliet. "You don't know what you will want later. You are thinking only about what you want right now."

The phone is ringing. The women leave it be.

"Hello? Juliet? If you're there, can you pick up? Please? I need to talk to you."

Mike's voice calls to them through the machine, gentle, a version of his father's, but without the chronic marijuana cough.

"Juliet, um, I know. I know what's happening. Dad called. Please pick up. Can I come to you? Or will you come home? Please. I love you."

Grandma Grace's lips quiver with tears she refuses to shed. Aunt Caroline lifts shaking hands together into a position of prayer, pressing fingers against chin, sodden with tears.

The apartment is too damn white. There is nowhere to hide, thinks Juliet. She stands out like a raging wound, dirt under her fingernails, sun-cracked skin, flame for hair. She just barely evades the thought: Would the baby have my hair?

"I hear you." She sits at the table and says to the machine, "I hear you, Mike."

Grandma Grace, who is nearest, lifts the receiver, speaking into it as she crosses the room. Her voice is steady and betrays no emotion. "Hello, Mike. How are you?" From the receiver's upper end she uncollapses a long metal antenna.

"I want to see you too," Juliet whispers into the heavy plastic shell, turning away, hunted by the generations in the room; the antenna swats dangerously. "But I'm not keeping it. Just so you know."

What he says in reply is only hers, and she will not share it.

"I will put the kettle on," says Aunt Caroline, her voice lifting, making of the statement a question, to which Grandma Grace does not reply. Instead Grandma Grace walks silently down the hall to the linen closest to snap sheets and count comforters. She runs a whining vacuum cleaner in the spare bedroom where Juliet has been sleeping. They hear her in the bathroom slamming cupboard doors, working, working, working.

"Juliet." Aunt Caroline removes the plate of uneaten pasta and replaces it with a cup of unsweetened Very Berry tea.

"Don't," says Juliet. She is surprised by her own tone: harsh, not kind. She opens her mouth to soften, to apologize, but

Caroline shakes her head in disappointment and stares up at the blank television, which Grandpa Harold affixed to the ceiling like the televisions in hospital rooms. Now that he is gone, Grandma Grace has cancelled the cable, but the television remains, prepared at any moment to rip out the screws and crush whoever lingers beneath.

Grandma Grace enters the room, rage all around her like a blaze, bends her long, graceful bones and yanks open the pullout sofa. "You can sleep here, Caroline," she says. "It's about as comfortable as the rack."

Gloria's plane lands in the morning and Aunt Caroline volunteers to collect her. Mike says he will grab a cab from the airport; he is calling from standby in Toronto.

When they come through the door, Caroline has been crying, the evidence all over her face, but Gloria's eyes are clear, her skin taut and lightly tanned, her travelling outfit a casual, flattering, unwrinkled shift that shows off lean arms and calves. She does not hurry, but comes directly to Juliet, who is hunched in some discomfort on a chair at the kitchen table, there being nowhere else to sit; before her, an uneaten bowl of cut exotic fruit arranged as if in a Dutch still-life.

Wordlessly, Gloria strokes Juliet's hair and face and pulls her into her rib cage, humming a low tune that Juliet does not recognize, that may not be a tune so much as a response to the moment: a flight of the voice, an answer. This is the longest Juliet can recall being held by her mother and touched with such tender regard. That may not be fair, or true. But it seems so.

The tenderness is too much, a crush of weight, and Juliet hears herself breaking beneath it, dissolving, undone. Wild sobs are a release, but there is no relief, and almost immediately Juliet resents with intensity the scene she is creating. She is doing what her mother wants her to do: she must be made hysterical in order for Gloria to calm her.

Juliet shudders. Her tears are scant. She has slipped to the floor and kneels in her mother's embrace, breathing the scent of lavender body lotion and an expensive hair product that holds in submission her mother's carefully untended locks. She sees that her mother's hair is streaked lightly with threads of pure white. When did that happen?

"Oh, my baby, how I love you," says Gloria.

Juliet thinks, She only loves me because I need her.

"I remember when you were small enough to sleep curled on my chest. And now you are a woman. If I close my eyes, I can see you as you were, right at the very beginning, when all we had was each other."

Juliet lifts her head out of her mother's lap. "And Dad."

"And your father. But he was busy studying. I would bundle you into your little snowsuit and pull you along the sidewalk on a sled. We got more snow back then. The banks were up to my knees and the stroller wheels wouldn't roll. So I tied you onto the little sled with a red scarf to keep you from falling off."

Juliet knows this story.

"But you were so strong. You were already the strongest little thing, and you rocked back and forth on the sled and screamed and screamed until you were purple, and I don't know what people thought of me. But out I'd go anyway. It was that or lose my mind. Do you remember, Mother? We were living in Canada?"

Juliet can't see Grandma Grace, who stands somewhere behind her.

"And of course you finally grew big enough and strong enough to tip over the little sled. A faceful of ice and snow. You looked like you'd been attacked by killer bees. And instead of coming for a visit, Grandma Grace kept asking for a baby photo, so when does your father decide to take one and send it down to Pennsylvania?"

"Enough," says Grandma Grace. "Leave the child be."

"She loves this story. It's one of her favourite baby stories."

Juliet lifts her head out of her mother's lap. "I'm not keeping it," she says. "We made the appointment."

"Is this true?" Gloria looks at her mother. "Of course, it's your choice, Juliet. Of course."

"There is no concern," says Grandma Grace stiffly, "about money."

"Money is the least of my concerns," says Gloria.

"While you are here, you will visit your father," Grandma Grace tells Gloria.

"You say that like I wouldn't."

Grandma Grace's nostrils flare.

"We'll all go together," says Gloria. "Today."

"Not me," says Juliet.

"And how is your new husband?" asks Grandma Grace.

Juliet, Gloria, and Aunt Caroline stare at her in confusion. Gloria bursts out laughing and Aunt Caroline follows; she is the elder by three years, but in Gloria's presence she is always behind, anxious to catch up. "You mean mine?" says Gloria.

"We've been married for two years; he's too old to be new. Unless there's some other horrible secret Juliet's keeping."

Grandma Grace's lips quiver. She will not smile. "Where did I go wrong, raising you two?" Her question is plaintive, fury revealed as sorrow. "You will come along too," she says to Juliet, a return that draws fresh mirth from her daughters. An inescapable order is amongst them: mothers, daughters, sisters. Each is losing the struggle to be other than who the others believe her to be.

Juliet does not go along.

Instead she goes to the bathroom, sits on the toilet, and stands to discover blood. It is warm and then cool on her thighs. An ache in her lower abdomen, which she has been ignoring while ignoring all the symptoms of her condition, grips with urgency. Juliet sits back down. Her legs are shaking. She reaches for the toilet paper and unrolls a long loop, unravelled across her thighs and onto the floor like a sash. She can hear the voices of the women in the living room, dulled by the white carpet. She thinks of the white carpet. The pain is a shimmer, a smear. Nothing. She's imagined it.

She stands again, and sits.

She thinks, If only my flight had been a week later. No one here would ever have known.

She is back in Nicaragua, in a *barrio* in Managua, a city unrecognizable from the map of her childhood. She is circling the sprawling city, swooping over verdant mountains and blasted volcanoes. She is twenty-one. She believes the body can express what the mind cannot.

She is back in the bedroom she shares with four Nicaraguan sisters, and with their arguments, which she cannot fully understand. She has no sisters and she wishes to understand. She is so certain she will find what she is looking for — here, in this country, in this city that glimmers with magic, with music and elation, with something lost that she believes can be found. Here.

The pain grabs.

She is back in Managua, in the office of an American nun, who says to her, You will not stay. The truth is too painful to keep; irrefutable, it devastates and confounds. She is an undeclared arts major volunteering abroad for a term. Her Spanish is weak. She has never been needed less.

She is in a white bathroom in Florida, on the western peninsula. She is losing an early pregnancy. It is an event both commonplace and utterly extraordinary. She is unavailable for comment. She breathes heavily. She checks, but there is nothing specific to be seen in the water: unnamed tissue, blood.

She is glad that the door is locked. But she has forgotten that Grandma Grace is a woman of resource.

When they burst in, four of them, Juliet is not ashamed, naked as she is from the waist down, only perplexed. "How did you get in?"

Grandma Grace wields a hairpin.

"Young lady, you scared us all half to death!" Gloria kneels before her.

"I'm not a young lady, I'm an old girl," Juliet replies automatically.

"Oh! She's bleeding, there's blood."

The fourth is Mike. He knows he is not wanted, though the others insist on pretending that, even if not wanted, they are needed. But he goes, he steps backwards down the hallway, and where he goes Juliet does not know, and forgets to ask.

The bleeding slows. She is treated to Chinese takeout in bed and a hot water bottle against the belly. She senses that this is how she would be treated had she given birth to a real live baby: with a kind of reverent caution. But something is missing, along with the baby: the element of celebration, of joy and wonder.

She lies flat on her back in the Murphy bed. Slatted blinds are open to light cast by this day's setting sun, shadows settling thick across the carpeted floor. Everything in here is white; but it looks grey. Outside, humidity rises like vapour off the cooling swampland. Juliet feels herself rising.

She hears the apartment door open and close. She hears him breathing in the hallway, and she says, "Come in."

He enters and sits with crossed legs on the floor, facing her, their heads level.

"We'll have another one someday," he says to her.

They look at each other, and she thinks, I have a secret. Everyone else in this apartment thinks one thing has happened today, when in fact something else has. The thing that appears to have happened is something she would never have imagined happening to her. But the thing that actually happened leaves her even more breathless, its layer of mendacity a skein across her mouth, a lie she will have to sustain perhaps forever, to disguise faithlessness: her own.

It wasn't yours, she says to him silently.

He says, "I love you."

She says, "I know."

He says, "Marry me."

She says, "We're way too young."

"I just wanted to ask. It seemed like the thing to do."

"I'm sorry."

"I'll ask some other time."

"Okay."

She says, after a little while, "I want to be needed."

He says nothing. Perhaps he knows she does not mean by him.

The room slides towards darkness. His hand paws the sheet, looking for hers.

"I was needed for a little while, but it didn't work out," she says, as if she is talking about something that happened a long time ago, not today. "I'm not especially useful. But I want to be." She does not mean that she wants to be a mother. She does not think a mother is especially useful.

Still he says nothing. Her palms are pressed flat against her stomach and he is afraid to touch her there. She rolls away from him and wonders what it will take to roll back, to let him reach for her, to give of herself and her body, again.

The mysteries are deep and she cannot use them. They are closed to her.

She tells herself, I had a Nicaraguan baby, but the story doesn't hold. Even tonight, when she thinks she could tell herself anything and believe it, the story doesn't hold. A mother brings a baby to life and it breathes and kicks and screams. She has done nothing like this, most egregiously not even in her imagination. The possibility of *life* has not entered her mind during these last few weeks; she refused it utterly.

Yet she feels no guilt. Where is the guilt that she's certain she should feel? What should she do now?

She rolls the other way, back to him.

RED ROVER, RED ROVER

Sober, they talk about the dog. Esther and Teddy have a brand-new puppy, a St. Bernard with rolls of fat at its neck and a need to chew.

"Put your shoes up high or leave them on," says Esther as Juliet and Mike come through the door. She kisses each on the cheek and takes orders for drinks before they are halfway down the stairs.

Juliet keeps her boots on, wet with snow. They make her look taller; she is young enough in her vanity to think this matters.

"I've never had a boot I could wear with a skirt," she says. The puppy worries at her laces. She leans to stroke its scruffed head, and it bites her with fresh baby teeth. She closes its jaw with one hand and whispers, *no!* while Esther is distracted with the martini shaker. The puppy presses its ear into the palm of her hand. Juliet can feel it quivering with life that is almost too much for it to bear.

Drunk, the men take turns examining Juliet's ring. Altogether they are not a large party: four couples in varying states of fidelity. One pair is known to Juliet and Mike only by proxy, through Esther and Teddy. The woman is a model, emaciated but with breasts. Juliet and Mike have brought another couple, Dane and Laura, good talkers, sarcastic: their fights are entertainment.

Teddy and Esther are official. Juliet has never been more ravishing than at their wedding reception: a transparent dress, gold gladiator sandals, so intoxicated that she and the groom, without anxiety, danced together to a slow song.

Esther did not want an engagement ring.

"I had sex four times last night," Esther tells Juliet as they reach for the same bottle of wine. Juliet assumes she means with Teddy.

The man who came with the model grips Juliet's hand and peers drunkenly at Mike's offering. "Did he get down on one knee?" he asks.

"Yes," says Mike even as Juliet is saying "No."

Laughter.

"I designed the ring myself," Juliet says as the stranger bobs over her fingers. "I mean, we decided to get married months ago — well, probably years. The ring wasn't part of it."

"I did get down on one knee," says Mike.

"Maybe you did."

"Of course he did. He would," says Esther. "Teddy tried, but I made him stand up again."

Teddy staggers from the kitchen, in his arms a platter of homemade ravioli stuffed with spinach and ricotta cheese. These prove underdone, but everyone raves. Teddy folds Juliet's palm inside his own to better see the ring. He strokes her knuckles with his spare hand. Esther is watching from the other end of the table. Juliet pulls free. They are seated boy-girl-boy-girl, not by couple, at Esther's bidding.

Juliet stumbles upstairs to the bathroom. Something green is stuck between two teeth: spinach. She digs at it with a toothbrush from the cabinet; she hopes it is Teddy's.

I have a crush on this friend, Juliet told Laura in the taxi on their way here.

Laura shrugged. As long as you don't fool around.

Actually, Juliet whispered, this is worse than a crush. Like being sick.

Don't tell me, I don't want to know, Laura said.

Who can I tell? Juliet asked.

Tell Mike. Laura laughed.

Tell me what? From the front seat.

She thinks, He already knows. It is an assumption she makes often of him: that he can read her mind. It keeps her from worrying about the things she does not tell him.

When Juliet exits the bathroom, Teddy is waiting on the unlit landing.

"Oh!"

"My turn." He moves to brush by but brushes against instead, and they stall, her breasts pressing his ribs, arms stiff at their sides.

"I hear you had sex four times last night."

He glances into the bedroom with the dark duvet pulled over the pillows. He is thinner than he was this summer, when he danced with Juliet. Some days he cannot walk.

I had to marry him, Esther told Juliet. This is my life. I will look after Teddy, Esther told her. I am his wife.

Esther did not need an engagement ring.

Juliet and Teddy turn away from each other. Juliet waits for one moment outside the bathroom door, swaying, but Teddy does not switch on the light. Soon this apartment will be too much for him. Too many stairs. Juliet has never seen Teddy fall.

Even Dane admires the ring. "You've seen it before," says Laura in disgust.

"I'm just looking."

"You just want to hold Juliet's hand," says Laura.

"I'm looking at the ring."

"Look at mine." Laura is not really jealous. The couples have had this conversation and they share it now: how Laura and Mike could get married and live contentedly, if not passionately, while the marriage of Dane and Juliet would end — though who would wield the instrument? — in murder.

Juliet carries dishes to the kitchen. The puppy whines from the corner, where she's been confined to a cage.

"That looks so cruel." Juliet kneels, the back of her hand against the wire, the puppy's tongue wet on her skin.

"For her it's a cave. A safe place." Teddy comes in with a handful of forks.

Behind him Esther bends, crawls in her shiny beaded skirt across the tiles to join Juliet. "She's sad, poor little beastie," says Esther. "She needs a walk."

"What about the dishes?" says Teddy.

"Leave the goddamn dishes," says Esther. "It's a party."

For the walk, Esther squeezes the puppy into a little red sweater that her mother has knitted for it.

"When did you become little-red-dog-sweater people?" asks Mike. He has finished half a bottle of Scotch but is still not slurring his words.

Laura has to be pushed off the couch. "I need a nap."

Dane thrusts her arms through coat sleeves. "It's a party." Everyone is saying so, as if they'd all forgotten.

The model's boyfriend pukes in the street. Effluvium hits the tail end of a BMW, setting off its alarm.

"I should take him home," says the model.

The cold freezes nostril fronds, paralyzes lungs, and they cough as they run down the sidewalk, away from the noise. The model and her boyfriend flag a cab and are driven away.

"Remind me why we hang out with them," says Esther.

Teddy says, "You always invite them last-minute. When you can't think of anyone else."

"It isn't a party with only six people."

"Don't forget the dog," says Juliet.

"The dog," says Teddy. "No one else wanted to come to our fling."

"Not true," argues Esther. "I was deliberately selective."

They cross the street and skid along a hilltop that was crammed earlier this evening with families on sleds: mothers, fathers, children, sliding through postcard scenes.

The puppy is off her leash, barking and weaving, snapping at her sweater. She tears a corner and threads dangle. "Oh no, your little poo-poo sweater!" Esther attempts a mittened repair. The puppy growls and nips, rolling in the snow; the hole grows.

Juliet runs along the brink of the steep and slippery hill, away. Below, cars pass on a highway that is carved like a river through the sunken valley. Juliet pretends that it *is* a river and the noise and exhaust of the cars a constant tide pulling towards the unseen but believable ocean. Why are some things more believable when unseen?

And then, some things are less.

In the middle of a silent fountain a fat cherub rises, cheeks bulging to blow on a stone bugle. Neutered stone, it ridicules love, and the need for love. Juliet has run so fast that she is alone. She sinks onto the curved concrete rim, tugs off her mitten and bends over the finger that is blessed by the ring; but the diamond does not glisten as it should.

She hears their voices laughing and shrieking, spreading in all directions.

But here is Teddy.

He falls at her feet, breathless, and buries his lean, dark-skinned face in her lap, draws the exposed fingers into his mouth. She slips from the fountain's rim and into the snow, knees bared beneath the coat that is not quite long enough, boots that are not quite tall enough.

"We won't," she says. It is impossible to tell who presses whom into the cold.

"We could," he says, but he doesn't.

They examine each other as if there is time to spare, because they have never let themselves — artificial light from tall black lampposts, glare from the snow. They can't stop smiling; is it predatory, an animal's warning?

"You won't die." The lie splits her lower lip, right down the centre.

"It's degenerative," he says. "Look at me."

"I see you," she says.

Teddy's breath is bright, frozen heat. "In six months you'll be afraid of me. I'll be afraid of me. I want what I want right now."

She thinks, We are lit from beginning to end, until our light goes out. No one knows where the light goes, smoke rising oily and vanishing, a stillness and darkness that has to be seen to be believed. How completely the light is extinguished. How empty the body's house. She thinks, Life is light. It weighs next to nothing. No one can hold on to it.

Juliet closes her eyes, leans into him, tongues meet teeth, wet and cruel, the scamper of blood through veins, flickers on the skin like shock. His hands smother her ears, push her into the snow. She is fallen.

Sadness spreads like a leak, pooling inside her mouth.

"Hey, kids." Dane has found them. He kicks sparks of snow onto Juliet's boot, rests heavily on the fountain's rim and searches his pockets.

Teddy breathes on her red hand, crippled by the ring, as she pushes to sitting. Dane pulls out a crumpled cigarette packet.

"You don't smoke," Juliet says.

"And you're getting married."

"It's not what it looks like." Her knees are numb.

Teddy lurches onto the fountain's rim beside Dane. "It's exactly what it looks like," he says. "I'll take one, thanks."

The two men fumble with the lighter, heads bent together, united. Before tonight they had never laid eyes on each other. But Juliet floods with relief that it is Teddy sitting beside Dane on the fountain. She could not bear to sit with Dane and look down on Teddy in the snow. She would rather be the foolish one, the fallen one, under their feet. Her sacrifice is temporary but she is certain that it matters: it protects them inside a moral universe of her own creation.

"Esther," says Teddy.

"Oh my God, you're smoking? You gave him a fucking cigarette?" She snatches it out of his mouth and tosses it, spinning and flaring, and the puppy gives chase.

Juliet stands. "Do you have any idea how enormous that dog is going to be?" Stiffly, she follows the puppy. She finds the cigarette, glowing, undampened by fiercely chilled snow, and bends and puts it to her lips. Lightly, experimentally, she draws. The last thing his lips touched, she thinks, and the thing before that.

"Off the wagon?" Laura and Mike hold hands in their approach.

"I'm so drunk it doesn't count." But in truth, she's certain she's sober as sin.

"How is it?" asks Mike.

"Do you know when you're dreaming, and you find yourself in the middle of a cigarette, inhaling, even though you can't remember lighting it — it just happened to you? The cigarette found you, and you think, 'This is not happening. I will make this not happen, but already it's too late.' Do you know that dream?"

"Yes," says Mike.

"You think, 'This isn't me. I'm not doing this.'"

"I know that dream," says Mike.

One last drag, and Juliet drops the cigarette into the snow, kneads it beneath the surface with the toe of her boot. Gone, as easily as that, as easily as tonight will vanish.

Dane struggles to his feet, grabs Laura's free hand. With Mike on the other side, arms swinging, the three of them are children playing: Red Rover, Red Rover, let Juliet come over.

The puppy is at her laces again, tugging, growling; everything is a game. Love for the animal rushes through Juliet, for its newness, its capacity for destruction. She bends to the puppy's snarl and snap. She gathers its surprising and lively weight into her arms, against her chest: fur tough, claws smooth, rolls of fat around its ribs. It nips her ear, and a tooth catches on the tiny silver ring Juliet wears in the lobe, and the wince of pain gleams.

It is how her own lies catch her, when they do, off guard, bright stabs that remind her that she is alive. She thinks of what she is willing to sacrifice in order to burn, to feel her light burning. It is dangerous close to the fire, and she does not feel afraid.

Teddy is standing, Esther wrapped around his arm; or he is bent onto her and she is holding him upright. He is hungry — ravenous — against the stillness that is coming for him, and Esther would feed him anything he wanted, anything at all.

"Nightcap." Teddy's teeth are chattering.

"Please," says Esther. "Please, can we just go home?"

Juliet looks at Mike. He swings his arm, promising *I will catch you no matter how hard you crash.* She thinks, He knows, he knows, he knows. She is comforted. She backs up three steps and takes a run at them all.

OSCURIDAD

They drive northwest through green and fertile fields of bushy wheat, deceptive corn. Every lane has a sign: QUILTS. NO SUN SALE; EGGS. BROWN, WHITE; GARLIC SCAPES, GLADS, LAMB. Further north and off the main roads, unkempt properties — trailers and rusted car bodies parked in unprofitable bush — advertise firewood.

They are sailing on the burning wings of excavated fossil fuels. Think of the buried arterial forests marinating for millennia in anticipation of this moment.

There is a sign at the end of this lane, too. SOLD.

Mike slows the car to a crawl, windows open, the sound of wind shushing the corn, the hum of insects. The maple trees are dying, splitting, limbs crashed into the raspberry brambles along the lane. Juliet turns her face away from Mike so he won't see her emotion. She'd expected to feel nothing, and it is not nothing she feels after all.

On the front lawn, in heavy grass, Mike pitches their tent.

Juliet can find no keys hidden under stones or antique iron

axe heads. She walks all around the house, spying through any dusty window that she can reach. The rooms are mostly empty: a broom with broken bristles leans against the kitchen wall; a black garbage bag, half filled, slumps on the dining-room floor.

Juliet stands on the porch, hip against the locked front door, and bangs the wood with her fist. Her fury is primitive.

Approaching gravel dust, a diesel rumble, music pumping a deep bass line, and then silence. Emmanuel gets out, stretches. Their mother bought him the car and pays the insurance. He seems too young to be living all on his own, in an apartment shared by friends, working the night shift at a diner near campus. He didn't even bother applying to go to university: *I'm not smart like you. Yes, you are too — you are smart! Nah, it's okay, I don't care. I like my life.*

"Hey, Sis, breaking in?" Emmanuel greets Juliet with a hug that pulls her shoulder into his armpit. How is it that she is so much smaller than him now?

"No," she says.

"Yes, you were," Mike calls out.

Emmanuel lights a match and touches it to the cigarette between his lips. "I was thinking we could torch the place."

"Okay," she says. "Let's."

"Seriously?"

"Why not?"

"Let's do your thing instead," says Emmanuel.

Well, Kay didn't think of everything. She can't keep them out.

"Don't smoke in the house," Juliet says.

Emmanuel watches her descend down begrimed steps into darkness. The cellar is damp, the inside of a lung. Juliet chases a spider's web out of her hair and it winds around her forearm like gauze. Another skims her lips.

"I'm going in," she calls to Emmanuel, who does not reply. The door at the top of the rickety stairs is closed but has no lock. She opens it and steps into light, into the house that has become, over the years, her father's house; into the narrow hallway between kitchen and dining room.

She receives the strangest memory as she pauses here, batting at her face — the web is tough and persistent. She remembers putting her hands on the wooden ledge, hip height, that runs along either side of the short hallway. She remembers practising over and over an invented acrobatic trick, palms on the ledge, swinging her legs into the air, higher and higher, aiming for the ceiling, aiming to twirl over backwards and jump down to land safely on her feet. It would have been the centrepiece of an imaginary show, the climax. She was always putting together imaginary shows for the entertainment of imaginary audiences — *admiring* imaginary audiences. But she remembers now that she never once twirled over and landed on her feet; the act ended after an attempt that threw her onto her back, crashed her through the air to the hard wooden floor, the wind kicked out of her lungs. She remembers the fall, and the slow-motion appeal of the fall, how she watched herself with mild perplexity: that this was happening and that it could not now be stopped.

It is the way one feels inside an accident whose ending has not yet arrived. She thinks it would be the way one would feel in an airplane tumbling towards earth. That the moments would stretch and the mind expand and time slow to contain all that was and could be, and will not be, in another beat, another beat and gone.

She winds through this memory in just the same way, slamming through, then vanished, and walks to the bathroom to pick away the spider's web. The wallpaper is peeling pink roses, luscious blooms exaggerated in all seasons, an eternal floral hell: someone else's heaven. The bathroom mirror has not changed — gold-rimmed, affixed above the cracked porcelain sink. *You again.*

Sixteen years rush past in fast-forward. She sees her family — her original family — the mother and the father and the brothers and herself, as if each were being pulled up a tunnel at great speed towards a miasmic light. They begin by holding hands, but one by one they disappear from each other, one by one, at a pace ever more terrifying.

Except for Emmanuel. She still has Emmanuel.

"Check this." He bumps up the cellar steps holding a box he has found. The two of them kneel in the front hall, lit by a lowering sun, and pull open the cardboard flaps crossed on top and caving in at the centre. Emmanuel sneezes. Juliet lifts out a wooden truck with bottle-cap headlights. It is missing two wheels.

"Juliet!" Mike is knocking on the front door. "Everything okay in there?"

"*Nica,*" breathes Juliet. It is like opening a grave, disturbing the totems of the dead. Crouched on her heels, she shudders.

Emmanuel just looks at her.

"Nicaragua. This was Keith's truck; we played with it out back in the mud in Nicaragua. I made houses out of palm leaves.

Keith caught lizards and took their tails off because he said the tails always grow back, but I don't know if that's true. We made the port of Corinto out of mud. We spent hours out there, rain or sun. You broke the wheels when Mom made us share."

"I would have," says Emmanuel.

"You were just a baby," says Juliet. "We were probably mean to you."

"You weren't," says Emmanuel.

"Can you remember?" She is surprised.

"No," he says, "but I know you weren't. Keith wasn't, you weren't."

She will weep. What faith. Does it matter if faith is misplaced? They were mean to him, she knows, picking silently through the remnants of the incident. Keith made him cry after the wheels got broken and Juliet went and told, though their mother took Emmanuel's side, which just made the two of them howl, Unfair! We're never going to share with that baby again and you can't make us! He wrecks everything! That's how mean the two of them were, even Keith.

Juliet prefers Emmanuel's version, but she knows better. It isn't always better, knowing better. She keeps it to herself.

Mike knocks again. "Hello? Anybody home?"

Emmanuel unlocks the door and throws it open with a flourish: "Where have you been all my life?"

But Juliet has no time for their jokes. She is sick with seriousness. This is who she has become: Juliet, running down to the shore to throw stones and stir up the waters; Juliet, standing an inch too close to demand answers to questions that have none, or that, answered, cause pain, burn like a lit coal she will hold in her hand, deliberately wounding herself.

She cannot *make light*; she dismisses lightness and its shallow pursuit of laughter. Stupidity, blasphemy: what is the point?

"What are we looking at?" asks Mike.

Juliet drops the truck back into the box and closes the flaps so he can't see, sending up a puff of decay and rot. Emmanuel defers to her; he stays silent.

"The past," she says.

She won't always be like this.

She hears herself saying, to a fellow grad student, "My father's body is in that building," as they stroll past on their way to get a cup of coffee. She's said this on several occasions this quiet, bleeding summer, not always when passing the same building; she doesn't require of herself accuracy when the truth remains the same.

It is true that her father's body lies in the bowels of a large stone building on campus, preserved and in use, but not by him. "He donated himself to medical science. Well, technically, his girlfriend did the donating, but it was what he wanted."

She looks for clues in the spectrum of gut responses — pity, fear, revulsion — but what she receives is so mild, so Canadian, so determined not to be shocked. Oh, how generous; he must have been an extraordinary person. To which Juliet must reply, Yes, he was; it was just like him, so in character; and she is prevented from pursuing her line of follow-up questions: Does this strike you as normal behaviour? Is this what normal people do to their children after they die? Do they go to the same damn university? What if I want to switch to nursing?

As if that's what's stopping her from stepping out of the concrete shoes of sixteenth-century popular English literature and a thesis she will never finish, doomed by thoughts she is unable to think, the weight of failure dragging her down, down, down to the bottom of a dead lake. As if someone else is to blame.

Nurse. Registered massage therapist. Yoga instructor. She has considered all of the above, investigated programs and costed out notions, and returned, always, to the library, to its heat, the fragrance of dried pages like pressed leaves, its quietude. Something else is present here, too: *oscuridad* — the Spanish word for darkness, which Juliet believes contains so much more than its translation. The *oscuridad* in here mirrors her own: one tiny darkness amidst the darkness of a multitude of minds seeking illumination, dead and alive, trapped in dormant words. She thinks she can hear the *oscuridad*, her cheek pressed to the fake wood of the carrel she has earned; she can hear it, even though the library's lights are forever on.

The air inside the tent holds flecks of dying sunshine as Juliet unrolls sleeping bags. Through thin walls she sees the flicker of first flame, hears Emmanuel's car stereo picking up a local country station.

Not one mosquito has penetrated the tent's zippered flap. It is hot, but the intensity wicks away quickly as night closes in: August in southern Ontario. Knees folded, head bent, she gazes through the mesh screen door at the farmhouse in silhouette. Looking at the house, she tries out the words, as if to shock herself, *My father's body is in that building*, and hears as if for the first time what she's really been saying all along: "My father is dead."

He is not supposed to be dead, and she is not supposed to be crouched, past dusk, in a tent on what was once the grass he would cut with a riding mower. Maybe if he'd pushed the damn mower; maybe if he'd been a vegetarian; maybe if he'd walked down the lane every once in a while to pick up the mail rather than driving in his car, which he loved; maybe if he hadn't loved his car quite so very dearly; maybe if he hadn't carried his sadness inside but had shared it everywhere, like Juliet's mother; maybe.

Then again, maybe not.

Near the fire, Emmanuel plunders the woodpile — their father's woodpile.

Mike offers a blackened veggie dog soaked in ketchup and nestled in a white bun from the gas station down the nearest highway. Juliet stands like a statue on a stump of sun-bronzed wormy pear wood and devours the meal; a handful of Cheezies for dessert, elbow-deep in the crackling bag.

"I brought marshmallows," says Emmanuel.

"I brought whisky," says Mike.

"Wash it down," says Juliet.

In his last year, fighting, her father tore down the falling garage. He dismembered the rotten pear tree with a chainsaw. He went to battle against the killing black walnuts. The woodpile sprawled, festering — the farmhouse was not fitted with a woodstove. The uneasy barn was his final project, and he burned the damn thing to the ground; but that was an accident, that's what Kay told Juliet. Kay, the girlfriend, the one Juliet's father would never marry, for reasons he kept to himself.

The concrete barn walls remain, blackened, half-collapsed, summer weeds flourishing as tall as grown men out of the ash-rich soil.

From her vantage point on the stump, Juliet points past the long-abandoned garden, to the east, where untended bush spreads, trees growing out of standing water, a tangle of swampy wild.

"Do you remember?" she says and lifts the plastic cup of lukewarm Canadian rye. "Keith was going to build a ship and sail it through the bush, with a pirate's eye patch, and a plank."

She is talking to herself. She is the only one here who remembers; who could.

The house is open, and there is something to be said for indoor plumbing.

On the threshold, Juliet does not hesitate. She is not afraid of ghosts, not the ghosts of the ones she knows. She would call them out of the walls: *Are you here?*

She lingers in the unlit bathroom, before the mirror that turns her into silhouette and phantom. The toilet fails to flush. She will have to warn the others: no paper. She isn't thinking. She is in *oscuridad*. She walks all around the shadowed, cramped rooms, ascends the steep stairway to the airless second floor.

She asks again, quietly: *Are you here?*

She calls to her father, so recently present, and she calls

to her brother, present nearly half her life ago, to them both. This is such a sad house, stupid with sadness, walls thick with the living seeped into stone, and stilled.

A scurry answers behind plaster and lath.

But really it's the only answer she expects in a place reeking of mothballs and mouse dirt, the settlement of lunar dust thick as fur on every surface: vermin, termites, the creatures that arrive after death to break down the remains, the life that feeds off the natural process of dissolution, of undoing.

Keith slept in this room. Its window overlooks the swampy bush. He slept in this room until he was too frail to make his way up and down. She sees her father holding her brother in his arms and swinging him down the steps: one large man with flyaway hair, one child of twelve puffed with drugs that are failing in their task.

The things that fail.

Juliet strokes the wallpaper beside the doorframe. A shape in the unseen but remembered pattern is raised velvet. She reads its outline with her fingertips: horse and rider; she remembers it is of a ferny green. She gives in to the urge to place her cheek against the velvet, a century of softness impervious to change. She is not a woman carved on a prow, pushing through the stormy waters; she is a woman lashed to a prow, seasick, exploring the wilds against her will.

She says out loud: "What am I doing here?"

"I brought gasoline," says Juliet.

"You didn't," says Mike.

"Okay, I didn't," she says. "But I saw a gas can in the basement, and there's the gas station down the road. It would be easy."

"Arson?" says Mike. "I don't think *easy* is the choice word to describe arson."

"It's ours. We can do what we want to it."

"It's not yours. It's been sold. It belongs to someone else now. It's waiting for a new family. You don't know who they are. You don't know what they hope for from this place."

"Fuck them," says Juliet. "Just . . . fuck them, whoever they are."

"Wow," says Emmanuel. "Whoa. I mean."

"What purpose would it serve?" Mike touches her, hands on both shoulders, and she spins away from him.

"Fuck you too."

"What good would it do?"

"We have nothing," she says. "Me and Emmanuel. He left us nothing. Less than nothing. He didn't even let us bury him."

"What's in the box? You have that," says Mike. "You can take it. No one even knows it was ever here."

"Oh, brilliant, thank you, that's awesome. Permission granted by the morality police. Well, I don't want it. What's in the box? Toys. I don't need toys. Do you need toys, Emmanuel?"

"Yo, I'm like, whatever, it's not."

"Emmanuel needed toys when he was a kid. He doesn't need toys now."

"Well. Maybe we'll need them, someday," says Mike.

And Juliet looks at him dry-eyed, as if she suspects he has a fever. She says, "You can't change my mind by dragging our completely imaginary unborn children into the mix, so don't even try. Here you go, kids, here's a box of rotten old broken-down crap to play with, here's some past I'm going to force you to care about; go ahead, enjoy your imaginary mother's sad little collection of burdens which she should have fucking burned years ago."

"So burn the box," says Mike.

"I saw that coming," says Juliet; but she didn't.

"I don't need it," says Emmanuel. He has stepped away from her, backed away out of the light thrown by the bonfire. "I don't need anything in it."

Juliet thinks: He's afraid — *of me*.

She never wanted that. She never wanted any of this. She's making a lot of mistakes, swinging away in the dark here, crashing away in the darkness of her mind's eye.

What she sees, what she wants, is the farmhouse absorbed by a wash of flame, the twisting of beams and clapping of heat, the devouring urgency of fire. She hears the noise of it, as loud as a freight train, shaking the earth. And she knows, she craves, the insignificance of its absence afterwards, where fire has been and taken everything away.

What remains? The smoking of its insides, the emptied-out cellar into which Juliet would drop the cardboard box to rot in a steady falling of grey midday rain, exposed to the sky, placed at the centre of an impromptu grave. She wouldn't cover it over. She'd let it waste away to nothing under the careering seasons: fall bashing into winter crashing into spring blasting through summer exploding against fall, around and around in a whirl, and the grass and weeds sprawl and choke out the foundation and the swamp creeps nearer and a wild orchard of pear trees erupts and the surrounding fields fall fallow, and it is still and quiet and no one will ever come here, not on purpose. Only a curious child might explore, a child they no longer make these days, an obsolete child: children are never allowed out alone the way she was, and Keith too. It will have to be them, then, Juliet and Keith, cutting across marshy fields and stepping into a mess of fallen pears, bees everywhere — *don't move, they won't sting if you don't move!* — and seeing red sumac huddled in a patch around some unknown emptiness. They would have to look in. They would creep to the cellar's edge and look down. Mud and branches and weeds. They would see the mouldering cardboard box and the faded thin wood of a painted toy truck. Both would want to climb down. They would jump without guessing at their fate, without regret. The walls so steep they'd never climb out again. There they'd stay, at play. Who would find them? Who would rescue them?

No one. She wouldn't let anyone rescue them.

"Juliet?" Mike is calling to her, holding her by the hand. She's turned to stone. No, she won't always be like this. The farm is sold, the house is empty, there are babies to grow and stories — good ones — that will carry her through and away, and she will not always be like this. *Oscuridad*, all around her, inside and without, *oscuridad*.

"Juliet? Juliet? What do you want to do?"

GIRLS

It was in all the newspapers, the kind of story people are drawn to. Sensational. This was before your father was born. The newspapers printed a photograph of the children standing in three rows in the yard — the photograph had just recently been taken, which seemed so very fortunate. It was probably the only photo ever taken of the boy. They've circled his head. Here he is, the littlest, the child who went missing. When I look at it now, I see that it isn't a very good photograph. We're all squinting in the sun, and he looks the same as the others. Not so fortunate after all.

There I am, in the back row, towards the middle. I wore my hair in a bun in those days. I could be one of the children, don't you think? And possibly a boy. I never photographed well.

Mr. John Dietweiller took the picture. He wasn't to blame, but he bore the brunt of it. It was an awful time. I wrote a letter of resignation, but Mr. John Dietweiller, bless him, replied by offering me a better position. He helped cover my secret when it was of no consequence to him. He was a kind man. He died of a blood clot to the heart, I heard, not so many years later.

This was in West Germany, in the village of Bad Dürkheim, in the French zone. The war was over and the Germans were starving. Our agency kept forty children in the house. These were not orphans. They came from overcrowded families in the surrounding villages and towns. We deloused them and gave them new clothes and fattened them up, batch by batch. I was a young woman, younger than you, not yet twenty. I did the jobs that the others didn't want to do.

I was the one who replied to the letter from a Mr. Warren Smythe. We received many letters from strangers, writing to express interest in German affairs generally and in our mission specifically. We replied to all with an invitation to visit, and more than you might think came. The agency relied on donations, and most visitors were moved to give.

I don't remember writing that particular letter of invitation. It was like any other, though I tormented myself afterwards with the belief that I was directly to blame. It was my way of thinking around the other evidence — the real evidence — of my guilt.

I do remember that the morning of May 4, 1950, was unseasonably warm. The cook complained of the heat and I wondered whether she would last the summer; but it wasn't the heat, really. She was coming down with a fever and she was terribly contagious, though none of us knew it.

Late afternoon, just in time for supper, the doorbell rang. I answered it. A man was standing on the doorstep of Weinestrasse S. 30. He was clean-shaven and wore a striped suit and a hat. Under the hat his hair was bright red, the colour of a new copper penny. He had a wife, too. And he had my letter of invitation.

"Mr. and Mrs. Warren Smythe," he said, as if we'd been expecting them.

Of course I invited them in.

Mr. John Dietweiller gave Mr. and Mrs. Smythe the tour. Two classrooms, dining room, and kitchen on the first floor; dormitory rooms on the second floor, plus the small room that Anna and I shared. The guest room was on the third floor.

Mrs. Smythe thought we were an orphanage. But that was a mistake many people made. Mrs. Smythe . . . what did she look like? Her face is long gone but I remember what she wore: matching brown dress and veiled hat. She looked very smart, and I did not. I remember that bothered me that evening. I felt shabby in my sensible shoes and my apron. Our aprons went up to our chins in those days. It saved us washing our dresses so often. I did not like the way Mrs. Smythe made me feel. I was not used to it.

But that was nothing compared to the way Mr. Smythe made me feel.

Oh, Juliet. I have never told anyone this story. Are you sure you want to hear it?

In the morning, Mr. Smythe took me aside. His wife was delicate and bothered by noise and could he trouble me to carry meals up to her room? I said yes. I always said yes in those days.

The cook — she was from the village — went home after lunch, sick.

I made supper with help from the older girls; extra work, but I enjoyed it. I liked working with the girls. Most were bossy and sturdy, despite their hard situations, and I liked them for it.

We sat down, forty at the table. There were so many children and they came and went every three months; over the years I have tried and tried to recall especially the littlest, but I can't. Instead I've made him up in my mind, I think.

Mr. Smythe sat beside me. He held my hand during grace.

I was younger than my age; I had never been held by the hand in quite that way. I knew instantly that it was something different, new. In every girl I've ever counselled, I've seen myself: a girl holding a strange man's hand under the table. Girls. There is something so fragile about them, beneath the surface. They want to be loved. They want something to love them back. They get lost inside their want. They could drown. Seated beside Mr. Smythe, his warm hand around mine, I wasn't thinking of the children, the individual precious children in our care, not at all. I was thinking of myself.

I remember that after the cook took sick, so did several children, and then several more. Anna and I were too busy to bother with Mrs. Smythe, so we sent up one of the older girls, who told us that Mrs. Smythe spoke German better than her husband. She was very friendly. Lots of questions.

Juliet, I am telling you all of this for a reason. The reason is Mr. Smythe. He was a man who was easy to like. Anna liked him too. He was easy to like if you were a girl, but Mr. John Dietweiller did not like him, not at all. I believe he tried to warn me: not with words, but I saw him watching me in a way that I resented. Mr. Smythe sought me out, you see. His questions were minor, but he was interested in my answers: how many children were in our care, where had they come from, were the families eager to send them to us, had I always spoken such fine German. Flattery. Mr. Dietweiller recognized what I could not.

Mr. Smythe caught me on my own.

The house was quiet and he startled me on the stairs. He wished to talk, privately. I had known him less than three days, but time was compressed and accelerated because of the fever spreading through the house. I was so busy, so full of purpose and certain of my usefulness. We walked together to the bottom of the stairs and into Anna's classroom. It was dark. I pulled the door shut behind us so our voices wouldn't wake the children. More were sick, and they slept restlessly.

Mr. Smythe wanted to stay on longer. I said it wasn't up to me. But I was secretly pleased that he might think so. He was holding my hand. I did not stop him. Who was Mr. Smythe? I never thought to question his story. He was an American minister. He was between churches. He was looking to serve and had not settled on how or where.

None of this may have been true. The only certainty is that I will never know.

Nothing concerned me, not in that moment. Who was holding me by the hand in Anna's classroom? I would have answered, in awe, *a man, a stranger: Mr. Smythe.* I let him touch me — he was gentle — my arms, my face. The house was very warm. Kisses. I could hardly breathe. I was not thinking of Mrs. Smythe. Perhaps I wasn't even thinking of Mr. Smythe, only of myself. I didn't turn my face away. I wanted to see what would happen next. So many girls do. They are lonely; they long for adventure — exploring the limits of their own bodies, what greater adventure? I never judged a girl, never; not even myself. My body knew what to do, and in some way I believe that I was brave enough to follow it. That it is a kind of courage. Foolish courage, of course, reckless and danger-ous, but in its own way, yes, brave.

Everything was over almost before it began. He waited for me to stand up and sort out my dress. He gave me his handkerchief.

And I told no one. I have never told anyone.

I just went to my bed. Anna tossed and turned, and by morning she was too sick to rise. Half the house was sick. At breakfast, Mr. Smythe said that Mrs. Smythe was also taken ill. He behaved as though I'd dreamed our meeting. I did not know that this was common behaviour for men. I was grate-ful to him.

He offered to stay and help. Mr. John Dietweiller agreed, but begrudgingly.

Mr. Smythe swept out the classrooms. I sent him to the market.

I took down my hair. I forgot that I was homely; I forgot myself. I was happy, I think.

It was warm, and getting warmer. I took Anna's brush and brushed through the tangles. There were no mirrors in the house but I wanted to see myself, because I knew that I was changed, somehow. I looked at my reflection in the side of a pot in the kitchen, but I was distorted. I picked up a spoon, but I was upside down.

Mr. Smythe found me. The potatoes were at a rolling boil. He was watching from the doorway and he did not look, after all, like what had happened in Anna's classroom had been a dream.

He came to me. "You're warm," he said. "Flushed."

Well, I was. I was already sick.

One of the older girls entered the kitchen before we could jump apart. That snapped me back to sanity. I went to dump the pot of potatoes. The girl fetched a pitcher of water.

As soon as she was gone, I said, "You will have to leave. You cannot stay."

"Don't think I will hold anything against you," he said. "Don't think I will tell anyone anything. Don't think that of me."

"Who would believe you?" I said. I hardly believed it myself.

"But you're lovely," he said. "I think so."

That is how easily a girl can imagine she is in love.

And that was their last evening in the house and the last I saw of Mr. Warren Smythe.

I didn't come to supper. I was taken with the fever.

In the morning it seemed he had done as I'd said. They were gone, Mr. and Mrs. Smythe. Can you guess? They had taken our littlest.

Mr. and Mrs. Warren Smythe were never found. The child was never found. He was never found alive, but then he was never found dead, either. Briefly it became an international news item — one of my sisters clipped this photograph from the local paper, back home in Ontario — but that didn't mean much effort went into solving the crime. I can see the boy's German parents — not their faces — heads bowed. The boy was one of nine, and not the youngest. I like to think that he grew up somewhere safe, loved by people whom he believed were his parents; I like to think that he was wanted and chosen by Mr. and Mrs. Smythe, who perhaps could have no children of their own; that he never found out where he'd come from. He might still be living today.

It was wrong of me, but in the months and years after his disappearance, I rarely thought of that little boy, of his actual breathing, living self. I was caught up in a different story altogether. In the back of my mind it seemed that someday I would find out what had happened to the child. But no. I don't think so. The answers are gone, impossible to track down. And now I think of him often — not Mr. Smythe, I mean, but the littlest. He is like my own child, my son, who never found out where he came from either.

One vanished, and the other arrived.

Juliet, he never asked: I swear that this is true. Your father never questioned, never doubted what I told him, because, I hope, he knew that he was loved and wanted. I believed, and lived out the belief, that that is all a child needs to know in order to grow and to thrive. I may have been wrong. It is too late to know, now.

If a person is going to keep a secret, a person should have a very good reason for keeping it. I can't think of a very good reason anymore.

Juliet, will you please nod yes? Please, if you understand what I am telling you. I don't know what should be done with this. Maybe nothing. Maybe it is enough that you know too. You'll know where to put it. You'll know what to do.

Look at you. Granddaughter. I'm proud.

DISRUPTION

It is one of those very hot days in late summer when even the sky wants to lie down. Humid and languid, two children and their mother pool together and believe this might last forever: that is what the mother believes. Blue plastic Popsicle stems litter the porch steps behind them, and cut grass sticks to their hands; the children sun-flushed, compact, prepared to be delighted by the smallest surprise, and the mother, Juliet, at ease.

Shaded by their patch of young birch trees, they watch the cars go by. It is rush hour and the asphalt throngs. Across the street seems miles away.

Juliet is waiting, though without purpose, without knowing that what she waits for is a little twist of wire in the grass, sharpened silver, that will cut her life wide open.

Across the street are brick houses converted into student apartments. One has lost its original façade entirely, risen

to three storeys, and taken over the entire lot, a sign perma-
nently erected in its yard advertising rooms for rent. Oddly,
this is the least vulgar, its walls sheltered by healthy trees,
bicycles locked along its drive. The next house over is
deformed by barnacle-like additions in cheap yellow siding.
The buildings share a caretaker who spends her days, in all
weathers, outside.

Juliet feels as if she knows the woman, their relationship
supported by hand signals and smiles and indecipherable
greetings called across the noisy street; but Juliet doesn't even
know her name.

The woman dyes her hair orange; the colour does not look
unnatural on her, cut to her jaw. Juliet guesses her age to be
about forty, though at moments she looks younger, and then
again older. She lives in the uglier of the two buildings, the
front yard of which is paved. To improve the space she plants
bright annuals in the patch of earth between sidewalk and
street and in pots set on the pavement, which is where she sits
in her lawn chair to read books — not magazines, not newspapers. Juliet is not near enough to see the titles.

The woman is nowhere to be seen just now.

Instead, as they sit under the patch of birch trees, waiting, expecting nothing more than to count the passing cars
and to remark upon their colours, a girl emerges. She bursts
forth, rent with screams, out of the rotten mouth of the uglier building. She is deeply untidy, feet shod in dirty flip-flops,
hair tangled and straggling, her body neither fat nor thin.
Juliet does not recognize her, but there are many tenants and
they come and go. At first she thinks her no more than a
teenager, but as the girl howls and stamps around the paved

yard, she ages, until she is as old as Juliet herself: approaching thirty, sailing past.

She is dancing with rage directly across the street from them.

The children have never seen anything like it. They sit quietly and watch and feel no danger. Finally, Lucy, the eldest, says, "I know that lady. She lives at Earl's house."

"Shh." Juliet is surprised. "Our neighbour Earl?"

Earl lives across the street too, in the only unconverted house on the block. Like the caretaker, he enjoys sitting outside, and can often be found where he is now: on his porch steps, smoking and sketching in a notebook. He has no apparent occupation and a houseful of cats, but his property is tidy, his yard raked, his sidewalk swept; in winter he has crossed the street to help Juliet shovel her walk. Though it seems he and the caretaker would have much in common, they are not friendly with each other.

"Yes," Lucy says, "she lives in the basement."

"Are you sure?" Juliet whispers despite the noise of the traffic. "I think he lives all by himself."

"Daddy and me saw her in the morning! A long time ago."

This could mean yesterday or a month past.

"I believe you," says Juliet. "I'm just surprised."

A taxi slows and turns into the paved yard just as the caretaker appears, hugging an overflowing garbage bag. She throws it from porch to pavement and its contents spill. She throws another bag, and another, with great calm and in utter silence, her fixed smile less cheerful than demented.

Earl rises, stretches, wanders down the sidewalk, as if the timing of his approach were accidental. The girl flies at him, weeping for rescue, but Earl tilts his head, only half listening. Smiling, the caretaker gestures to the taxi driver to open his trunk, and the girl flies back, kneeling and wailing and shoving things into split black bags.

The caretaker comes to Earl and they stand together in the landscaped yard between their two residences.

"What are they saying?" asks Lucy. "Why is that lady crying?"

"I don't know," says Juliet. Walter, not yet two, crawls onto her outstretched legs like a slug and presses his head to her stomach, where inside there beats an extra heart, though none of them know it, not yet.

Juliet thinks, We are invisible.

The caretaker bends to pluck a weed from a lush bed. Whatever Earl says to her, it isn't solicitous. It takes him about two seconds to say it. The caretaker folds the weed and puts it into her pocket.

"Where will she go?" Juliet says out loud.

"What's happening?" Lucy turns to her mother.

"We really don't know," says Juliet. At this moment the caretaker is sturdily stuffing bags into the taxi's trunk while the girl fights her. *Tooth and nail.* A thin scratch of blood rises on the caretaker's cheek.

"Why not?" cries Lucy, but Juliet has no answer for her daughter. She thinks, It is better not to know.

The taxi driver slams the trunk until at last it catches. His expression is closed. He wants assurance he will be paid, nothing more. Again the girl approaches Earl, arms outstretched. He holds her off with what looks like twenty dollars. The taxi driver shakes his head: it might not be enough. So Earl brings out another bill.

The girl collapses into the back seat, but she is silent only for a moment. As the taxi waits to pull out of the driveway, she seems to catch fire. She rolls her window down and emerges, dazzling with fury, rising as if from the sea, terrible and prophetic and bright. She fixes directly on Juliet, as if she's known all along that they've been watching, mesmerized, consuming the surface of her story, silent accomplices to her misery.

Juliet knows: she stands accused.

And then the cabbie catches a break and squeals out between a silver minivan and a white sedan, and the girl is gone. Earl scuffs back along the sidewalk to his house, not in any particular hurry. The caretaker has gone inside. Presently she emerges with a broom and sweeps the paved area where her chair belongs, as if it has been soiled by the girl's spilled clothing, a diseased thread here, a scar of fabric there.

Into the silence, Walter says, randomly, "She a mommy." He does not often speak. He says it again: "She a mommy."

"Who?" says Juliet, and then, "No. No, they're not mommies. They're just ladies. Girls. Women." She feels this strongly: she wants the sun's gaze and the pool of birch shade and this forever afternoon just for herself and her children, the solidity of family immunizing them against the forces of chaos and confusion, of mistakes made badly and publicly, of breakdown and uncontrolled display.

"She a mommy, she a mommy, she a mommy."

"Yes," Juliet says, to stop him, and in saying it she knows it could be true. Mothers are everywhere. Everyone has one. The caretaker and the girl who left by taxi — their bodies might know everything that Juliet's knows: the clutch of love, the slippery molecules of joy, the anticipation, the endless promises and ripping guilt.

The thought opens her like an axe.

She is sitting under the patch of young birch trees on one of those very hot days in late summer. Blue plastic Popsicle stems litter the porch steps behind them. Cut grass sticks to her hands. Her children's warm bodies sprawl nearby. She is waiting. She is waiting for a girl — a stranger — to tear out of an apartment building across the street.

The girl is screaming, she is casting about for help, and no one will help her.

Juliet stands. She does not hesitate. She takes her children by the hand and walks to the street's edge and waits for a break in the traffic. They cross.

As she approaches the girl, she calls out, Are you okay?

The girl rages. No, I'm not fucking okay.

Can I help you?

No. The girl pauses. Well, cash. Cash.

Juliet has a flattened ten-dollar bill in her pocket. Her children watch silently as she passes it to the girl. Behind them, bags thrown off a porch land like dull explosions.

Let me help.

The caretaker smiles. This is none of your damn business. If you knew what shit she was pulling in here — she's crazy. She's certifiable.

You're the fucking crazy.

I wouldn't touch those if I were you. She's sick.

But Juliet bends and gathers a thin T-shirt, a pair of cut-off sweat pants, a neon green windbreaker, and folds them neatly.

Why are you doing this? says the caretaker.

Because, says Juliet, I couldn't just sit there and watch. She points to the birch trees across the street, and there they are, sitting and watching, the mother, the children, protected by the wall of family, enthralled.

You can't be there and here.

I know, says Juliet. I think I am in the middle of a decision.

That's not how it works. Look at us. You can't choose one way or the other; you drift, we're all drifters, it all happens invisibly, by accident; even if you think you know where you're going, you don't know what's going to fall into your path, what's going to trip you up, what you can't stop no matter how hard you try. You don't control the weather.

And all along, it's all in here. In your head.

And in here, says the girl, pressing her heart. In your body.

And in here, says Earl, walking slowly up the sidewalk towards them. His hands are cupped. Juliet can't see what he's holding.

They stand on the paved earth and the taxi arrives. The girl says she doesn't need any more help, thanks.

But where are you going? asks Juliet. And are you going to be okay? How can you go like this into the world, with nothing, with no protection, how can you do this? Aren't you terrified?

The girl does not answer. She climbs into the back seat and slams the door. But she is silent only for a moment, and then she rolls down her window. She climbs up and out, dazzling with passion, rising as if out of the sea, and she says, Juliet, that is how every last everyone goes out into the world. And no, she cries, I am not afraid!

EPILOGUE

DANIEL ORTEGA'S WRISTWATCH

Pick up all the little pieces that do not fit. There are at least enough for one more story. You have Daniel Ortega's imitation gold wristwatch slipping sideways, too large for the slender bones of his wrist. You have children at sunset, and a lost island, and the pitch of your mother's laughter as she returns from an evening out. Laughter has woken you, and comforts you deeply. Your father laughs in return. They are laughing together.

But you can't find what you are looking for.

What are you missing? Is it your grudge, your urge to confess, your rage, your trouble, your righteousness? Can't you leave the little pieces to shrink and wither and drift, to be knocked to the floor by a child's elbow and accidentally vacuumed up?

No, you can't.

So you pray. You practise. You work. You stretch your body regularly and lie upon the floor hearing your heart pound in rhythm with your lungs. A month is like an hour, and an hour is a month. You live for years until it comes to you: how you have loved sifting the little piles for clues and premonitions.

You don't want to come to the end.

Tell me: Do you remember what it feels like to be young?

Your birthday has come and gone, and you measure your age on your hands in two outspread suns. The symmetry of numbers enchants. You have memorized the multiplication tables in your new language, and they are forever cast in this form: *ocho por seis, cuarenta y ocho; ocho por siete, cincuenta y seis*.

The natural world is both literal and magical. You make a camera with your fingers, framing every scene you want to keep: *click*. One of the grown-ups has taught you this trick, because real cameras and film are rare. You believe in the technology; you take hundreds of pictures with your hands. On car rides you close your eyes and drift through the album in your mind. Many photos are of horses: thin, bony, stark in deep, dry fields of grass. You are drawn to sunsets and water. You take a picture of the dank and rotting house you and your brother have constructed against a concrete wall: stinking palm branches, swarming with minuscule flies. Here is the front porch wall against which your bare feet have crashed and stopped you, hard, when sliding the slick red tiles in a rainstorm.

Why keep these things? You do not think, the way a grown-up would, *This too shall pass*. You gather not for need or market value but for pleasure, much as you and your brother collect bottle caps and, later, when he is sick and you are not, the shared loot of coins and stamps and baseball cards. You enjoy arranging them in symmetrical piles according to characteristics and rules based on your own interests: by colour, or type, or year, or by an arbitrary and personal hierarchy from favourite to least. Their existence is comforting, and the pleasure of placing them in your own order pulls you towards the ground, sits you deeper inside calm and solidity, and self.

You think none of these thoughts. Without agonizing, you do what feels right.

You cup your hand to catch the wind and catch the wind and catch the wind in the back seat of a cramped car bumping around blind corners on a jungled mountainside green with the rainy season. To your left, a tangle of trees and rocks beyond the sheer drop into valley. To your right, a wall of crumbling boulders. Should a bus loaded with strangers surprise your dad around the next corner, where will he turn?

We're all going to die! But you shout it as a joke, as full of mirth as if shouting *I'm alive, I'm alive, I'm alive!*

The car, rushing with air and noise, slips into a cloud come down to earth, milky and cool, and the road disappears, and horizon, and form. Through broken floorboards wispy tendrils seep in like words erased before expressed. You are trying to catch the wind in your hands. It is all around you, all over your skin.

A voice says, This is what a cloud looks like from the inside.

You have imagined walking on a cloud, kicking out the window of an airplane and leaping, light as a ballet dancer, onto marshmallow softness. If you were a grown-up you might be disappointed to discover that wet fog is the true nature of a cloud, and not what you'd imagined. But you are young, and you believe in many things at once. The cloud in the sky retains its froth, even while you shiver with delight to find yourself inside a real cloud here on earth, breathing its humid coolness, admiring its shroud, gazing upon a changed and lost world, your cheeks damp.

Do you remember when your parents knew everything?

Your mother is ever so slightly in love with Daniel Ortega. Your mother and father dress up fancy and go to a dinner and dance attended by the Sandinista leadership. Your mother is smoking a cigarette when Daniel Ortega, the president of this country and hero of its revolution, approaches her table. In one smooth movement, she and another woman, also smoking, pass their cigarettes to a friend. The friend sits coolly, delighted beneath his moustache, a non-smoker holding two lit cigarettes between the peace fingers of his right hand, while Daniel Ortega inclines his head, pulls your mother to standing, leans in to kiss the air brushing her cheekbones.

Daniel Ortega's wristwatch slips from under the green cuff of his uniform and catches the bones of his wrist: it is too large for him. Your mother believes this is proof of his humility. She needs no further evidence.

Why do you?

Escape. You are not getting away from it all, or running away, or leaving it all behind; that is what a grown-up would do. You have entered another dimension, elementally free in thin shorts and T-shirt, the wind lifting your braids and lake spray light on your lips. A fisherman pilots the motorboat that is taking you and your family to an island among many, a place you've never been.

You disembark; the boat tilts with weight dispersed. If you fall into sweet green water it is as warm as your own blood. There are sharks in this lake: the only freshwater sharks on the planet, and you would like to see one. The fisherman catches fresh fish for your lunch and guts them, roasts them over fire. Your dad slings a hammock between trees and relaxes, a large man in short swimwear; he drinks rum and Cokes with your mom. Your hands grip rope hanging from a branch and you swing out over the water, drop down, plunging all the way under, drenched as a sea rat.

It does not rain until late afternoon. There are hundreds of tiny islands in this lake. You could live here, with fire and a hammock and a net for fish, or sharks. Everyone imagines it, even your parents.

Your parents are talking about a dream, but you are not. You are talking about something that could actually happen. You are talking about possible worlds, parallel lives, the ones you will live in throughout your life, slipping sideways and through the membrane that separates the noise and substance of your finite life from the sweet, calm inertia of your forever lives, the ones going on beside you, drifting and holy and unchanged despite the passage of time.

You are on the boat; your face is wet. The boat rocks to a lull and you step onto this island and you are here again, warm, barefoot, wiry, at play with your brothers, and your parents are here too, without a care for the day, without grief or rage or blame. This is not an illusion. This is still happening, and you know that it is, because you can find it in your mind as easily as closing your eyes and letting go the rope, the fibres scratching your palms as you hang for an instant between sky and water, as you fall through and under and hold your breath, your knees folding to meet your belly, your hands spread in front of your face and your eyes wide open.

Where are you right now, if not here, too?

The stones beneath your feet are cool, wide, washed by the warm salt water of the Pacific Ocean. Your bare soles are tough and your toes grip the slippery rock effortlessly. All around you breathes the humid falling of night. Earlier, following the afternoon rains, you ran the solemn wild shoreline believing you could catch the rainbow left behind, and now, a phosphorescent thunderous sky of layered orange and black draws in as you watch, exhilarated, belly full of fresh fish and fried rice eaten at a thatch-roofed shack way back there. Flies landing on the lip of your glass pop bottle; blowing them away.

Your brothers stand beside you. You pause in a ragged row and look at the same sky.

Click.

Three children silhouetted against a pure palette, vivid shadows.

The waves beat a steady wash against the rocks, and out there someone is crawling the water — your dad, though he is not a strong swimmer. Behind you, when you turn to shore, a grown-up's heavy black camera swings around his neck; whose, you cannot remember. There are so many of them, and you feel such intimacy, such knowing, it seems you should recall with absolute clarity who stands where and does what; but the details are mutable. Anything you put down on the page will be wrong.

You are here.

You spring out of the camera's frame, splash into the waves, crouch, slip your shoulders and head backward and down until your face goes under and comes up, rushing with salt water, tilted to the sky. The tides carry danger. You don't know what *undertow* means but feel it viscerally, in the body, a quiet power beneath waiting to grab you and pull you under, where no one will hear when you open your mouth.

Your hair is wet rope and your bathing suit clings to your stomach, and it is almost time, almost, to leave, but no one wants to go.

So you'll stay.

You'll pick this up and keep it, as the photograph is kept, printed and framed and packaged and mailed to a new address in another country, where it hangs on the wall by the stairs, a little askew no matter who tries to straighten it. It is a beautiful photograph. Guests remark upon it.

You think, I don't know where that picture ended up.

You look to the pile on your desk, but while you were typing it has scattered. The windows are open, and a breeze pulls out like tide receding from shore. You see Daniel Ortega's wristwatch in the teeth of a squirrel scrambling across the street on a wire. Your mother's laugh has been caught by a girl passing on the sidewalk below, a cellphone pressed to her ear.

The tide pulls.

You cover the keyboard and stand. You climb onto the window ledge — it isn't high. Without pause or hesitation, without listening for the cries of your children, you spring

onto a shifting cloud and, toes pointed, leap on strong legs
to another and another and another, higher and higher, until
this house is a red and black speck and the trees are smudges
of smoke and the sky is an ocean, and you swim like forever.

ACKNOWLEDGEMENTS

This book would not exist had my parents not chosen to follow their hearts. For giving their children an unforgettable gift of an experience, I thank Linda King and Arnold Snyder first and foremost.

Though I never set out to write a book about siblings, I've come to cherish *The Juliet Stories* for its portrayal of that particular relationship. My brothers and sister are the most talented, creative, interesting people I know, and I hope my love for them shines through in this book.

In 2006, with support from the Canada Council for the Arts, I travelled to Nicaragua with my family to do research towards a book that was not *The Juliet Stories*. I want to thank my Spanish teacher Isabel Cisterna for preparing me for that adventure. And I want to thank Sharon Hostetler for hosting us while in Nicaragua and for agreeing to be interviewed; our conversation changed the direction of the book entirely. I came home knowing that I was going to write a story much closer to my own. But it would be nothing like a memoir.

Throughout many drafts and versions, the writing of *The Juliet Stories* has been a delicate balancing act, pushing away the real past while seeking truth in invention; I hope I got it right.

I'd been looking forward to writing these acknowledgements for a long time, and now I'm terrified of leaving someone out — because it took a crowd to lift this book. My agent, Hilary McMahon, has been with this project for as long as I have, and she's seen it through every stage, always with invaluable suggestions and encouragement. I was also helped early on by Barbara Berson. *The New Quarterly* came to my rescue at a particularly low point in the writing process when I was coming to grips with the term "labour of love." They recommended the stories for an Ontario Arts Council grant, and later published three in their magazine; *enRoute* and *Rhubarb Magazine* also published stories that appear here. I would like to thank the Ontario Arts Council for assisting in the development and polishing of this book. Finally, I would like to thank my editor, Melanie Little, and the entire team at House of Anansi (you, especially, Sarah MacLachlan). Sarah saw not only what this book was, but what it could become. And Melanie and I clasped hands and took a big brave leap together into the unknown. Damn, but I'm proud of what we made. Thank you.

In addition to the editors and mentors who guided the direction of this book, it could not have been written without help from friends and family, many of whom volunteered their time to look after my children during chaotic and necessary "writing weeks." I live in the best neighbourhood imaginable. Among others, thanks to Janis, Nathalie, Zoe,

Marnie, and Nina. And thanks to loving babysitters Amanda, Silvia, and Mehrnoush.

I saved the best for last. My husband has dreamed every dream with me, and he never, ever gives up hope. If there's anything a writer needs, it's someone nearby who kindly and stubbornly refuses to give up hope. Our kids are pretty awesome too. Thank you, Kevin.

November 2011

ABOUT THE AUTHOR

Carrie Snyder is the author of two books of short fiction.
Her second, *The Juliet Stories*, was a finalist for Canada's
Governor General's Award and a *Globe and Mail* Top 100
book. *Girl Runner*, her debut novel, has been shortlisted for
the Rogers Writers' Trust Fiction Prize.

Carrie lives in Waterloo, Ontario with her family
and blogs as Obscure CanLit Mama.

carrieannesnyder.com
twitter.com/carrieasnyder
facebook.com/carriesnyderauthor

Also by Carrie Snyder

'original and moving . . . it has something of the quirky charm of *The Unlikely Pilgrimage of Harold Fry*'
Daily Mail

'a joy to read'
Independent on Sunday

Aganetha Smart was a poor farm girl who could run like the wind, but this was rural Canada in the 1920s when girls didn't run, they didn't compete or dream of the Olympics and they certainly didn't win.
Aganetha Smart was about to change all that.

'The book hurtles through the 20th century in rich technicolor . . . a real page-turner'
We Love This Book

'extraordinary . . . a wonderful story of a free spirit forced to make difficult choices'
Sara Gruen, internationally bestselling author of *Water for Elephants*

GIRL RUNNER

CARRIE SNYDER

TWO
ROADS

LOVE SONG

THIS IS NOT THE love song of Aganetha Smart.

No, and don't talk to me of being weary and claiming one's well-earned rest.

All my life I've been going somewhere, aimed toward a fixed point on the horizon that seems never to draw nearer. In the beginning, I chased it with abandon, with confidence, and somewhat later with frustration, and then with grief, and later yet with the clarity of an escape artist. It is far too late to stop, even if I run in my mind only, out of habit.

You do what you do until you're done. You are who you are until you're not.

My name is Aganetha Smart, and I am 104 years old.

Do not imagine this is an advantage.

I have outlived everyone I've ever loved, and everyone who ever loved me. Nor have I aged well. Just look at me.

I am surrounded by strangers. By day, I am propped in

a wheeled chair in a room that smells of chicken fat and diapers. By night, I am lifted into a rigid bed and tamped down with a blanket that stinks of bleach. This pattern has held for much longer than I care to estimate. I am a bit deaf — though not so deaf as they think — and not-quite blind, so I'll admit that my descriptive capacity may be lacking. It is entirely possible that I am living in a cathedral of light and sleeping in a vast canopied bed, and cannot appreciate it. But I suspect otherwise: my sense of smell is perfectly intact.

As for speech, the words do not exit my mouth entirely at my command. It is only at great cost that I make myself clear. So much easier to loop lazily, mumbling a string of disconnected yet familiar phrases, the ones that wait poised at the front of the tongue in case of emergency, or occasion for social nicety: "Well, now, I don't know, but why ..."

It's a barrier, I won't pretend.

I'm in a state that appears simple. Pared down. Reduced. Boiled clean away.

What astonishes me is how little remains. What proof? A rattling shoe box of scorched medals and no one to claim them. My name at rest in a column in a forgotten record book. Daily blasts of words, produced on deadline, inked onto newsprint, out-of-date by dinnertime.

My achievement is to have lived long enough to see my life vanish. Who will write my obituary? This is not something I fret overly about, mind you. But there it is.

It is too late to change tactics, to go wide around trouble, to save my best burst of speed for the final stretch. There's no starting this race over again. And still I run. I run and I run, without rest, as if even now there is time and purpose and I will gain, at last—before my spool of silence unwinds— what I've yet to know.

VISITORS

"COMING, AGGIE?" FANNIE SQUEEZES my fingers.

We walk the dusty lane, her hand around mine. Fannie is not like anyone else. She moves like water in a muddy creek. We stop to gather wildflowers, ripping their tough stems free, the delicate flowers expiring in our hands. Tall grasses vibrate with heat. We cut a path through the raspberry brambles and along the edge of the front field, planted with corn, the corn taller than my head, taller than Fannie's too.

Fannie's hair is falling out of her bun. Wisps halo her. I look up into her face, like the face of the moon, looking down into mine.

We are going to the graveyard. We are always going to the graveyard.

"Here we are," Fannie says in a comfortable way. I climb the mossy split rails. Dark and grooved, the wood is cool and damp against my knees. Fannie enters at the gate.

"Hello, everyone," she says. "Hello, boys. Good morning, Mother."

I leap from the fence and drop the dying wildflowers. My job is to clear away the crabapples that fall from the overhanging trees. Fannie hitches her skirt, swings it out of the way, and kneels on a grave to pick it clean of weeds. That is her job.

I throw handfuls of crabapples, making noises like guns firing, like grenades exploding, like I imagine war to sound. Our brother Robbie is at war—my half-brother, Fannie's full.

Fannie pats the grass to call me closer. I chew open a crabapple, spit it out.

"Born too early," Fannie begins. I know her stories by heart. "Born too early," she repeats, waiting for me, sitting now on her bottom, arms gathering her legs into her bosom. "Their skin was thinner than crepe, blue as baby birds."

She's got me. I kneel and brush the grass over the twins, buried together in a tiny square coffin. I can almost see its outlines under the ground, of thin dark wood pressed on all sides by the weight of the earth.

"Were they boys or girls?" I ask. Fannie is waiting for me to ask.

"Boys, of course."

I already know, but her answer still gives me a shiver. This is a graveyard of dead children, all boys, my half-brothers. I am relieved to have been born a girl.

The twins: the first and second babies born to our father Robert Smart and his first wife, who was Fannie's mother—not mine—and whose name I know was Tilda. The twins lived for a few minutes each, not even an hour, let alone a day.

Next born came Robbie, who is alive and well and fighting in the mud fields of France. His letters home are scant on details, but for the mud. He writes that his feet are always wet, and that the boys suffer from foot rot. Some of their toes turn black.

I would like to know more about this. I am thinking about it now.

"Do their toes fall off?" I ask Fannie.

"Whose toes?"

"The boys in the war, in the mud."

"Robbie doesn't say."

"Can you write to him and ask?" (I don't yet know how to write.)

"I think we have nicer things to say in our letters, don't we? Robbie doesn't want to think about his toes falling off."

"Maybe they've already fallen off."

"He would tell us."

But I wonder: would he? I look forward to inspecting his feet, surreptitiously, when he's home again, whenever that may be. The newspaper says our boys will be home by Christmas, but Christmas is a long way off.

After Robbie was born, along came Fannie, and then Edith, a string of good luck.

Fannie is older than Edith, but Edith is no longer at home with us. Last fall, she married a man named Carson Miller, and they live across the cornfield, on the next farm over. I like to close my eyes and see Edith standing under the arbour built by our father for the wedding — I think she looks beautiful and I don't understand why my mother grieved over the bareness of the arbour. In my mind, Edith stands alone holding fresh-cut late-blooming flowers, her newly sewn dress tight at the wrists and close at the neck, a raven blue hue.

Fannie moves to the next grave, pulling me along with her. I poke at the initials in the flat stone, scraping away flecks of moss with my fingernails.

Here is another boy. After Edith was born, the string of good luck came to an end.

"Fever," says Fannie, her fingers plucking at minuscule weeds. "Only six months old."

But six months isn't *only*, and I know it.

Edith's baby is already six months. I get to haul around his squirming protesting self as often as I please. I might go whenever I want, so long as I tell Mother — she likes to send along a basket of something: fresh salt buns, or a ball of butter, or beans and tomatoes from our garden. At home, I am the youngest and I like the novelty of being in charge of "Little Robbie," named so as to tell him apart from Robbie, my brother, and Robert, my father.

I feel torn, on visiting Edith's. There is something

unfinished about the house and yard, and it feels different from home. Strange.

Edith's vegetable garden is half the size of ours, and weedy. The flowers grow scanty in their beds, as if they've given up trying. The house is cramped and smells of damp and dirty laundry and soup.

Edith greets my surprise arrivals with an irritated "Oh, Aggie," flushed and hurrying, her hairline damp with sweat. She never sits down, and she never offers me a cookie. (Maybe she doesn't bake any?) She hands off the baby and rushes to other business — not baking cookies — muttering to herself.

Little Robbie and I go a long time without seeing her — it is like she's disappeared — until he is howling and I am hot and cannot soothe him and my arms ache and I feel like howling too. This is when Edith pops into the scene: "There you are!" Annoyed, as if she's been looking and looking everywhere for us.

So I might go as often as I like, but I don't go very often.

Fannie is shifting her weight slowly from the baby who died of fever to the next grave, the grave that grieves her most of all, the one we've both been moving toward: little James.

"It was haying time," says Fannie, drawing out each word slow and plain. "Maybe he was hot and wanted cooling down. Maybe he was lost. He was only two years old — how did he find his way across the back field to the pond? Drowned before we even knew he was missing, that's how fast it happened. That's how fast it can."

Neighbour boys fishing at the pond discovered James floating facedown in the water, and they pulled him out and ran screaming to the farmhouse, carrying him between them.

When they set him down in the yard, little James was not yet stiff, the life fresh out of him.

"I was seven years old," says Fannie. "Older than you. The neighbour boys—they're in the war now, but they were just boys then—Jerry and Jack—I can hear them hollering. They laid him on the patch of grass by the summer kitchen door. Everyone came running, my mother falling down over him, trying to lift him, telling him to breathe, please, breathe. And then I knew he must be dead. So I ran and hid in the barn, in the mow, under the straw. The shock of it. It broke my mother's heart."

For a moment I forget that when Fannie says "my mother," she means the first mother, not mine, and it jolts me to think, even for a breath, even mistakenly, that my own mother's heart might be broken by anything.

None of my mother's babies are dead; none of the graves are hers to mourn. I believe this is because my mother gave birth only to girls, three of us: Olive, then Cora, and me, Aganetha, last of all.

I have decided that my mother is nothing like the first mother. The first mother—*Tilda*, I mouth her name—is fuzzy around the edges, shrouded in black netting from all her years of mourning. The stories about Tilda are not really about her. She is in the background, weeping for her dead babies, and then, suddenly, she's buried too.

"Puerperal fever," says Fannie, but that is not what I hear, and so I imagine the first mother purple from scalp to toenail when she died.

All of this happened almost at once: little James drowned, our brother George came early—"So tiny we kept him in a drawer"—and the first mother died.

I imagine Fannie hiding under the straw past dusk, refusing to come out, like a kitten in a nest. Who pulls her out? Fannie doesn't say.

The neighbour men came to finish the haying. Father sat in silence at the table and ate whatever the neighbour women laid before him. Fannie and Edith, aged seven and six, spooned milk into the tiny new baby's mouth—my half-brother George. Everyone watched Father eat and eat and eat, like he had a hole in his stomach through which the food was falling, and they wondered whether he would ever speak again. (He must have; he married my mother before the next spring.)

Nothing so sad has ever happened to me.

"It was James drowning that killed my mother," says Fannie. "I don't think it was George at all. George wasn't to blame."

I know what she's going to say next, and I wait for it.

"I was supposed to be watching him, Aggie. Watching him was my job. What was I doing instead?"

We are nearly done. In another moment, I'll go back to gathering and throwing crab apples. There is just one more thing Fannie needs to say as we kneel here beside each other.

Thin yellow hair lifts from my scalp. I can't see my own face, looking up at my sister's, and don't know that it is wildly freckled, and in my silence looks long and carven. Fannie is both smiling and serious.

"I'll never stop watching you, Aggie. I promise."

There.

It is the clearest air. The quietest sky. The hummingest bugs. The sun shines.

TWO
ROADS

Stories . . . voices . . . places . . . lives

We hope you enjoyed *The Juliet Stories*. If you'd like to know more about this book or any other title on our list, please go to www.tworoadsbooks.com.

For news on forthcoming Two Roads titles, please sign up for our newsletter.

enquiries@tworoadsbooks.com

TwoRoadsBooks